MW01089313

Death

at the

White Hart

Death
at the
White Hart

CHRIS CHIBNALL

PAMELA DORMAN BOOKS | VIKING

VIKING
An imprint of Penguin Random House LLC
1745 Broadway, New York, NY 10014
penguinrandomhouse.com

A Pamela Dorman Book/Viking

The PGD colophon is a registered trademark of Penguin Random House LLC.

VIKING is a registered trademark of Penguin Random House LLC.

Map illustration on pp vi–vii by Sally Taylor represented by Artist Partners, www.Artistpartners.com.

Designed by Cassandra Garruzzo Mueller

LIBRARY OF CONGRESS CATALOGING-IN-PUBLICATION DATA
Names: Chibnall, Chris, author.
Title: Death at the White Hart / Chris Chibnall.
Description: [New York City] : Pamela Dorman Books/Viking, 2025.
Identifiers: LCCN 2024050150 (print) | LCCN 2024050151 (ebook) |
ISBN 9780593831571 (hardcover) | ISBN 9780593831588 (ebook)
Subjects: LCGFT: Detective and mystery fiction. | Novels.
Classification: LCC PR6103.H53 D43 2025 (print) |
LCC PR6103.H53 (ebook) | DDC 823/.92—dc23/eng/20241024
LC record available at https://lccn.loc.gov/2024050150
LC ebook record available at https://lccn.loc.gov/2024050151

First published in hardcover in Great Britain by Michael Joseph, part of the Penguin Random House Group of Companies, Penguin Random House Ltd., London, in 2025

First United States edition published by Pamela Dorman Books, 2025

Printed in the United States of America
1st Printing

The authorized representative in the EU for product safety and compliance is Penguin Random House Ireland, Morrison Chambers, 32 Nassau Street, Dublin D02 YH68, Ireland, https://eu-contact.penguin.ie.

To Madeline, Cal and Aidan
for more than words can express

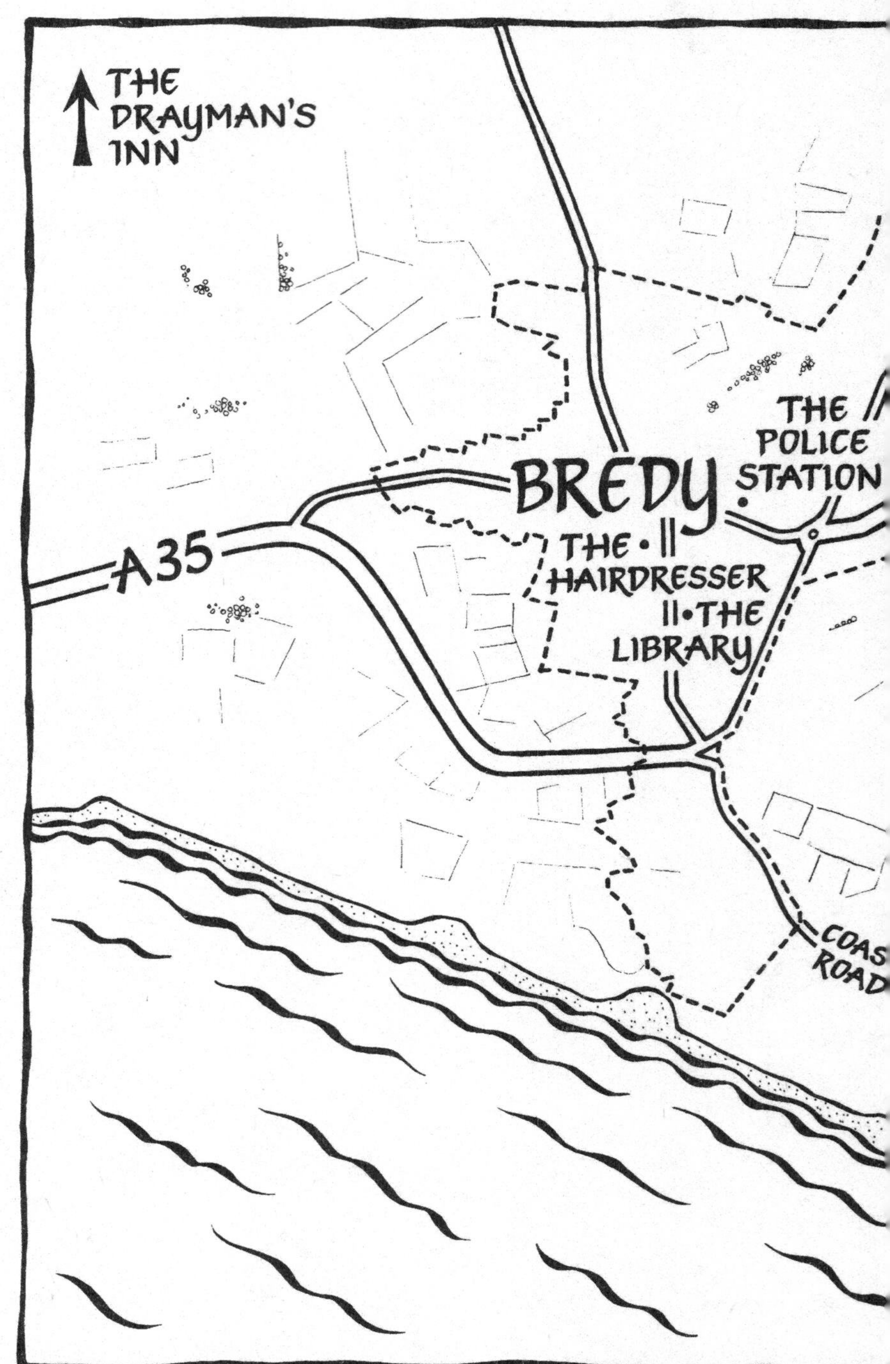
THE
DRAYMAN'S
INN
BREDY
THE
POLICE
STATION
THE •
HAIRDRESSER
•THE
LIBRARY
A35
COAS
ROAD

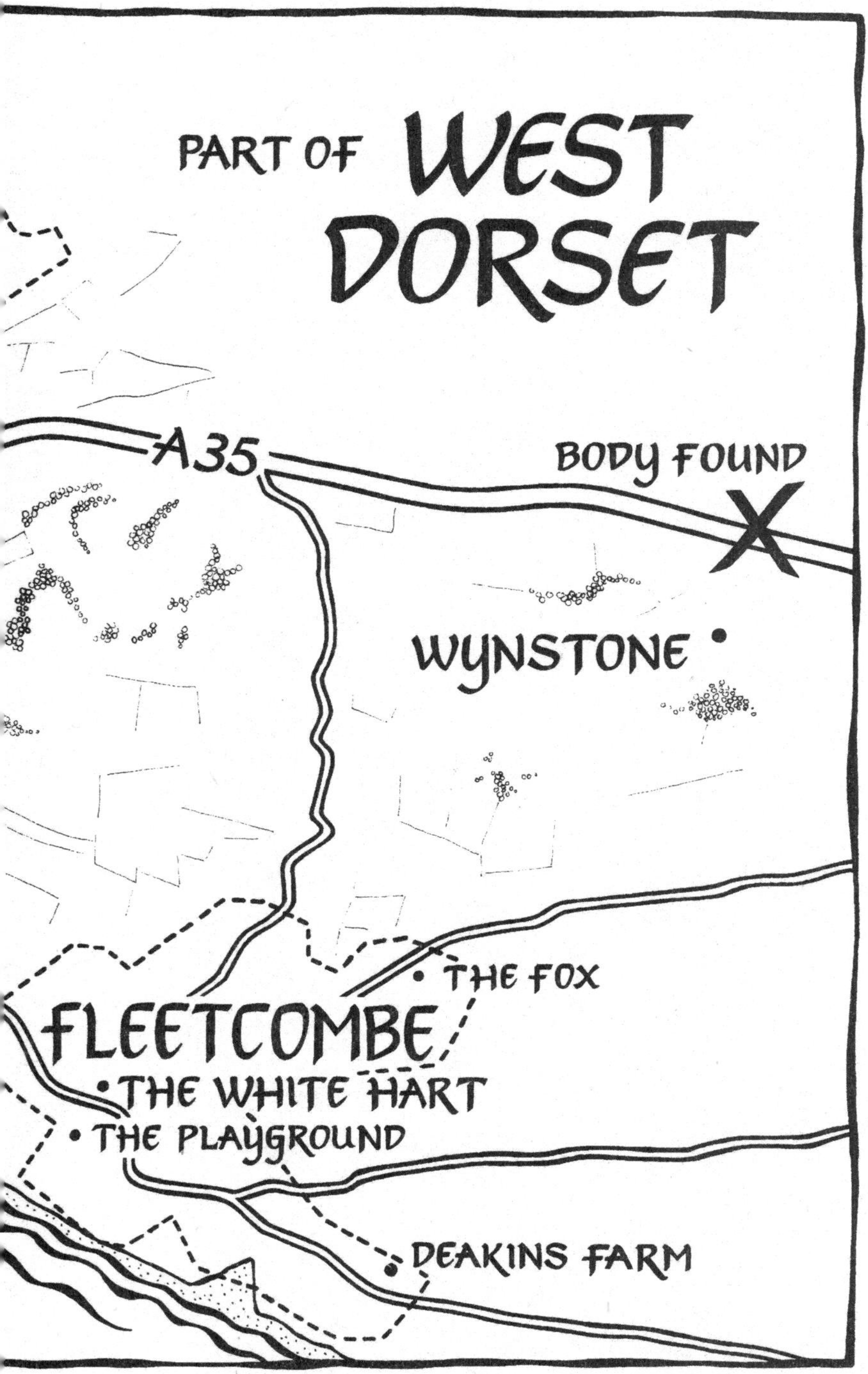

PART OF WEST DORSET

A35

BODY FOUND

X

WYNSTONE

THE FOX

FLEETCOMBE

THE WHITE HART

THE PLAYGROUND

DEAKINS FARM

Death

at the

White Hart

CHAPTER ONE

It was dark when Ewan made the return journey.

He felt a familiar relief driving past the sign for Dorset. Ewan and Devon had never got on. As his car grumbled along the empty moonlit road, he fought to keep his mind on what was in front, rather than where he'd just been.

Think about positive things, he told himself. With a bit of luck, the remnants of last night's not-too-dreadful lasagne should still be knocking about at home. Maybe he could find a cold bottle of cider to go with it. A 2 a.m. treat.

As much as he tried to focus his mind on the road ahead, it kept drifting back to the image of his funny, startling mum in her prime, whirling daftly about the kitchen, making him giggle in front of half-eaten fishfingers. The woman he had just visited was barely an echo of that. A shell, reliant on care provided by others. Ewan scratched at his beard, trying to rub away the stab of guilt.

Be more like the dog, he told himself. The dog lives in the present; only alert to now. That's how to cope. (Back home the following afternoon, Ewan shares this thought with his wife, who says, "The dog shits in the garden. Are you going to do that as well?" and turns her attention back to eBay.)

As the car lumbered over the brow of the hill, Ewan took in the glistening coastline beyond. This was the best section of the drive, any time of day or night. Now, on this September midnight stretch, the world was his alone.

He exhaled, in the manner he'd learned from a long-deleted mindfulness app, appreciating the view of the inky-black water dappled with diamonds of shimmering moonlight. The curve of the bay to his right.

His eyes drifted back to the road, a shocking stab of panic—

—something in the middle of the road—

—you're going to smash into it!—

He swerved—

The car pulling out of his control—

Sharp, hard brake—

Slam. Jolt. Stop.

Breathe.

The bodywork ticked and creaked in protest at the emergency halt. The engine had stalled at his carelessness.

Ewan checked himself. Spike of adrenaline subsiding.

First thought: *maybe it's a deer.*

Second thought, as he peered through the windscreen: *that's not a deer.*

Ewan's shaking finger fumbled at the car's hazard lights button.

He got out of his car and began to walk hesitantly toward the unmoving shape in the middle of the empty A35, oblivious to the fact he'd left the door open, not hearing the alert repeatedly pinging, nagging its now-absent driver. Ewan didn't notice the flashing hazards turning the dark of night intermittently orange. He was too distracted by the object ahead.

As he approached it, Ewan felt for a moment like he was looking down on himself from above in the night. A tiny lone figure in a vast vista. The smell of grass and sea salt tickled his nostrils. The silence of the night air deafened him.

Ewan approached the object placed across the two lanes of the road. He had not hit it. Momentary relief, immediately compromised by the realization of what the object was.

Not a deer.

A dead body.

A dead man. A dead adult man.

Sitting upright on a high-backed wooden chair. Trussed to it. Seemingly naked, his lower half placed inside an old sack, tied at the waist.

Left here. Like he—*it, the body, the corpse; bloody hell, a corpse*—had been put here, placed deliberately. The chair bisecting the white lines down the middle of the road.

Arranged.

But the arrangement of the corpse on the chair was not the most startling thing.

Attached to his head was a huge crown of deer antlers.

Ewan reached out instinctively to touch them but then realized he probably shouldn't. He pulled his arm back.

He took his phone from his pocket. Hesitated. Was this a 999? Bit late for an ambulance now.

He dialed anyway and told the operator he thought he probably needed the police.

CHAPTER TWO

As the call came in, the bedside clock read 03:17. Nicola Bridge was not asleep.

She had managed just under four hours, waking around 2:42 a.m. Since then, she had been lying still, refusing the urge to pick up her phone or turn a light on, instead keeping her head on the pillow and examining the new ceiling. The light from the hall—they still kept it on overnight, despite their son, Ethan, now being seventeen, a habit from his childhood years none of them yet wished to break—was coming through the gap in the door, casting a narrow shaft of light across the floor and the end of the bed.

Nicola had not yet managed an undisturbed night in the new house. Seven weeks and counting. She didn't think it was the house. The house was fine. The bedroom was fine. She even hoped to like it, in time. But she found herself jolting awake around three o'clock every morning.

Angry.

She had always been a light sleeper. That only increased with Ethan's birth, when she had found herself more sensitive to night noise, alert to the needs of her new son. In the years since, undisturbed nights had become panaceas enjoyed only by others, including Mike. When they first got together, she had boggled with admiration at the way he slept:

rarely moving, seemingly at peace. He claimed never to dream, either. She had found that suspicious.

She'd learned to live with her own nocturnal wakefulness. Previously she had even liked having the dark to herself. The silence meant she could think, sometimes about work, sometimes about life. It occasionally brought clarity or a new perspective. That had changed since the move. Her 3 a.m. thoughts were no longer ones she wanted to be alone with. Quite the opposite.

She could feel the anger rising as she lay there. The sweep of bed-bound emotion usually followed the same pattern. Anger would become resentment, which would slowly slide into self-doubt, guilt, ultimately falling into a pit of profound existential dread, before once again rising up into what she could only describe as a seethe. Her heart would be racing once she hit seethe mode, and this was the moment she would attempt to regulate her breathing.

Some nights she would be lucky and get back to sleep by five or so. Others, she would lie there till seven, having at some point shoved in earphones and started listening to her playlist of songs which took her back to being seventeen and full of hope.

The question that tugged at her, the undertow of every concern as she lay there in the early hours of every morning, was simple: *have I made the right decision? Have I been a fool?*

Her ceiling-staring was harshly interrupted by the buzzing on the bedside table. Nicola was still in the habit of laying her phone, switched to vibrate, on a soft flannel overnight so that any call would disturb only her, as the lighter sleeper of the two. The flannel now was moot, but she hadn't changed the habit. She grabbed the phone quickly, feeling it buzz in her hand, answered the call and took in the urgency of the voice on the other end of the line.

Detective Sergeant Nicola Bridge listened to the description of what she was being summoned to with rising incredulity.

As she attempted to slip noiselessly out of the bedroom and into the light of the landing, she crashed into two as yet unpacked moving boxes and swore. Ethan must have moved them out of his own way as he stumbled to bed, repositioning them as a trip hazard for anyone else: the oblivious self-regard of a seventeen-year-old expressed in cardboard.

The door of the spare bedroom opened a crack and a bleary-eyed Mike peered out.

"Sorry, sorry . . ." whispered Nicola.

"Everything all right?" he mumbled back, still half asleep.

"Got a shout," she said, holding up her mobile as documentary evidence.

Mike nodded. "Go safe," he said, and retreated mole-like to the darkness of the spare room, softly closing the door.

I'm glad *you're* sleeping fine, thought Nicola uncharitably as she headed downstairs.

At least, she thought as she drove westwards through the night, this hadn't happened during the day. An obstruction at the top of the A35 just past Wynstone, where the dual carriageway funneled into a single lane, would bring traffic to a standstill during daylight hours. The A35 was the main artery taking travelers west, shadowing the coast. It got busy fast and blocked even faster. With a bit of luck and effort, an incident at night could be cleared before the morning traffic began.

At the site, she got out of her car into the chill night air, clasping the tea that was her lifeline. She took in the white tent SOCO had already erected, an incongruous beacon in the dark, atop the hill. She looked around: fields either side of the carriageway. The sea distant. Road diversion barriers already in place, warning flashes of yellows and blues illuminating the dark. A fresh-faced young uniform officer she didn't yet know the name of was standing ready to direct the currently nonexistent traffic around. He smiled at her, hopeful for acknowledgment, the keenness of youth undimmed by the early hour. "Let's hope we're not still here at rush hour, eh, Skip!"

Nicola smiled back. "Were you first here?"

At this his undaunted smile faltered, replaced by a shadow of unease. "I was, yeah. Bit of a weird one, if I'm honest."

She moved on and past him, perturbed by the way his face had clouded.

Outside the tent, she pushed her long arms and legs into the white scene-of-crime hazmat suit. She had been taunted by girls at school that she was a rake. Bony Maronie. Later, told by men that she was svelte. Once, sylph-like. Even now, at thirty-eight, she was never sure which to believe.

In her own view, she was tallish, five foot eleven (she could still remember being relieved in her late teens that she had remained under six foot, as if it had been inculcated into her from early on in her life—*had it?*—that there was nothing worse than a tall woman), and thinnish. She had good bones: *wonderful bone structure*, she had once been told by a photographer taking her portrait for a professional profile. On her best days, in the rare stylish clothes she kept for even rarer posh nights out, she would confess she could feel briefly elegant. On her worst days, in baggy or ill-fitting workwear, spindly. Most days: between the two.

Gloves. Shoe coverings. Medium-length dark hair tied back, hood up. Ready. She liked the structure of the process: a ritual during which her mind set itself. Observe, process, analyze. *Don't miss anything.* She could already see the difficulty of scene preservation, the possibility of contamination. How many car tires had already whizzed across this scene?

Nicola strode in through the entrance flap of the tent with a nod and a courteous smile to the scene-of-crime officer working. Older woman, fifties at a guess. Nicola hated not having been back here long enough to know everybody's name. But before she could introduce herself, she saw it.

A man's body. Seemingly unclothed; lower half covered in an old hessian sack. Arms bound behind his back. Lifeless gray face streaked with blood which had trickled down from the top of his head. Eyes were open, staring ahead, unseeing. Scruffy dark hair ruffled. In his forties, or well-worn thirties, at a guess. He was placed upright on an old wooden chair, his bound arms locking him in position.

On his head had been placed what Nicola, who admittedly knew little about wildlife, assumed were stag antlers. Seemingly bound into place with rope which had been criss-crossed in an X pattern back and forth over the back of the head and face, distorting his features. It was gruesome.

Nicola looked to her SOCO colleague quizzically. The woman raised an eyebrow, as if to say: *messed up, right?*

"Reeta Patel—don't think we've met."

"Nicola. Bridge. Detective Sergeant," Nicola replied. All the right words, but not necessarily in the right order.

The body resembled a trophy, on a poor man's throne. Sightless eyes, trussed up, and a crown of antlers.

Nicola walked around it, slowly circling, looking at the object, peering at details as if it were an installation in a gallery.

Her level of unease was rising. A gnawing feeling was establishing itself in the pit of her stomach. Clearly this was not a minor incident. Utterly uncharacteristic of this area, where major crimes were few and far between.

Few and far between. That was the whole point in coming back here.

"Time of death?" Nicola asked Reeta.

"Three or four hours ago, maybe less. Dumped here, not killed here. Too soon to be sure on cause, but the back of the head has evidence of blunt force trauma. The blood seems to be from the deer scalp, rather than his."

Nicola could already feel herself dividing into two states of being. The first was detached, professional, factual: OK, major incident. She knew the last murder in the west of the county had been more than a decade ago.

The other state was human and emotional: a life had been ended. A few hours ago, this man was going about his day, presumably with no inkling of what was to come. The people who loved this man would not yet know they had lost him. The ripples of this death hadn't yet begun to spread. Soon they would affect everyone who'd known him.

Killed somewhere else, deposited here. Trussed, transported, left.

Where was he killed? Why move him? Why here? And those antlers. Why antlers?

Most importantly, who was he? *Was he local? If not, where was he from?* Where should he have been right now in the normal run of things? The normal run which was now a distant and alternative reality.

"No ID, I presume?" Nicola asked, stating the obvious, given the absence of clothing.

"Not on him, no," said Reeta, humoring Nicola. "Not that we need it."

"How d'you mean?"

Reeta Patel looked back at Nicola, grim. "We know who this is."

CHAPTER THREE

Less than four hours later in the small market town of Bredy, some five miles from where the antlered body had been found, Frankie Winters finished disinfecting the razors and scissors and arranged the display of products they'd brought in from the company van on arrival that morning. Frankie stared at the empty black leather chair, still absent a client.

Frankie looked at the clock: 7:47 a.m. The chair should have been occupied since seven thirty. First Wednesday of every month, that was the appointment. Regular as clockwork.

But not today.

Not after last night.

It was bad. Frankie knew it was bad.

The door opened, the bell tinkling.

"All right?" A lad Frankie didn't recognize, couple of years older than them, probably. Frankie put him at twenty-threeish. He peered, sizing Frankie up.

Frankie flicked on the big, beaming smile. "Hi, mate!"

An upward flick of the head passed for hello. "You do skin fades?"

Duh. "Oh yeah."

"How long's the wait?"

Frankie gestured round the otherwise empty shop with a grin. It was a small site, smartly kitted out with the latest equipment. Frankie kept it glistening.

"You're in luck. Had a cancellation, so I can do you now. Wanna hang your coat up there?"

The lad looked around, taking his North Face off awkwardly. New surroundings, not sure where to put things. Frankie knew the type, saw them in here most days. Outwardly a little cocky, but not that practiced at life. Probably been to the same hairdresser all his life. Now, in this new place, a recent opening, he was nervous and didn't want to signal it.

"You always open this early?" he asked as he placed the coat on the rack.

"Wednesdays and Saturdays," said Frankie, spinning the chair toward him. It had been Frankie's suggestion, knowing plenty of market workers, tradespeople and teens who griped about hairdresser opening hours. The boss had initially balked and later recanted. Frankie knew the idiosyncrasies of this town.

As the new client sat down, Frankie fluttering and fastening the apron around him, he said, "Just a skin fade. Long on top. I don't want the nose- and ear-fire thing."

"Got it," said Frankie.

"My mate got proper singed at a place last week."

"Not here?" queried Frankie.

"Oh no, not here," came the hasty response, a mixture of twenty-something laddish bravado and a desire not to upset Frankie. The fear of a bad haircut from an accidental insult played across his face. Frankie knew that look.

"I was gonna say," said Frankie, continuing to establish authority, "we're all proper trained."

"It was over Weymouth," said the lad.

"Weymouth—what d'you expect?" smiled Frankie, gratified to see this new client grin and relax.

"Exactly! That's what I said to him."

He was looking at Frankie in the mirror now as Frankie set to work, selecting the shaver setting.

Here we go, thought Frankie.

"Where do I know you from?"

"Dunno."

"Did you go Fairfax?"

"Mm-hmm." Frankie started work. Felt his eyes on them, like this was a Year 7 maths problem to be solved.

"When d'you leave?"

"Five years ago."

"After A levels?"

"No. Did a college apprenticeship." Frankie brandished the shaver and smiled. "So I don't set fire to people."

"So, if you're twenty-one now—"

"Soon—"

"Right, you'd've been two years below us then. What's your name?"

"Frankie."

The lad's brow furrowed as he silently began to ransack his memory. Frankie kept working, not making eye contact. Frankie had finessed this conversation over many haircuts. Here we go.

"But I used to go by Alice."

The lad looked in the mirror, staring now at Frankie. Checking the features beneath the short bleach-blond crop-cut.

"Alice Winters!"

"Frankie Winters, now."

"Yeah! I knew I recognized you!"

Long silence. Frankie worked away at the lad's neck. They had navigated this conversational slalom many times: one of the delights of identifying as non-binary in a public-facing job. Frankie could almost hear him thinking what to say or ask. Then:

"How long you been Frankie?"

"Four years, give or take."

The lad nodded. Frankie knew this was the moment things went one of two ways.

"My cousin did the same. She used to be Jessica. Now she's—no, sorry, now *they're*—Jack."

"Ah, right!"

"Nine months since. My sister's still not really sure."

"It takes some people a sec to get their heads around."

He was looking hard in the mirror, at Frankie absorbed in their work on the back of his head. "D'you get much shit for it?"

Frankie looked up, met his gaze. "Not really." This was the second pivot point, when the conversation could sometimes become a bit more tricky. Frankie had strategies to deal with that. They watched for a half second as the lad took this in.

He half nodded. "That's good."

A minor flood of relief washed through Frankie's body. They gave no outward signal of it. "Yep. It's mostly the pronouns people get worried by."

"Huh. Yeah. Same." Frankie noticed with gratitude that he'd finished with that subject now, lost interest, and was looking around the shop, when he remembered a juicy nugget. "Oh my God, you heard they found a dead body?"

Shit.

Frankie paused, but didn't look up. "No. What's that?"

"Out on the A35 by Wynstone, early this morning."

The back was taking shape. "Jeez."

"Yeah. Left in the middle of the road. Summink weird about it, apparently."

"How d'you know all this?"

"Bloke two doors down is a community support officer. PCSO. He only does it for the gossip. He tells us all sorts of things he shouldn't. Bloke in his forties. That's all he'd say. He does that; he's like guess what I know, and then he'll be: oh, I can't tell you. He's a bit of a twat, if I'm honest."

As the lad was talking, Frankie could feel cold beads of sweat dot their forehead. They had started to use the scissors on the top of the lad's head. Frankie looked at their hand moving. The hand was shaking.

Frankie was instantly back in college: *It is never desirable*, said the lecturer as she berated a hungover and nervous student, *for a hand holding a deadly sharp instrument in close proximity to a human head to show signs of losing control. Shaking hands are what we do everything to avoid.*

Frankie's forehead tingled. They stared, focused, willing those scissors to become calmer, more controlled. No, shit, it was getting worse. It was in the blood now, in the veins. The feeling, the coldness, the panic. Now the feeling was in Frankie's eyes. They were pricking.

A few more trims, get the length right, keep going.

Frankie was fighting a losing battle. Paused. "Sorry, d'you mind if I go and blow my nose a sec? Worried I'm gonna do a massive sneeze." Frankie's smile was full wattage. Only their eyes, gaining redness by the second, betrayed them.

"Course." The lad, oblivious, reached under the apron and pulled his phone out.

Frankie walked calmly through the screened-off arch into the tiny bathroom and locked the door. Sat on the lid-down loo, heart racing.

It was all they could do not to lift the lid and vomit into the bowl.

CHAPTER FOUR

Ninety-four deliveries. Today of all days.

Ninety-four deliveries timed to the minute, his day parceled out in every sense, laden with high customer expectations. People were waiting in or rushing back because they'd been notified: *your parcel is on its way! Your delivery driver is: Eddie.*

Timings are approximate, went the disclaimer. Yet Eddie knew customers who tracked him all the way, all day. He felt their eyes, the taps of their fingers on their keyboards or phone screens, on him throughout the miles. He sometimes felt his essence, his very being, reduced to a pulsing blue dot on a screen, inching forward along the gray lines of a road. Track your parcel, track your delivery, track your driver. Tracked, tracked, tracked.

It was, Eddie had realized as the optimistic uplands of his first month faded into the starker reality of a second month on the job, not ideal for an older man with his blood pressure. He measured it daily, after that business a few years back. He knew that this was not the best job for an easily stressed man of sixty-one with a fuse that could border on the short and a face that could quickly turn beetroot. "Gammon!" a disgruntled woman in her twenties had yelled at him last week when he told her it wasn't his fault the bag containing her clothes order was ripped open at the top.

Eddie tried to hide his anxiety, externally. He smiled. He whistled. He waved. He projected jaunty. *You're next! Eddie is on his way with your parcel! Eddie has delivered your parcel! Take a moment to rate Eddie!*

Take a moment to rate Eddie.

If Eddie were to take a moment and rate himself right now, he thought he would give himself a big fat zero. Only because it was impossible to rate a negative number. If he had that option, he would rate himself negative five out of five. Eddie's intestines were twisted with self-loathing this morning. He despised himself right now.

Cold, hard panic was setting in. He had too much to think about. He spent his trip to the filling station trying to figure it all out. And failing. He was still turning mental cartwheels as he loaded up the van at the depot. He had not showered, merely chugged three gobfuls of mouthwash before leaving the house. He stayed as far away from his supervisors as possible while stacking the van. As he headed straight back to his home turf of Fleetcombe for the first delivery, he clocked his own pale, haunted expression in his rearview mirror.

What did you do?

Concentrate on the driving. Concentrate on the work. An absence of concentration could prove catastrophic.

Fleetcombe. His family had lived here for seven generations. *The ancestral seat*, as he would often jokingly refer to it. Eddie drove slowly, carefully, past the village sign, which was keen to remind everyone that it had been the runner-up in the Village in Bloom competition in 2017. Eddie could remember the rivalries and arguments that had occurred in pursuit of that momentous gong. The night before it was awarded, they'd been tipped off they'd won, so they'd had a celebration. The next day the prize actually went to Netherstock. There was the whiff of controversy, dark mutterings about a bribe, and the villages had been enemies ever since. Over some stupid bloody flowers, thought Eddie.

The September sky was a crisp and clear pure blue, offset only by storybook cloud wisps. It was the type of day that perfectly illustrated why the village had once featured on a program about people relocating from the city to the countryside. It conformed perfectly to the idea of the chocolate-box English village. Even better: it had proximity to the coast (half a mile up and over the cliffs eastwards) and the thriving market town of Bredy five miles west. Though the television piece had been some fifteen years past, Eddie had been told by Alan, his estate agent mate down the pub, that most buyers from out of the area would still start by saying, "We like the look of Fleetcombe."

Having spent all his sixty-one years here, Eddie agreed they *should* like the look of it. The village, which spread out from a center where the two pubs, church and school were located, housed no more than eight hundred or so people. Around three hundred houses, mostly built in the eighteenth and nineteenth centuries, a good portion of them still topped off by thatched roofs. The thatchers did good business in Fleetcombe. If you wanted your roof sorting, the waiting list was daunting.

The primary school was small—around fifty pupils—and fed into the secondary school in Bredy. There had been a post office two doors down from the school for a long time, but it had gone when the last owner retired and had been unable to convince her family, or anyone else, to take it on.

And then there were the pubs. The White Hart and the Fox. Each pub had its locals, and a different offer. You had to choose. The White Hart, run by Jim Tiernan, was livelier: a skittles alley, ever-changing real ales, standard pub grub, an ongoing rotation of live music and sports on the TV. The Fox, now run by Ayesha Barton, had higher aspirations:

more foodie, more welcoming to families, bigger car park. The patrons of the White Hart thought the Fox had ideas above its station. The patrons of the Fox felt the White Hart could attract the wrong sort of people.

Eddie was a White Hart man, though these days if you got barred from or became disenchanted with one pub then you could easily make the other your new regular haunt. Neither pub was so busy that it could afford to turn people away. Everyone, deep down, knew that Fleetcombe couldn't really accommodate both for much longer. Question was: which would go first?

Eddie pulled up outside his long-time pub of choice, turned the engine off and stared at the building. This *would* be his first delivery of the day, wouldn't it?

You've only yourself to blame.

That feeling of dread took over again, gnawing, nagging.

He took a deep breath and flipped open the door, jumping out from the driver's seat. He strode to the back of the little van to retrieve a small brown cardboard parcel.

He stopped at the pub door, hesitant. Banged on the door. Waited.

No answer.

He banged again, waited another moment, then pulled out the block of "sorry we missed you" notes from his top pocket and started to write—

"Eddie." The voice behind him made him jump.

He turned to see Irina walking over from the small car park, car keys in hand. Forty years old, Ukrainian, and looking right now like she'd had very little sleep. Very attractive, thought Eddie, then told himself off. *She's twenty years younger than you, behave.* He put on his best public-facing smile. Paper over the dread.

"Morning, Irina! Up and out early?" For a second, he wondered whether Irina was wearing the same clothes as yesterday.

"Why's he not answering?" demanded Irina.

Eddie shrugged. "Will you sign for this?"

Irina took the e-device off him and used her fingertips to scrawl a massive X.

Eddie grimaced. "It's supposed to be your name."

"It's bullshit. I don't have to put my name—who says?"

"Fair enough. Thank you." He thought he should make small talk as he handed over the small parcel. "Didn't see you last night?"

"No," Irina replied curtly. He waited for more detail, but none was forthcoming.

"Everything all right?" Eddie regretted asking but couldn't stop himself.

Irina looked at him. "What the fuck has it got to do with you?"

Eddie's gadget buzzed, rattling in his hand. "Anyway, must get on."

They parted, Irina unlocking and disappearing behind the pub door, Eddie into his van. He heard the door being locked again.

Eddie sat in his seat for a moment. Placed his hand over his heart. It was going like the clappers.

He started the van and went to his next delivery.

Ninety-three to go.

CHAPTER FIVE

How about we start again from the beginning?"

Detective Constable Harry Ward understood that Deakins didn't like him. He was trying to find a way to change that, but the bearded, bulky farmer standing a few feet away in the next field, across several strips of barbed wire and hedging, was not giving an inch. In fact, he seemed to be very much enjoying sticking to his infuriating guns.

"Which beginning is that then?" smirked Deakins. "The beginning of all these shenanigans? The beginning back before I was even here? Or the beginning of all existence?"

Harry was also beginning to understand, as the coastal air whipped around him, that he had been stitched up. Again.

"Oy, Westlife! One for you, your part of the county!" the duty officer had called cheerily as he walked into work earlier that morning. Harry knew the duty officer understood how much Harry hated the nickname. It had stuck ever since they'd been introduced on Harry's first day and the duty officer had leaned back, unimpressed, and said, "Bloody hell, you just stepped out of a boy band?" Fourteen months later, and he was heartily sick of being sent on fool's errands, where a detective was not even required. Was this the best use of resources or time when the force was so strapped for both? Harry would fume to himself as he drove.

This was not Harry's first trip out here. As he got out of the car this morning, he'd heard Deakins shout, "You again, is it?" with great amusement.

Harry Ward was very much over being the source of other people's amusement.

He adopted what he hoped was the calm tone of a patient parent negotiating with a particularly stroppy toddler and smiled beneficently at Deakins. "Mr. Deakins—"

"Nothing you say to me will make a difference, boy! Cos this goes back too far. We got over a century of this to put right, and how would I look to people round here if I was the one who surrendered?"

What? Why is this already getting out of my control? What are we even talking about? Harry felt that any conversation with Deakins quickly became a slippery eel desperately writhing out of Harry's hands. He tried to keep a grasp on it.

"It's not a question of surrender—"

"That's exactly what it is! Surrendering my family's rights, what we can do on our land, to you and them—"

Patient parent. "Let's just take any emotion out of this—"

Nope, that just riled Deakins up even more. He went puce, as if Harry had insulted his mother. "Emotion is all I have! The emotional bond of my family to this place. Look at it. Go on. Go on! Look!"

Deakins pointed insistently. Harry looked, just as he had many times before. It was an extraordinary vista. The patchwork of fields sloping gently down to the shingle beach below. Sea cabbage dotting the foreshore. And the clear turquoise horizon of the English Channel beyond, rippling with the breeze this morning. The sun was shining. The sky and water were partners in blue. Harry could see fishermen trying their luck for mackerel, toddlers squealing and running, driftwood sticks being thrown for dogs. An elderly couple walking arm in arm.

"I'm here to talk about the fire," said Harry.

"Told you all: it weren't me," said Deakins.

"I didn't say it was you," responded Harry, as calm, neutral and non-confrontational as he could manage.

"It's what you think, though, isn't it?" Deakins could not wipe that shit-eating smile off his weatherbeaten, stubbled face, as if he'd provoked this fight for something to do. "Always something you're trying to get me on, you and them. Ooh, take down that fencing, remove the barbed wire, can't have your tractor there, don't do no digging and stop moving animals across that land. Trying to cook up an excuse, aren't you?"

"An excuse for what, Mr. Deakins?"

Deakins's bushy eyebrows rose and his face contorted, his mouth coming into a comic-book "o" shape as if he'd been told a particularly good joke. "Don't pretend you don't know! You rush out here on any tiny little thing, same this time as the last."

All right, Harry had reached his tolerance level for Deakins's bullshit. "No. Last time we spoke, you'd been haranguing walkers who had the right to access across your land."

"I don't remember that," huffed Deakins defensively.

"Well, I do, because you threatened to shoot them, and they believed you. That's why I came out."

"No one takes a joke anymore, do they? Bloody woke!" Deakins beamed, before adding after a moment's consideration, "I would shoot 'em, though. That'd learn 'em!"

Harry wondered if he was fast becoming one of the few people Deakins ever interacted with. When Deakins was getting lonely and craved company, did he cause a bit of trouble, knowing it would result in an official visitor? Harry persisted with his task.

"A large fire was set, sometime last night, on the field adjoining your neighbor's land. *Your* field. The smoke and flames caused a lot of concern. Your neighbor's very upset. Says you're trying to annoy him."

"Lives his life upset," said Deakins. "Cos he thinks it might get him something. But it won't. Hasn't got 'em anything for two hundred years and won't get 'em anything now."

"So you have no knowledge of how it started?"

"Oh, I can tell you how it started!" said Deakins, leaning forward conspiratorially. "Someone got a load of stuff, piled it all together and set a match to it. Or . . ." He left a moment for dramatic effect: "aliens."

He leaned back, grinning at Harry.

Harry had been around people like Deakins all his life. Harry's father knew Deakins's father. The family had a reputation. Best left alone. Because they were nutters.

"Thanks for that," said Harry.

"Don't know who, and you can't prove it was me. Anyone can get in that field. It's probably him. Because it suits him, doesn't it, Mr. StickUpHisArse?" Deakins was peering at Harry now. "Hold up. You're Ward, right? Joseph Ward's lad?"

Harry sighed. The endless games. "I am, yes."

Deakins's eyes sparkled in mockery. "Bloody hell. You got one more brain cell than the rest of your family, then."

That was enough for Harry now. "No fires! If you remember anything about the fire, contact me. And if you threaten your neighbor again, we'll take further action."

Deakins grinned and said, "No need to get worked up, boy. Let's just take any emotion out of this."

Harry would've liked to punch Deakins then, but his phone had begun buzzing. He looked at the screen: DS Bridge. His new boss. "Thank you, Mr. Deakins," he said tersely. "I have to take this. I'll look at the site of the fire on my way out."

Harry felt the eyes of the unmoving Deakins on his back as he walked away.

Nicola Bridge was straight to the point. "Can you meet me in Fleetcombe?"

Harry was approaching the remnants of the fire, looking at them, realizing his mind wasn't fully on the call. "Um, probably. D'you mean now?"

He instantly regretted every word that came out in response. There was a frosty silence from his new boss.

"Yes. I do mean now. Where are you?"

"At the Deakins farm. It's about three miles east, just off the coast road."

"We have a suspicious death."

"Wow."

Harry would think about these words for many years to come. When he was told of a murder, he said "wow." *Why did I say "wow"?*

He knew why he said wow. Since joining the police, the work he had been given had been mundane, low level. There was not a lot of crime in West Dorset. This was a biggie. And, for a split second, Harry was not thinking of the victim, he was thinking of himself.

Finally, something to get my teeth into.

He would regret that thought and word for a long time. If only he hadn't said "wow." Maybe she hadn't heard.

"Did you just say 'wow'?" Nicola's tone was incredulous.

"No," lied Harry. "It's very windy here."

"Body was found on the A35. I've sent you details, and a dropped pin. Meet me there in fifteen."

"Copy that."

Don't say "copy that." Not on the phone. Just say yes.

Harry had not had much to do with Nicola Bridge since her arrival.

He was intimidated by her. She was experienced, with a ferocious reputation. *She'll have you for breakfast, Westlife.* She had made her reputation dealing with organized crime. No one really understood why she was joining the soon-to-be Three Counties Police. *Either she's had enough, or she's in disgrace*, went the gossip. *This is where careers come to die*, grinned one old-timer.

The call ended. Harry checked his emails on his phone. Nothing yet: the signal was weak out here. As he waited, he stopped by the remains of the fire. It had been large, constructed. Lots of damp wood, thought Harry. Some plastic fertilizer bags in there, which would've created nice black smoke. It was very deliberate.

He poked around: mostly ash. He'd done his diligence. This had been a fool's errand, and now he had a proper one. The email downloaded. Harry looked at the set of the images taken on a darkened A35. He took a second to process what he was seeing.

Wow.

CHAPTER SIX

Unprepared.

The word rattled around Nicola's head as she drove into the village of Fleetcombe. The word bounced around her mind, all but blocking out the newsreader burbling on the car radio.

The word that would not shift had begun as self-excoriation: scolding herself after opening the boot of her car, having finished for now at the crime scene. She had looked round the car boot for the bulky bag she kept there, containing a couple of changes of clothes for exactly times like these. The big bag which always sat next to the box with walking boots, wellingtons, black shoes and battered trainers inside.

Both were missing. She had not replaced them after the move, when the car had been emptied and piled high with household objects.

Rookie error, she told herself.

Unprepared.

She had not met her own standards. This bounced around her psyche as she drove, slowly metastasizing from self-directed disappointment—*absolute basic procedure; how many years have you had those things in there?*—to the larger professional doubts that had begun to linger as she went about her new job.

Things she had not been told before she signed her contract: the force she thought she was joining—Wessex Police—was suddenly about to become one third of a new force, Three Counties Police, covering *all* of Dorset, Devon and Cornwall. This, she was told three days after signing, was the result of a "strategic review" and nothing whatsoever to do with Wessex's chief constable leaving due to alleged improprieties and a catastrophic budget shortfall. Oh, also, Nicola would only get half the number of staff she had been expecting. Oh, *plus*, had they also mentioned that the swanky new HQ, three years behind completion and £15 million over budget, wouldn't be ready for another two years minimum. So for now, she and her two other CID officers would be stationed in a disused bank building on Bredy High Street, next door to the run-down local police station. High ceilings, big spaces, no heating. *Just temporary*, she'd been assured on her first day as she looked round, stunned.

Unprepared.

Her call with DC Harry Ward hadn't helped. She could've sworn he said "wow" when she told him it was a suspicious death. She'd struggle to think of a less appropriate response. And he'd tried to cover it up by blaming the wind. This case was going to need thoughtful, precise handling, not puppyish enthusiasm.

Unprepared.

The placing of deer antlers on the head of a dead body was occupying the majority of her mental bandwidth. Antlers. Why place antlers on a dead body? *A warning? A message? A joke? (Some joke.)* She worried what it meant, and couldn't help but go to the worst-case scenario (the job had taught her, from brutal experience, always to run the worst-case scenario): serial killer in the offing. This crime did not present as an unplanned explosion of violence or a crime of passion. Rather, the ritualistic nature of the display spoke of premeditation. The body had not been accidentally deposited: it had been left, meant to be found, in the middle of a main road. There was a brazen, fearless aspect to it which Nicola found extremely unsettling.

I do not want this. Now is not the right time.

She had returned here from her beloved Liverpool after half a lifetime away to get life back on track. This would not help.

Nicola gave herself a talking-to: *don't make this about you.*

Unprepared.

As Harry got out of his car in the White Hart car park, Nicola looked at him properly for the first time. Ten years separated them, Harry still luxuriating in his late twenties. She'd picked up that his work nickname was Westlife, which seemed to say as much about his colleagues as it did about him. At least be up to date and call him One Direction, she thought, especially with that name.

She knew he went to the gym every morning before work, because he would shove the gym bag under his desk on arrival and slurp down a mud-colored protein shake as breakfast. He was, admittedly, toned. He was also, admittedly, good-looking. Well styled and coiffed. More pertinently, however, he was inexperienced in the job: a recent recruit from the Professional Admission scheme, designed to bring in graduates with life experience of other industries. When Nicola realized, a week or two after her arrival, that he had been one of those described to her as an experienced detective, she had ground her teeth in annoyance.

If the job wasn't as described in the brochure, then Harry Ward was the poster boy for that deception, perpetuated by those who had enticed her here.

"I can't babysit you," Nicola said to Harry by way of greeting.

Ouch. Hello to you, too, thought Harry.

"I don't have time, and I don't have the headspace, not with a murder like this."

"Understood," said Harry.

She said "murder," thought Harry. His first murder. He nodded respectfully to Nicola, trying not to show any enthusiasm. Trying to prove he was a serious human being, as his heart raced with a burst of excitement. Was it callous to be excited? Was it inhumane to feel motivated by the prospect of being able to do what he'd joined the service for?

He wasn't sure. He hoped not.

"I'm here to work. I'm here to learn from you," he said.

It felt necessary to be so stark. He worried she had already taken against him, and he wasn't sure why. From a misplaced word on the phone? Maybe she didn't realize how intimidating she was.

"I'll do whatever's needed. I'm not an idiot. I'm not gonna say or do anything stupid."

She looked at him, her eyes piercing into his soul. "Did you say 'wow' when I told you there'd been a suspicious death?"

Harry thought about his answer for half a second. "No."

She persisted. "Seriously. Did you say 'wow'?"

"No!"

She took another look, then nodded. "Ever done a death knock?" she asked him.

Harry shook his head.

"Only way is the hardest way: simple, clear and direct. It'll feel callous, but it's worse if they come away confused, or not understanding. Use short, factual sentences. Show empathy, but don't get caught in their emotion. Get in, deliver the information, make sure they understand the next steps and the support on offer."

Harry was confused. "Are you saying I have to deliver the news?"

Nicola looked irritable. "No! I'm just—I'm just telling you how it's done. For when you have to do it. You said you wanted to learn!"

You said you didn't have time to babysit me, Harry thought, but didn't say. He could see she was already exhausted and realized she had probably been up all night. And her explanation of how to deliver bad news was the first bit of professional mentoring he'd had in months. Water for a thirsty man. He kept quiet as she carried on.

"I need you to watch for reactions. Keep an eye out for anything relevant."

"How many times have you done something like this?"

She took a moment before responding. "I stopped counting."

Her single phrase laid a blanket over that whole conversation. He realized she was dreading it. After a second, Harry spoke again.

"Can I ask . . . why antlers? Why leave him in the road?"

"That's what we have to find out." She handed him a piece of paper with a phone number and a name on it. It was clear she expected him to make the initial calls, asking the next of kin to meet.

He knew she knew he did not relish doing this. She had set him a tiny test and he was determined to pass.

He felt her watching him as he dialed.

CHAPTER SEVEN

Blood was always stubborn.

Patricia removed the king-size sheet from the drum of the washing machine. The bloodstain was still there. She had tried cold water, leaving it soaking while she went for her morning constitutional over the cliffs, but it had not shifted. She glanced at the clock, concerned that her list of tasks did not fit into the time she had available. While she was out walking, her next guests had decided, at short notice, to ask for an early check-in. She always wanted to do all she could to help her guests. Of course she did. That was the person she was: helpful and obliging wherever possible. Plus, it helped the rating.

She looked at the sheet: it would have to do. She would hang it out to dry, regardless. As she stepped out of the side door and pegged it on the line in the Fleetcombe sunshine, Patricia mused that more and more people wanted early check-in now, despite the fact that check-in and check-out times were clearly marked on the property profile. Patricia thought that these requests were mostly down to Americans. Patricia had only been to America once, to New York. That had proven enough: she had sat, morbidly fascinated, listening to Americans order their food in restaurants. Every single person wanted something changed from the menu, something left out, something additional, something on the side. Some people didn't even want to eat it in the restaurant, despite it being a restaurant. This, Patricia felt, had now become the norm, everywhere. No rule was set, no policy was unquestioned anymore. Everything that once was rigid had become flexible. Bespoke was standard. But if everything is moveable, how does anyone know where they stand? That's what she found confusing.

Throughout her life, Patricia had always prided herself on striving to keep up with the world. But this was not without problems. Take this whole venture. She had thought that renting out her house on Airbnb was the perfect early retirement plan. A guaranteed income, a way of extracting money from a property that was now too big for her. She had divided the detached thatched cottage into two, living in one half and renting out the other. All done through the apps. Her impressive career in data management had kept her interested in evolving methods of corralling and communicating information. The digital advance had excited her. She enjoyed technology: her phone was always up to date, she was an early adopter, a silver surfer. Her friends often asked her which apps they should have and how to use them, and Patricia obliged happily. She loved to be helpful: she loved sharing her understanding of technology and data. Data was reliable: a fact. One could not always say the same about people.

By way of illustration, as she walked round the front to check for weeds in the garden, she saw Eddie's van about to pass by. She raised a hand in greeting and walked over as Eddie pulled the van up, his window sliding down.

"How are you feeling?" Patricia asked Eddie, carefully.

Eddie seemed both surprised and relieved by her question. "Little bit rough, if I'm honest. You?" The question seemed cagey.

"Oh, just tired. Quite a night."

"Yeah."

Patricia noticed Eddie's expression shift, his tone unsure. "I'm glad to have seen you. I was rather worried when I left you."

She watched Eddie brush that off with a fake smile. "You never have to worry about me, Pat."

Patricia smiled back. "Hope it's not too long a day ahead."

"You know what they say: no rest for the wicker!" said Eddie, indulging his love of weak puns. "Must get on! I'll see you around!"

With that, the window slid closed and Patricia watched Eddie and his van glide off to the next delivery.

Eddie was the only person she let call her Pat without picking him up on it. She didn't like the abbreviation, but it seemed less offensive in his mouth. There had been a moment, within the past six or seven years, where Patricia had wondered whether there might be a spark of romance between Eddie and herself. They were both of similar ages, early in their sixties, and unpartnered. Eddie had a divorce in his past (rarely referred to now) and Patricia had never got over the line with a marriage. But the spark between them had never crystallized further, and she had not had the courage to push it. She told herself she was happy with how things stood.

He had looked exhausted. She herself was a little weary, after an unanticipated stint behind the bar last night. Still, she had to push on and get the house ready. When she considered becoming a host, she hadn't accounted for the fact that the app meant people could reach you day or night. To complain about bedbugs and demand instant fumigation, or tell you of a breakage of something that held fond memories, to alter a set-in-stone arrival time, to say they'd lost keys or a cupboard had fallen off the wall, or ask why were there no anti-allergy pillows or air conditioning (*this is Dorset, after all*), or heaters, or olive oil and, yes, the shower door had just shattered despite the fact that no one had touched it, certainly one of their teenage twins hadn't thrown the other into it and it was merely coincidence that they were both now in A&E with glass cuts to their feet and hands.

She had anticipated—*hoped*—this arrangement would be better than carrying on working. It turned out that running the property was *the same* as working. Occasionally she wondered if removing herself from the company, and from something she was recognized as being good at (though she noted the nuanced difference between being *recognized* as exceptional and being *appreciated* for it—another reason to make the change), had been the right decision. But then she reminded herself that she was her own boss now and could go cliff walking anytime she liked and had more freedom than in all of her previous life.

She realized her tiredness was affecting her mood. She also thought that she was perhaps a little bit down, a little bit *wounded*, that the last guests in had recently marked her down a star for communication. She hadn't felt that was fair, and it affected her rating. People affecting data.

Her phone was ringing. She pulled it out of her pocket, hoping it was not the guests letting her know they were arriving even earlier and could she accommodate that? No. It was a call. She didn't really want a call right now: it was not a convenient time. Except: number withheld. She weighed up whether to answer. Sometimes the withheld numbers were important and official; other times they were scam calls. She got too many of those. She answered anyway, ready to tell them she knew what they were up to.

Patricia Tiernan listened to the voice on the other end of the phone. It belonged to a DC Harry Ward. When he'd finished speaking, she told him she'd prefer if they didn't meet at her property as she had paying guests arriving. She would come to the White Hart pub.

Patricia Tiernan hung up.

She stood very, very still in her front garden in the autumn sunshine for a long time.

The sheet fluttered in the breeze.

CHAPTER EIGHT

From her vantage point at the top of the covered slide, the girl had watched the woman wait in the parked car, perhaps doing some work. That was the sort of thing adults did. That, or stuff on their phones.

A while later, she watched as the woman got out and met a man who had arrived in another car. The two of them talked and looked serious. She decided they looked like police officers, but without uniforms. She had seen enough TV to know the difference between these and police in uniforms. CID. She had wondered if this might happen. It was sooner than she'd thought.

She looked down from her perch, surveying the playground. It was quiet this morning. Two younger children—maybe four or five, might be brothers, might be friends—on the swings, with a man she thought must be their grandad who was beaming and making "whooo!" sounds with every push. She liked how pleased he was. She wished she had a grandad like that. Hers was long gone, and he'd never pushed her on the swings anyway.

On the other side of the playground a young couple was cooing over a toddler who looked about two. The kid was jammed on a little metal rocking-horse thing that moved backward and forward. That section of the playground didn't interest her anymore: it was for more babyish children. At nine years and three months, she preferred the more grown-up bits. She watched the parents either side of the laughing, squealing two-year-old being rocked gently back and forth. The parents were smiling and holding their arms out anxiously, as if anticipating that the child would fall at any second. They looked delighted and terrified at the same time. She saw that a lot here. She did not remember people ever holding out their arms to catch her in the event of a fall.

The playground sat on the corner at the edge of a large field with a vantage over both main roads through the village. It had been improved about two years ago, with new swings, slides and static jeeps and horses, along with a huge rope climbing frame. Since then, she had gradually made the playground her second home, spending more and more time here. Her main home wasn't a good place to be. It was an uncertain place, and it felt unsafe. She felt safer at the top of this slide, at the back of the playground, watching other people play and the world go by. She didn't have to listen to the noises coming through the wall from her mum and her boyfriend. She didn't have to smell the smells of smoke and vape and vodka. She didn't get told off for feeding herself here. She wasn't told she was in the way. She didn't feel people resented her being there.

The slide was her best place. The little sheltered roof over the top of the slide meant that not only was she less visible but that if it rained or was windy she could avoid the worst of it. The rope frame was her second favorite. She could get right to the top and lodge herself there, with a great view of the world, but she was very noticeable. Which was fine for a little while, but not for an extended stay. She preferred not being noticed. It was safer.

Lately, she spent the bulk of her days here. Everyone assumed she was part of someone else's family. If anyone questioned her, or suspected that actually she was here alone and asked after her well-being, she would tell them that her mum had just gone to the shop and would be back soon. She liked it when people asked, and she always felt a pang of disappointment when they believed the lie so easily. Most people came and went quickly. Twenty minutes or half an hour. An hour, tops. She wasn't their concern.

Sometimes she came here at night. The playground was different then. Different people, different things going on. Houses lit up, curtains left undrawn, lives exposed. She watched people going in and out of the pub. Late at night, when the pub had closed, the street outside the pub would sometimes get noisy. Sometimes scary. She would watch hidden in the dark, eyes staring out from the sheltered seat at the top of the slide.

She watched as the two people who might be police officers knocked at the door of the pub. The woman called Irina came to the door and let them in. Shortly after, the old woman from up the road walked toward the same door and let herself in with a key.

After this, nothing. The village was calm in the Wednesday-morning sunshine. She wished it was dark and the pub curtains were undrawn. She would like to be able to see inside.

She wondered if the police would come over and ask her what she had seen. She wondered what she would say if she was asked. She had learned to her cost that even when you do tell the truth grown-ups don't necessarily like to hear it. The truth can make people unhappy. She didn't know why this was, she only knew from experience that it was true. Her grandmother used to say, *Least said, soonest mended.*

She would say the least, and it would be mended soonest.

She tried not to think about the horrors of the night before.

CHAPTER NINE

Less than fourteen hours previously, several hours before he was found dead, Jim Tiernan looked around the White Hart pub—his pub, the pub he ran; my God, how was it allowed that he, of all people, was able to run a pub, what was the world coming to, ha ha ha—and concluded that he would never understand this game.

Tonight, the place felt—what was the word?—*rambunctious*. It was a night when, inexplicably, all his regulars had decided to get on it. Something was in the ether. It wasn't like the place was rammed, but the energy was crackling, the chat and laughter and noise were increasing. Jim knew how it would go. The lines between social groups would soon disappear, people would start joining each other's tables, moving about the pub. Packets of ridged crisps and chili nuts would supplement the pints and chasers; olives with lemon and garlic, and salted, dried broad beans would be decanted from their large jars (Jim made good money on the stuff in jars). Oh, here we go: Eddie had just broached the idea of a pickled egg. Always a signifier! If pickled eggs were being taken, tonight could get rowdy.

Jim watched as Eddie dropped the pickled egg into a bag of ready salted crisps, as others grimaced. Eddie looked three sheets to the wind already. Egg into the ready salted—old-school move. No, wait, not "ready salted," he thought to himself, not anymore, that phrase betrayed his age. Harkening back to being a teeny child, in Mile End, and crisps that had no salt. You got a blue sachet in the bag, which you fished out, opened and decided how much to add to the crisps. Un-ready salted. Hence the name of the others. Nowadays, people asked for sea salt, often Cornish, maybe with cider vinegar, or with black peppercorns. Everything had an added descriptor; nothing was just itself. And you definitely didn't get to choose how much salt. Salt was ubiquitous. Even in the puddings. His most popular dessert was a simple vanilla ice cream and a jug of salted caramel sauce. Jim pondered to himself that he should've got in on salt, years ago. Those salt makers must be making a mint. Salted mint, would that work?

Keep your mind on the job, Jimbo. He worked the arm of the pump elegantly as he kept his eye on the entirety of the bar. What was the order he was in the middle of? Two IPAs, one Stella, one glass of red, one G&T. Let the IPAs settle before a final top-up (people round here did not appreciate heads on their pints and would accuse you of trying to short-change them if the foam took up too much of the glass).

He glanced to the side of the bar, where Deakins was sitting, watching. The definition of a pub loner. Whenever he came, he brought a battered banjo, kept it at his side. Occasionally he'd grab it and pick at it, as if to send out the signal *yes, I've got a banjo; yes, I can play it* and put it down again, returning to his pint, watching others. Smiling, but not, Jim thought, in a particularly happy way. Others gave Deakins a wide berth. There were many reasons why. Not least, local history.

There was the kid, Frankie, from the hairdressers'. Jim absent-mindedly stroked the back of his head, feeling the length. He needed a haircut, badly. He'd been told that earlier today. He grinned at the memory. Tomorrow morning, bright and early, he would be in Frankie's chair. As he was looking over, Frankie looked up and saw him watching, and smiled, slightly weakly, Jim thought. Jim smiled back and saw Frankie look anxiously at their watch. Waiting for someone. A date? They looked nervous. Jim wondered why.

Eddie had now consumed the pickled egg to both cheers and groans of horror. He caught Jim's eye and gave him a wink. Jim was relieved to see him happy. It wasn't always the case. Jim knew this because Eddie was a barstool confider. Eddie did not bear life lightly. He would order and install himself at the bar as if Jim were his therapist and the pint his admission: an invitation to lie on the therapist's couch and vent. He told Jim too much, about his work, about what he saw in other people's houses when they opened their doors to him, and also about his own life. Jim didn't want to know, but he was told anyway, and sometimes he lay awake thinking about what Eddie had told him.

Jim believed being a publican meant he provided a refuge: and the onus was on him to be an open ear, a receptive listener. Always sympathetic, never dismissive. People here thought that came to him naturally. It did not. He was not like that when the doors were locked. But for years now he had projected that persona during opening hours. It was a pretense, but his customers did not need to know. Nor would they care if they did know. Well, maybe if they knew about the events of today. That would undoubtedly exercise a few people.

As he looked around, Jim noticed a figure dumping a handbag at a table in the far corner. His sister, Patricia.

Oh God, here she came. Polite smile, lodged onto a stool to order.

"Slimline tonic, please, James."

Who came to the pub for a tonic but no gin?

As he got it for her she looked around and said, "Lively tonight." Then: "No Irina?"

Jim felt himself tense. *What the fuck has it got to do with you?*

"No. She's out tonight," he said. Don't get drawn in, he thought. Irina will be back. Wouldn't she?

Sure about that, Jimbo?

Patricia stared at him with an expression in her eyes that he couldn't quite place. Like she was boring down into his soul.

"Busy day?" she asked.

"Middling," he replied. "You?"

She said nothing and retreated to her corner. He did not need this tonight.

He heard their mother's voice in his head. *Be nice to your sister. She has your back. She will always have your back.*

What if I don't want her to have my back? he thought. What if my back is none of her business anymore?

He felt hemmed in.

He dealt with a flurry of drink orders, which took his mind off Patricia. As the activity around the bar quietened, a small figure heaved herself up onto one of the bar stools.

"Pint of beer, please, mate. Good old pint of beer."

The girl, who Jim knew to be little more than nine years old, maybe ten at a push, grinned at him.

Jim looked at her. He wanted to be disapproving, but he couldn't.

"Can I see some ID, miss?"

"There you go," she said, sliding a child's library card across the counter.

Jim picked it up, playing along. He could feel Patricia still staring. He would show her. See. He was happy and warm and playful and *liked.*

"All seems to be in order," he said, sliding the card back.

"Yes," said the girl. "People say how young I look for my age."

Jim looked at her, serious now. He knew the trouble she had at home. "Is it bad tonight?"

The girl nodded.

"I can't have you in the bar unaccompanied, I'm afraid."

"I know."

"Is there someone I can call?"

The girl shook her head. "No."

"Want me to take you back?"

She looked at him. "Would you do that?"

"Course. We have a deal, right?"

The girl nodded but looked unsure. "I don't want you to get in trouble."

"Look at this face. How could this face ever be in trouble?" The girl grinned.

"Don't you need to serve people drinks?"

"Gimme five minutes. But would you mind waiting outside?"

"I'll be on the playground."

"Righto."

The girl slipped down off the barstool and headed to the door.

Jim looked round the pub. Who could he ask to mind the shop? He couldn't trust Eddie, Frankie looked anxious, and Deakins . . . well, just *no*. Jim took a deep breath and approached his sister, and her slimline tonic.

"Could you mind the bar for a moment?" She had done it many times before. He trusted her with the money and she wouldn't take any nonsense. Most people in here knew her.

"Why, what're you doing?" asked Patricia.

She could never make it easy, could she? She could never just say: sure! Always wanted to know reasons, always assumed he was doing something stupid, or selfish. She still treated him like the younger child, and it drove him mad.

"I'm checking that little girl gets home safe," he told her.

Patricia raised a judgmental eyebrow. "Are you? Really?" she said.

"Yes!" he responded defensively. "I want to check everything's OK at home."

"Oh, I bet you do," said Patricia in a tone that made Jim want to slap her.

Calm, Jimbo. Calm.

"Will you do it, or not?" He had reached the limit of his patience with his sister now. Whatever she was hinting at, he didn't have time for it.

"How long will you be?"

"As long as it takes!" Dear God, this was taking so long.

Patricia shook her head at him. He felt there was something she wanted to say but was biting her tongue, for now. He would probably hear about it tomorrow. In full. But he was grateful to see her walk past him and take up a position at the bar, brandishing a welcoming smile. That ability to put on a facade ran in the family.

There was the sound of a banjo from the corner. Deakins. Jim groaned inwardly. He didn't want any trouble, where someone asked Deakins to stop, or to play a request, and Deakins took offense and—well, it would all kick off. Except . . . a couple of people were cheering, encouraging voices getting louder. Deakins paid no attention, the intensity of his focus solely on his banjo. And Jim, never the banjo's most fervent admirer, had to admit to himself it added something: an atmosphere, a life, a sense of party. The evening was becoming a blast.

And just for a second, Jim Tiernan felt a surge of pride. He had made a success here. It had been unlikely, at the start. He had needed an escape and had found one. He had evaded his past. He didn't love his present, but it was better than the alternative. From here he could plot a way forward, if he could keep those bastards at the brewery at bay.

In the microsecond that passed, he thought once again about how much he knew of this village and its inhabitants. He knew all these people by name, he knew their lives and their lies, their secrets and delights, their joys and their shame, their finances and their addictions. He knew who would order what, often before they did (he would sometimes find himself clenching his teeth as regulars dithered, looking across the range of drinks before settling on the same order they made every time). He knew their everything. His pub was a refuge for all: the gregarious and the loners, the socialites and the weirdos, the enemies and the lovers. It was a community within a community. A haven.

As he was heading toward the door thinking this, it opened and a burly, bald-headed man in his late thirties walked in.

Jim felt his body go into fight-or-flight mode. A defense mechanism, in response to the surge of fear that had smacked him hard in the gut.

But the man walked straight past without looking at him and headed for the table where Frankie was sitting.

Time had slowed down for Jim. He couldn't help but look back at his sister, at the bar. Her head angled, like a dog quizzically assessing what was happening. Jim turned back to see the man at Frankie's table look over. He looked Jim Tiernan directly in the eyes.

The man tapped the face of his watch, while looking at Jim.

Tap tap.

Time's up.

CHAPTER TEN

Fourteen hours later, as she looked round the silent White Hart pub, Nicola was assailed by a sudden memory: of being in this bar before, many years ago, on a disastrous date.

It felt smaller than she remembered, maybe because that night she had wanted it to swallow her up, like a tiny figure in a big sea. The ceilings seemed lower now—had she got taller since then? That would be mad—and the wooden beams felt more imposing. The large slate tiles on the floor looked a recentish addition. She recalled a worn and beer-stained carpet back in the day, with the rest of the interior displaying an overreliance on Formica. These days it was a higgledy-piggledy, careworn, wood-and-slate-tile local pub with an open fireplace.

There were two women seated, apart from each other: Patricia Tiernan, who had wanted to meet here, and Irina Bortnick, who claimed to live in the pub. Nicola noted their body language—they did not seem close friends.

"I'm Detective Sergeant Nicola Bridge and this is Detective Constable Harry Ward. I'm afraid a body was discovered early this morning on the road near Wynstone."

Silence for a second. Both women stared at Nicola. She continued, "We believe it's the body of James Tiernan."

The silence stretched out.

Eventually Irina said, "How do you know it's him?"

"We've had a preliminary identification," replied Nicola.

"Was it a car accident?" asked Patricia.

"We're awaiting confirmation of the cause of death."

There was no screaming or keening. Neither woman sunk to her knees. They both sat there, silently. Patricia nodded, as if to herself, while staring into the middle distance. Irina wiped away a silent tear or three.

"I'm very sorry. Specially trained officers are on their way to support you. DC Ward and I are investigating the exact cause of death, and we'll need to speak to you both in due course. In the meantime, we do need someone to make a formal identification."

Irina looked to Patricia, who stood up briskly, as if to disguise her pain.

"I'm the next of kin. Where are you parked?"

Nicola took Patricia, while Harry stayed with Irina.

Patricia did not speak on the journey. Nicola would check every so often in the rearview mirror, but Patricia was completely still, staring out the window, her mind elsewhere.

At the hospital, where the body was being kept, the identification was swift, bloodless.

It was just the body now: five foot seven, slight and wiry, the antlers removed for forensic analysis. Nicola wasn't intending to tell Patricia any details surrounding that just yet.

"Do you recognize this person?" asked Nicola.

Patricia nodded. She leaned in slightly. Examining the dead body of her brother as if it were a lab specimen rather than a beloved.

"This is my younger brother, James."

"Thank you, Patricia. You have our condolences."

Patricia nodded.

She did not speak in the car all the way back, but the look on Patricia's face as she gazed out the window was stricken. Nicola knew from experience that there were moments when people's unspoken emotions changed the temperature of a space. Patricia's mood silently flooded the car. Bereft, broken.

As they turned into the car park, Patricia came back to the present moment, as if waking from a reverie.

"It wasn't suicide, was it?"

"We don't believe so. But we are treating his death as suspicious."

Nicola looked in the rearview mirror. Patricia was looking back, realizing the implication.

"You think someone killed him. Deliberately." Her eyes met Nicola's in the mirror. "Are you telling me Jim was murdered?"

"Was he in any difficulties you know of?" asked Nicola.

Patricia laughed, taking Nicola by surprise. "Was my brother in any difficulties? Only all his life. You'd be better off asking when *wasn't* he in any."

"Did he confide in you about anything, or anyone, recently? Any names we should be looking at?"

Patricia was quiet again, as if running through a rogues' gallery. "I'll have a think."

As she was readying to exit the car, Patricia said, "Do I have to go back in and talk to Irina?"

"No. We can update her."

"I'd prefer that." She paused for a second. "Someone will have to tell the brewery. They'll want to know why the pub isn't open. They'll need to plan their business. I don't have to do that, do I?"

Nicola recognized this moment, when the shock of grief made a relative obsess about practical minutiae. "No. We'll make sure that happens," she confirmed.

They got out of the car, and Patricia stood there for a moment. It felt to Nicola like Patricia was slowly sinking with the weight of it all. She looked for all the world like a lost and bewildered little girl.

"We were all in there, last night. I was behind the bar."

There was a silence. And then she added, plaintively, "He was my little brother. And I didn't save him."

CHAPTER ELEVEN

Harry did not want to fail the first solo task set for him by DS Nicola Bridge. She had told him to take a statement from Jim Tiernan's partner, Irina.

You know how to do this, you've done it plenty of times before, it's no big deal. Take notes, ask the simple questions, pay attention, don't mess up.

He sat with Irina by the window in the silent pub. He had made them both tea. Irina vaped, staring out.

When he handed over the mug, he said, "So you're from Ukraine, originally?"

Irina didn't look back from the window. "He asked me to marry him once, you know. On holiday. He was drunk. I told him he had to ask when he was sober." She paused, considering, maybe even reassessing a memory. "He never did. I think he thought I would say no. That because I asked him to do it sober, it was no. But it wasn't."

She looked plaintively at Harry. He felt she was regretting the response she'd once made to Jim.

"You married?" asked Irina, breathing out vape.

"No," said Harry.

"Girlfriend? Boyfriend?"

"Oh, er . . ." Harry hesitated, unsure how to respond. Irina picked up on it.

"You ask me questions about myself. I can't ask anything about you?"

"Single. Split up with my girlfriend a few months back," relented Harry, though inside he felt panicky as he wondered what Nicola would say if she knew he'd revealed that. It was a good thing, right? It helped to connect with someone, at a difficult time. Or was it bad that he was revealing personal information to a possible suspect? Was she a suspect? His mind roiled for a moment, before he brought it back under control. *Everything is fine. Keep going.* "Did Jim have a phone?"

Irina nodded, "Old one. Nokia, I think. He never used it. He said he didn't need modern tech in an old pub. It drove me crazy. Was always just left on the counter, or by the bed."

Harry nodded and noted. "When did you last see Jim?"

Irina's face changed. It hardened. She saw what he was doing. Not listening, but questioning.

"Yesterday afternoon."

Harry nodded, wrote that down. "Not last night?"

Irina paused before speaking, as if weighing him up.

"I was out." Her eyes had a sparkle of defiance in them, like she was daring him to ask more.

"Anywhere nice?"

"Driving."

"Right. Where did you drive to?"

"In the Vale, round and about. Sometimes I drive. Put my music on, drive for hours."

The Vale was a sparsely populated bowl of fields and farms some twenty miles wide, inland from Fleetcombe. It was indexed by crisscrossing single-track lanes. You could get lost there easily, blinded by identical high-hedgerowed lanes and narrowing tracks.

It was also, thought Harry, somewhere you could go to get *deliberately* lost. Or say you were.

"Anyone with you?"

"No."

"Anyone see you?"

Shrug. "Don't think so."

"What time did you go for this drive?"

"Half five, six."

"OK. And what time did you get back?"

"This morning."

Harry's pen paused over his book.

She noticed it, tried to fill the space—the first time she'd done that in all the time they'd been talking. "I slept in the car."

Harry checked his notes, looked at her. Left a bit of a gap. Let her watch him.

"Was there any reason for that?"

She shrugged. "I didn't want to come back. It's not so bad. Find a lay-by. Watch the stars. Have music on. Fall asleep."

"Long time to be out."

"Yeah."

She wasn't giving any more detail. He persisted.

"Did you stop anywhere to eat or drink or use the loo?"

"Yeah, sure."

"Which?"

"I had food and drink in the car. I pissed in some hedgerow down one of the lanes. Don't ask me which one."

Harry kept her gaze. "Did you have your phone with you?"

"Sure. But it died. Didn't have a charger with me."

"Can I ask why you didn't come back here last night?"

Harry watched Irina choose her words carefully. "Sometimes, Jim can be a dick."

She put down the vape and said, "I know. No alibi, right?" She stared at Harry evenly. "You think I killed him?"

Harry wasn't uncomfortable meeting that gaze. He noted that her defiance levels had risen. She was showing him who she was.

"We can't eliminate you from inquiries until we have corroboration on your whereabouts."

She stared out of the window. "So you don't eliminate me. What can I do?"

Harry felt that wasn't quite the declaration of innocence he might have expected.

The upstairs of the White Hart pub was a mess. It had not seen love for a long time, thought Nicola as she ascended the stairs. She had arrived back at the pub, having escorted Patricia Tiernan home, informing Harry that SOCO were on their way: she had decreed the pub should be treated as a crime scene for now, given it was where Jim Tiernan had last been seen.

While Harry kept Irina downstairs, she took a look round, kitted out in forensic shoe coverings and gloves. The building was old and cold; it smelled of damp, must and beer. Lovely. Nicola noted cobwebs above her, off the beams. The wooden stairs creaked, and worn patches of carpet adorned the middle of each step.

On the darkened landing there were a number of doors open. A bathroom with a smell of moldy shower curtain. Two rooms with boxes and packing crates inside, along with three suitcases, two of which were open. There were beds in both rooms, unused, no duvets or pillows on top, just the bare, exposed mattresses.

At the far end was the master bedroom. A door was open off to the left: an en suite bathroom. Built-in wardrobes. A big double bed in the middle of the room. Duvet scrunched up, unmade, on one half of the bed. Couple of pillows on the floor.

Men's clothes were discarded by the left-hand side of the bed. A knackered old mobile phone was on the bedside table, switched off. On the other side of the bed was a bottle of vodka. A drawer open with bras and knickers spilling out. There was a dressing table with a mirror on that side of the room. It was stacked with makeup and a bottle of scent marked "Pour Femme." Nicola clocked lipstick-marked tissues in the bin.

Irina had warned Nicola "we're not tidy people." Nicola would concur. But if there had been a struggle up here, or anywhere else in the pub, there were no obvious signs. No broken banisters, blood marks on doors or window frames, cracked or broken windowpanes, no scuffed-up carpets or rugs. No evidence of theft: Nicola had asked Irina what to expect in each room, and the contents matched Irina's overview. The cash safe had not been broken into; no one had absconded with last night's takings.

More to the point, there was no evidence of forced entry that Nicola could see on any of the doors or windows.

Had Jim Tiernan left of his own accord? Had he gone to meet someone, been killed and then left on the road? Murdered here by someone who had access, and then moved? Or had he let someone into the pub and been coerced into leaving against his will?

But the one question which kept thudding through Nicola's mind was: would Jim Tiernan's killer strike again?

CHAPTER TWELVE

Move fast, Nicola.

As she stood rattling off commands in the middle of the disused bank now housing a makeshift incident room, Nicola pushed against the wave of tiredness washing over her and resisted the overwhelming urge to yawn. *Not a good look.*

"Trace all transactions in the White Hart for that night. We need full details of, and statements from, everyone who was there. His sister says Jim was there till closing time, but he stepped out at one point. His partner, Irina, wasn't there; we need more intel on that next time we speak to her. Who was the last to leave? When was the last time anyone saw Jim? We have his phone and an old laptop he used for work—we'll need both analyzed. Also, I want information from all ANPR, all cameras, any domestic or doorbell cameras between the White Hart and where he was found dead. If we locate drivers, see if they have dashcams. Talk to the man who found him—let's be sure we can rule him out. Remind everyone you speak to that they must not speculate on social media, or off it."

"It's a lot of work," muttered Mel, harbinger of doom.

"Yes, it is," said Nicola, resisting the temptation to add *because someone's been murdered, dickhead.*

Nicola had not worked with Mel before. He was a skeletal figure with a bald pate and an energy that could charitably be described as dour. She did not see how he was going to be an asset and that made her even more angry than she already was.

"I need more than two officers, ma'am," Nicola had said on the phone to her boss earlier that morning.

"You're lucky to have that. Now, we need you to be the reassuring face of this, Nicola. Get a statement on video over to Corporate Comms so they can post on social." And with that, the DCI had considered the conversation shut.

Definitely not as shown in the brochure.

Nicola looked in the mirror of the ladies' loos, triaging her appearance with makeup. She was pale; she'd always tended toward pale, so tinted moisturizer. Dark bags under red eyes; eye drops might help a bit (or at least get rid of the bloodshot look). She had never thought of herself as vain. But she was representing the police, herself, and even the victim. She had to look like she was in control. She knew the killer would be watching. She needed to project *we're going to get you. You should be shitting yourself, mate.*

Face work done. She looked in the mirror—the best she could do with the weapons at her disposal.

She stood outside the back of the building, against an old stone wall. Harry was filming the statement on his latest-model phone, ready to be sent to Corporate Comms for review and issuing. They had been discussing where she should stand just a little too long when she snapped, "I really don't think it matters!" and Harry's expression had made her feel like she'd just kicked a puppy.

She added, “Let’s just get on with it,” to try and ameliorate the snappiness, but it just made it worse. She knew what was going on. The whole situation had exposed her inner emotional rawness. She was trying to disguise it, and failing. *Get through and rest, Nicola.* Reset. She was on the back foot, practically and emotionally. She hated it: she needed to be proactive and pushing. That was who she was.

Except, she asked herself as she waited for Harry to line up the shot, how do you know that? Who are you now, exactly? Who are you here, with all that’s happened? Why has this rattled you? Why are you so snappy?

She recited a standard form of words, familiar to her from experience. She had taken the decision to name Jim Tiernan. Better this was in the open, to stop rumors and falsehoods amassing online. The statement ended with reassuring words to the local community and a pledge that police presence would be increased in the short term.

When Harry stopped filming, he said, “Very good.”

“Thanks,” said Nicola.

“Want to do it again?” asked Harry, instantly regretting it.

“Why would I want to do it again?” said Nicola.

“I dunno.” Why couldn’t he find the right words around this new boss?

“Is it OK or not?!”

“Yes.”

“So send it on, then.”

She went back inside, as Harry winced. He knew he had a lot to prove to Nicola Bridge, and so far he was making a right mess of it.

Texts buzzing. First, from Mike. It said **SEXY POLICE LADY ON MY SOCIALS**.

Nicola smiled, scrolled a bit and found a gif of a blushing woman with her hand on her chest saying, "Who, me?" She clicked and sent it to him. Smiling, proud of her gif ability.

Mike put a heart reaction. Nicola stared at it.

Is this what you did with her?

A few seconds later, another message from Mike: **You OK tho?** and a raised eyebrow.

We're trying. We're both trying. This is what we said we'd do.

Nicola breathed slowly through her mouth for exactly a minute. Not really OK, no. Unprepared. Compromised, even. Angry, probably. She resented these feelings, but now was not the time to go wading through them, or what lay behind them. That would not move this investigation on.

Her phone text-buzzed again, this time her son, Ethan. First contact in about three days, despite living in the same house. **you scare the shit out of me where do I confess.**

She texted back: **EAT SOME VEGETABLES.** Reply: **have allergies.**

She knew that was the end of the exchange and didn't try to extend it with further witty comments. She had learned this the hard way when, in the midst of one argument about dirty washing on the floor of his bedroom, he had berated her with his impression of what he called needy beg-friending: *oh please text me, oh please reply, even just an emoji, oh I can't breathe if you don't!* Having a late-teenage son meant constantly being in two states simultaneously: one of hypervigilance and worry, the other of being utterly ignored and at peace with it. It was a world of tension.

Another buzz. Shit. An old colleague from Liverpool. **So much for the quiet life, Nic!**

It sent her into an immediate spiral of doubt. What was she doing back here, with two officers and no resources? Her old team would pity her if they could see what she'd got herself into—she could hear the reactions: *what d'you expect, girl? Bloody country bumpkins, aren't they?!*

She could hear all of their voices and she feared they were right.

As she went back into the main office, Harry came striding over like an eager pupil.

"So, two things. Firstly, I've been thinking maybe the antlers are a symbolic gesture, like a deeper meaning. Cos deer are symbols of fertility, they represented gods in natural myths, they're embedded in many religions, have special meaning in pagan ceremonies. So, a deer can represent virility, strength, stamina. It's also a god of the forest, cos the antlers represent tree branches, or of the wilderness. It's supposed to be a peaceful, strong spirit, but also a creature that will go to battle to protect its herd. Then, also I thought maybe it's something to do with the name of the pub? The White Hart—a hart is a deer. Could be a connection, right? Also—"

Nicola held her hand up. "Gonna stop you there. Fascinating, and . . . good, but not now. Do the basics, gather the intel, find everything I've asked for. We'll start theorizing when we have a full picture of the victim's last day and a sense of who might have motive—"

"Yeah, that's what I mean, motive. I was trying to get inside of the head of—"

Nicola talked across him, despite being unable to bear it when someone did that to her. "Harry, I need to get some sleep."

And with that she slung her coat over her shoulder and headed for the door. Harry found himself following her. *Why are you following her?*

"Yes, no, sorry, wrong order. I've been doing the legwork, I meant to tell you that first. Jim Tiernan—he had a criminal record. Served nine months in Wandsworth Prison."

CHAPTER THIRTEEN

As the sun set, Nicola Bridge's social media statement made its viral journey across the many screens in the houses of Fleetcombe. Two uniformed officers knocked on every door, spooning out calm and reassurance.

It did not do much good. The local residents spoke about Jim Tiernan, the shock of his sudden death and what, if anything, it meant. They speculated about who might have done it. They speculated over why. Who had he fallen out with? What had he been doing? *Who* had he been doing it with?

Almost every discussion within the houses of Fleetcombe ended up in the same place: the dead man was one of them. Was the killer, also?

By the time 10 p.m. came, the village's streets were deserted. No drinkers stumbled home worse for wear. Only police officers made their way in and out of the White Hart. Four different sets of flowers had been left in front of the door, with cards carrying messages of shock and grief and wishes for the soul of Jim Tiernan. Somebody else had tied flowers to the nearest lamppost. Up the road, the Fox pub was also closed. The handwritten sign said it would reopen tomorrow as usual.

From under a tree on the deserted road opposite the White Hart, a small, lone figure watched forensics officers carry items to their cars: big paper bags, small sealed clear bags, boxes and containers. She supposed this was all evidence. She watched them load it all into two police cars.

Once the police had left, just before eleven, she wandered out from the shadows and weaved her way along the street, staying out of the sodium light cast from the lampposts.

She knew all the streetlights would go off at midnight, *cuts* her mother had said tersely when she asked why that happened. And then she would be happier.

She could not believe she was out on the streets again. Not after what had happened. But she did not really have any choice. It was too dangerous elsewhere.

She returned to many of her usual places. But everywhere felt different tonight. She could not explain *how* it all felt different, but she did know why. Just as she knew why she was avoiding one particular place tonight. She would never go back there ever again.

As she walked back in the direction of the playground, she saw ahead in the middle of the road the bloodied, flattened corpse of an animal. Its guts were splayed out. It had once been a fox, or maybe a dog.

Another dead thing. The crows would come for it in the morning, she thought.

She sat on a swing in a corner of the darkened playground, knowing she would not be seen there. She hoped there would be no repeat of the night before. But she no longer felt certain. Everything had changed.

Elsewhere in Fleetcombe, Eddie, the delivery driver, sat at his kitchen table, poring over a set of numbers written into his battered notebook. Numbers that instilled dread in him. Numbers that told a story. A story he did not want anyone else to know.

In a house round the corner, Frankie finally stopped doomscrolling, placed their phone on the floor by the charger and lay in bed, listening to the night. The silence was, for a moment, welcome. The talk in the salon had been of nothing but the White Hart today. Frankie listened as a set of footsteps passed by the door. Frankie tensed, half expecting someone to hammer on the door, demanding admittance. The footsteps drifted into the distance.

Five streets away from Frankie, Jim Tiernan's sister, Patricia, sat at a small faded white metal table on the patio of her small back garden. She had a blanket around her shoulders and was smoking for the first time in more than a decade, listening to the chatter of the guests staying in the other half of her house. Lights were on behind the blinds. Music was bubbling away. Patricia imagined there was wine. They have no idea, she thought. Nobody in the world had any idea how she felt right now, and never would. Alone did not even cover it.

Her phone buzzed. She looked at it, surprised, then got up and walked round the side to her front door. There stood a disconsolate Irina with a hastily packed bag.

"It's a fucking crime scene. I can't even sleep in my own bed." Irina waited for Patricia to make the offer and then grew tired of waiting. "Can I stay with you?" There was silence from Patricia. Irina persisted. "I have nowhere else."

Patricia Tiernan was unsure whether she was comfortable with this idea. But whatever misgivings she had, she could not turn Irina away.

"I only have the sofa," she said, and Irina nodded.

As the door to Patricia's house closed, silence shrouded the darkness of Fleetcombe once more.

CHAPTER FOURTEEN

Four miles west, on the outskirts of Bredy, Nicola was still thinking about Jim Tiernan's fraud conviction as she arrived home, shortly after 11 p.m., to find carnage on her front drive.

For a second, her body went into fight-or-flight mode. *Fuck fuck fuck. Who's done this?* The black bag of rubbish that somebody had put out on the curb had been torn open and its contents were strewn over the pavement and into the road. Their house was being targeted and someone had done this to scare them.

Then she stopped. Checked herself. This was West Dorset.

It had happened a dozen or so times in Liverpool. She had been investigating murders connected to organized crime, city-center gangs. They had found her address, slashed her tires, made harassing calls, sprayed graffiti. Once she had come back to find the shed in the backyard on fire. Ethan, at age twelve, had been stopped on his way to school and told to tell his mum to stop interfering in things that were none of her business. When that didn't work, men would suddenly be walking alongside her in the street, or a woman would sit next to her in the coffee shop and they would be talking to her about joining forces, about payments and life being made easier, so long as she just turned a blind eye or passed the case elsewhere. She still thought about those men and women, entangled with no choice but to do the bidding of someone above.

The threats had only made her redouble her efforts. But redoubling meant longer hours, meant not going home, meant not being there enough. And that had led to . . . well, that's why things had to change.

She looked down the deserted lane: this house was more rural and isolated than anywhere they'd lived before. Clearly an animal had ripped open the bag. No one was targeting them here—*were they*? Few people even knew them properly here yet. *We need a bit more time before people hate us that much*, thought Nicola. But she felt irritated at the thought that their new neighbors further down the lane might have seen this. *The people who live here are not locals*, this trail of animal-ravaged rubbish screamed. *Here is a house of idiots who don't know how life is lived outside a city!*

She opened the gate to their back garden and reached inside for the dustpan and brush she knew was there. She scraped the rubbish up, wincing as some of it (*food goes in the food waste, not the rubbish, Ethan!*) stained the road and pavement. She hoped for a little light rain in the night to wash the mess away, then retracted that hope as she remembered what it would do to her crime scene on the A35.

The mess cleared, she looked again up and down the lane. The silence and the darkness made her suddenly feel vulnerable, like she was being watched.

She looked up to the ink-black sky. The stars were clearly visible. She was not yet used to that—the absence of light pollution here. She felt tiny, and judged, as she suddenly felt the eyes of the heavens looking down on her.

She did not have faith, but she wanted to yell out, *I'm doing my best here*!

As she walked through the back door into the kitchen, the room felt like the aftermath of a storm.

Mike was at the kitchen table, Ethan was sat at a distance, on a kitchen counter. They both looked at her, as if caught misbehaving.

"Hey," smiled Mike.

"Hi, Mum," said Ethan breezily.

She could not have been clearer about the mood if she had found them rolling around on the floor punching each other. There had been some kind of conversational dust-up between father and son. She would put money on it. (She did not need to put money on it.)

It was one of her—what, abilities? Traits? Gifts? She never knew how to categorize it, but Nicola possessed antennae that could pick up atmospheres in rooms as soon as she walked in: the crackle of the dynamics, the pre-existing conditions. She had come to realize from a young age that not everyone had this. It was one of the things that had proved invaluable in her work: "the human lie detector," one boss had labeled her.

But what was a gift at work could be a curse at home. Sometimes, it's better not to know what other people are thinking. Because it can hurt.

"Everything OK?" she asked innocently.

She wondered what it was about, but thought she could guess.

"There's food," said Mike. "Did you eat?"

"I did not," said Nicola. "Thank you!" She looked into the pans on the cooker. A turkey chili and rice. On the table a bowl of salad and supermarket tortilla chips and salsa. One of her favorite combos.

Someone's making an effort, she thought.

"How were your days?" she asked her boys.

Ethan shrugged. "Fine. No, wait, terrible."

She knew that would be the answer. She felt responsible. "I'm sorry to hear that." She looked to Mike: "You?"

"Yeah, good," he said breezily. "Quiet."

They had met on their respective jobs, in their early twenties. Emergency service call-outs. She was a young uniform officer; he was a trainee firefighter. They would later joke to others that a serial arsonist was their Cupid. Over the course of a year, they ended up at the same scenes a handful of times. He asked her out, *and the rest is mystery*, as Mike would put it when regaling others with their origin story.

"Quiet is good," she said through a mouthful of chili. She gestured to the bowl with her fork. "This is also good! Thanks so much."

When the plan became to leave Liverpool and take a job as a detective in her childhood hometown, Mike had spotted a firefighting job in the county town of Dorchester, some fifteen miles away. He was four weeks in, and getting used to the slower pace, of work and life. *A country Scouse*, he called himself.

"Is it a murder?" asked Ethan from the counter as he swigged from a bottle.

"Can't talk about it," said Nicola.

"You mean yes," Ethan shot back.

"I mean I can't talk about it," Nicola snapped back, more tetchily than she intended. She watched her son's face fall. She was tired.

"Thought the plan was a quiet life," said Ethan, looking at them both accusingly.

"Shall I go and run you a bath?" asked Mike.

She could see Ethan looking at his father with contempt. She too found the overcompensating tricky. She hoped it was temporary, that it would calm down. "It's fine, I'll do it in a bit," she responded.

"It's no bother." Mike was on his feet and out of the room. She could hear him taking the stairs two at a time.

Nicola looked to her son. "Go easy on him," she said.

Ethan looked back at her angrily. "Why? We should not be here. I should not have to be here."

Nicola suddenly felt a wash of sadness flood her body. Her beautiful family, into which she had placed all her hope and love, had been disrupted. A poison had been administered, seeping into all corners. They were gambling that this move was the antidote. But how long would the antidote take to kick in?

Ethan was right: this was not the plan. The plan was the quiet life. The plan was to reset. A murder investigation was the last thing she—or they—needed.

Ethan added, "Oh, by the way, Grandad rang. He said why haven't we been to see him and Granny, they're only thirty miles away, do you think you're better than him now? He was laughing when he said it, but he sort of meant it, too."

Nicola's head dropped. She could do without parental guilt as well. She had definitely sold their return to Dorset to her parents as a brilliant move for everyone to be closer (rather than revealing the real reason). But her parents had moved further east along the coast five years back and were now irritated they'd made the move out of Bredy when Nicola had decided to come back. Plus, they were obviously expecting more regular visits, which, as of yet, hadn't happened. Just another consideration, thought Nicola. She felt like she had a lot of considerations in her life.

Mike appeared in the doorway. "Bath's ready," he said.

She worried that her son was now carrying as much anger as she was. And she worried she did not have the time to help him with that.

As she lay in the bath, closed her eyes and breathed in the aroma from the oil Mike had diligently added, she planned her next move. She set the alarm on her phone for the middle of the night. She messaged an instruction. She did not tell her husband or son what she would be doing, or that she was unlikely to be present for breakfast.

With her eyes closed, the image of a dead man's face framed by stag antlers filled her mind. *Please God*, she thought, this woman with no faith, *let there not be another body tonight.*

CHAPTER FIFTEEN

There were no stars now. It was 2:04 a.m. and the cloud cover on the A35 was low and oppressive, the barometric pressure heavy. Nicola could sense when a storm was due: growing up by the coast, it became part of your inner weathervane. In Liverpool, she'd been mocked for it. But she was rarely wrong. The pressure would break tomorrow, and the storm would come.

She glanced at the car clock as she drove. It was twenty-three hours after Jim Tiernan had been found. This time yesterday, the killer was moving Jim's body toward the place it would later be found.

She had taken what was essentially an end-of-day catnap of forty-seven minutes, having set her alarm to ensure she would be out at the scene, monitoring traffic, ensuring cars were stopped and questioned as to whether they'd made the same journey twenty-four hours earlier, feeling what it was like. *Noticing.* The mirror moments: twenty-four hours later, a week later, a month later. She hoped she wasn't still looking for the killer in a month's time.

Nicola parked just past the taped-off cordon, noting there were lights on within the evidence tent, lighting it up like a beacon. Mac, on sentry duty for a second night in a row at the cordon, handed her a piece of paper, keen to impress. "As requested!"

Nicola looked at his notes. Times, registration plates, names, addresses and two columns of ticks and crosses. The first column was marked "Yesterday?," the second "Dashcam?" Seeing Mac was due to be out here again tonight, she had spoken to him and given him an action to carry out. From the moment he took over, at 10 p.m., he was to stop every vehicle that passed, going in either direction, take the drivers' details and quiz them over whether they had made the same journey the previous night, and if so whether they had a dashcam fitted.

Fifty-nine vehicles between 10 p.m. and now—the majority of them before midnight. Only thirteen since, of which only five were in the past hour. The A35 was a ghost road post-midnight. The killer must have known this, thought Nicola. That increased the probability of them being a local. It still didn't make sense to her—why leave the body at this exact spot? She had asked Mel (who, she had already clocked, seemed to live for this sort of request) to check whether this particular location had any connections to ritual or folklore, but so far he had found nothing.

Nicola thanked Mac, congratulating him on his rigor, and stuck her head into the evidence tent. To her surprise, Reeta was in there, in full protective uniform, on her knees, examining a piece of road. Nearby, the table was full of bagged-up samples. Reeta looked up at Nicola.

"You too, huh?" She smiled, the two women acknowledging that both of them should be in bed, instead of working out here.

Kindred soul, thought Nicola, nodding at Reeta as she verbalized the question she knew was bugging both of them. "Why here, why this time of night?"

"And you thought if you were here, you might make more sense of it."

"Girl can dream," said Nicola, grinning, and she was gratified that Reeta grinned back. She clearly shared Nicola's work ethic and tenacity. She wondered whether Reeta had a family. "You got the resources you need?"

Reeta looked directly at Nicola. "We'll make it work. Just wanted to double-check a few things." That was a clear no. Nicola understood—between here and the scene at the White Hart, Reeta and her team were overstretched.

"Let me know if there's anything I can do," said Nicola.

"How much sleep have you had?" asked Reeta.

"Oh, loads!" said Nicola with a smile, and left her colleague to continue.

Nicola stood in the middle of the deserted carriageway, allowing her eyes to get used to the darkness. Being here now, twenty-four hours later, was the closest she could get to replication, or time travel. She wanted to have a sense of what the killer had seen and smelled and heard, one night previously. The weather, she noted, was beginning to get cloudier but otherwise felt much the same. She breathed in deeply, taking a tug on the night air, filling her nostrils and lungs. She looked at the distance from the roadside to the verge. She checked round three hundred and sixty degrees. Nothing but fields in the line of sight—completely unoverlooked.

The road was still empty. The body must have been driven here. It was too far to carry on foot without risking being seen, even at that time of night. So then the body must have been moved from a car to the middle of the road. It wouldn't have been easy to haul him into place there. Was more than one person involved?

Why was it so important to the killer to leave the body here with antlers on his head? What was the message? Who was it for? Jim himself? Other people? Her? Was this someone who wanted to play games with the police?

She heard movement in the field to one side of her.

She froze. Animal? She peered into the night. Foliage moving. Twigs snapping. She looked in the direction of the noise. The thick dark offering up no clues—

She looked back to where Mac was stationed—should she call him over? But that would surely warn whoever it was off—if it was a person; could easily be an animal—

No, there was a figure—moving there—almost sweeping the field to the side of the road, as if searching for something—

She walked toward it, slowly, as silently as possible—she couldn't believe that this was the killer returning to the scene of the crime. Had they made the most basic of mistakes?

She was getting closer, and still the figure had not heard or sensed her. If she could get close enough, she might be able to take them down. She was slight but muscly, and the kickboxing training she'd done ten years ago was still fresh in her memory—

The figure crouched—had it found what it was looking for?

She slammed her torch on—and yelled, "Police, stay where you are!"

The figure froze—didn't try to run—as Nicola got the torchlight to find its intended target.

"Sarge?" Harry moved forward from the field. "What you doing here?"

"Harry? I could ask you the same!"

"Wanted to have a poke around, further outside the scene. I've been combing the verges. See if anything was discarded. Thought it'd be good to do it at the time of the night the body was found. Didn't Mac tell you I was here?"

Nicola exhaled. "He did not. I thought you were the bloody killer there, for a sec."

Harry said, "I'm worried Forensics don't have the manpower or budget for a scene as big as this. Kept worrying we might miss something."

Not so naive after all, thought Nicola. Where had he come from, before joining? Some business? Which business? Somebody said his family ran the butcher's in Bredy. Was that his only life experience?

Together, they set up some lights and worked their way along each side of the road, where the carriageway met the verge, one hundred meters either way. They worked silently, easily. After two hours, they had found nothing. Nicola looked across to the far side to see Harry yawning.

"Enough now. I'm calling it. Long day tomorrow."

Harry nodded, disappointed. "I thought being out here might trigger something. It's a needle in a haystack, isn't it?"

Nicola looked at him, realizing. "Which is most likely the point. Leave the body at a scene that's open to the elements, likely to be contaminated quickly."

There was a moment's silence when they both stood in the middle of the deserted road, sensing the wide-open space all around.

"Go on. Get some sleep," said Nicola after a moment.

Harry nodded, headed off. She could see he was downhearted, like he'd felt he might make a breakthrough out here, in the dark, in the early morning. But also, also . . . that was fine. He wasn't as flaky as she'd feared. He'd come out here determined to get something done. She could work with that.

She didn't know how long she stood there thinking. But she again had the feeling of being watched. She looked up.

Ahead of her, in the middle of the road, a hare was standing, poised. It was looking at her, stopped in the dead center, on the white lines.

The hare stared at Nicola. Nicola, statue-still, looked back at it. It cocked its head a fraction of an inch, like it was looking into her deepest soul.

It's a fucking hare, she told herself.

She had never been this close to one, never seen one stay this still.

Were you here? What did you see?

She caught herself. *You're tired, Nicola. Go home.*

As Nicola returned to her car, someone was watching.

Someone else had come to check on things. Someone who had assumed that, though the area might be cordoned off, nobody else would be here. Someone who had felt a surge of primal fury at other people's presence. Someone who did not want Nicola, or Harry, or Reeta to ever work out what happened.

Someone who told themselves: *it's not done.*

You have to continue to be clever.

CHAPTER SIXTEEN

Morning came too quickly. Lack of sleep was beginning to gnaw at Nicola. She looked at Harry and noted he was looking bleary-eyed as well, with a day's worth of stubble on him. Not a bad look on him, though.

In their quest to understand who Jim Tiernan was, they began with an 8:30 a.m. appointment at Wilson's brewery in Bredy. A Victorian redbrick building with a large chimney, the brewery had been going strong for two centuries.

Nicola estimated Christine Wilson, the brewery's head, to be in her late fifties. Smartly, practically dressed in a trouser suit (understated but a clear power signal), with minimal jewelry, medium level of makeup and expensive-looking hair. Christine had the air of a no-nonsense Tory wife, not afraid to get stuck in to whatever was in front of her and moving through this world as if she owned it, which she essentially now did.

She told them briskly they'd have to join her on her morning inspection of the brewery. "It's important everyone sees my face at a moment like this," she explained. "Uncertainty and fear are the enemies of productivity and good business." As they walked, she explained how the business had been passed down to her as the family concern. She was proud of the fact they were one of the few truly local, truly independent breweries left in the country, and prouder still to be the first woman to run it, although this had apparently been a bit of a scrap, at the beginning.

They went from the office to the floor via the stores, and then to the delivery warehouse. Christine required few prompts and kept talking throughout. Nicola noted that Christine knew everyone by name, touched their arm when checking how they were and asked after some of the workers' family members. Nicola wondered if that was all for show, for her and Harry.

Christine ran through the history of the White Hart. "It's been a tricky site for us historically. There isn't really enough business in Fleetcombe to accommodate the Hart and the Fox."

"Do you own the Fox as well?" asked Nicola.

"We no longer have that particular pleasure," replied Christine frostily. "The Fox was divested from our portfolio in the late 1920s, by my great-grandfather. People said it was a mistake at the time, and it feels even more of a mistake now. They're a Free House"—she all but spat that phrase—"and since they made a concerted effort toward a premium food offer, they've become something of a destination. People come from far afield for their food now. So I can't pretend I don't look at the Fox with some degree of envy. Even tried my damnedest to bring their landlady, Ayesha, into our fold. But she won't have it. It's a source of no little annoyance, I must admit. A well-run pub like that is a rare and precious thing."

"And how well run was the White Hart?" asked Nicola guilelessly.

Christine stopped walking, seemingly unused to her flow being interrupted. They had reached the floor of the brewery. The air was thick with the smell of malt, hops and yeast. Nicola did not like it at all—the sweet, burned, brown gloopiness was lodging in the back of her throat.

"Our business has transformed in the last twenty years," explained Christine with a teacherly air and a subtext of *I'll get to your questions when I'm good and ready.* "We've lost a quarter of all pubs in the country: fifteen thousand establishments closed for good. Wilson's has had to sell off a third of our properties."

"Wow. A third?" said Harry. Nicola noted that "wow." He definitely had said it on that first call.

"How often do *you* go to the pub?" Christine asked Harry.

Harry shrugged. "Once a fortnight, maybe less."

Christine winced. "A man of your profile, twenty years ago, would have been going three or four times a week. Maybe even a few lunchtimes, too. Ever go to the pub at lunchtime?"

Harry smiled. "I do not."

Nicola thought to herself that she'd worked with plenty of men who did and was glad that tradition was dying.

"As an industry, we've tried to keep up, but there is a point where you have to admit that people aren't buying what you're selling," said Christine.

"What's that got to do with the White Hart?" asked Nicola, steering Christine back on track.

"The state of the industry has an existential effect on the quality of people you can attract to work within it. Publicans have become less reliable. Thirty or forty years ago, you got a lot of married couples who stayed with the same pub for decades. Nowadays the turnover is much higher. For a start, couples don't stay together in the same way. Others, once they actually get into the nitty-gritty of running a pub, just run a mile. They think it's going to be all fun and mine-hosting, but it's not. It's bloody hard work. Physically and mentally, seven days a week, eleven till eleven minimum, often later on weekends now. Then, outside of opening hours, there's the cleaning, the maintenance, resetting, restocking, the accounts, the purchasing, the menus, the snacks. It's demanding and thankless, and once people realize that, they scarper.

We have a huge retention issue among our tenant landlords and landladies."

Christine paused for a moment, looking around to see whether anyone from her employ was eavesdropping. "I'll be honest with you: I wouldn't do it. Running a pub is merciless." Then, she caught herself. "Anyway. You want to know about Jim Tiernan."

"And how well he ran the White Hart," prompted Nicola.

Christine exhaled. "Well, we've had worse. We *have* worse. He can be erratic. Late accounting, strange ordering, high turnover of staff. But credit where credit's due: he built that pub back up. It had been on its arse, all sorts of problems—drugs, fights. He came in and, for the most part, built it back into a good local, a drinker's pub, with a simple food proposition. Nothing too clever or pricey, but he built loyalty. Somewhere you'd drop in for a pint or two, a couple of nights a week." She looked at Harry. "Well, obviously, *you* wouldn't. But there are still plenty of people who want that. That's the White Hart. That's what Jim has done. Overall, he'd turned what seemed like a dead site into a functioning, thriving local. And that really is going against the tide of the business right now."

She stopped, as if for the first time really registering the fact of Jim Tiernan's death. "One of our landlords, *murdered*. I don't think I've been able to process it. There's a lot of rumor going round. Something about antlers? Is it true?"

"How would you describe Mr. Tiernan?" pressed Nicola.

Christine shrugged, as if she'd never really thought about it. "Personable. Good smile, well deployed. Firm handshake, always looked you in the eye. These things matter for a publican—they're part of my scoresheet when interviewing. Got on with most people, didn't suffer fools. He ran things reasonably well. He knew he had to, as we'd given him the pub on probation, so to speak."

Nicola's ears pricked up: "What d'you mean, probation?"

Christine said, "I presume you know he'd been in prison. We'd looked into it, and he had good character references from four or five reputable people. He said the incident had been a misunderstanding and the police and CPS had been heavy-handed. Now, obviously, having a criminal record doesn't disbar you from running a pub. If it did, we definitely wouldn't find enough landlords."

"Was there ever any trouble at the pub?"

"A few minor scuffles in the early days. But that wasn't down to Jim. He was the peacemaker, sorting things out, barring people—that didn't faze him. And there was the break-in shortly after he took over, but nothing else."

Nicola felt the crackle of new information fizz through her veins. She remained composed externally. "What break-in was that?"

"A couple of weeks after he took over. Early on a Sunday morning, 1 a.m., something like that. Couple of thugs broke in, armed with iron bars. Jim was forced to open the safe, and they took the week's takings. He was beaten up quite badly."

Nicola glanced at Harry, who was scribbling furiously in his notebook. He looked up at Christine. "Did they ever catch the people who did it?"

Right question, thought Nicola.

"That's your area, not mine," said Christine sharply.

Nicola moved on. "How would you characterize his relationship with his partner, Irina?"

Christine thought for a moment. "Tempestuous," was her pointed reply.

"Can you give us any more than that?"

"I don't know all the ins and outs. But they argued a lot, sometimes in view of the customers. They were two people with strong opinions.

There was one occasion where it got a little physical—the reports I heard were that she shoved him and he fell, behind the bar. I had words, told him to keep any conflict away from the punters."

Nicola watched Harry writing away furiously. She also noted that Christine was watching Harry, possibly with an air of satisfaction, a smile playing across her lips. Nicola felt Christine Wilson did not like Irina.

"When did you last see Mr. Tiernan?" Nicola asked.

"The day before yesterday. We met at the White Hart to go through accounts, supplies, future planning."

"Was that usual?"

Christine Wilson paused for a moment. "Look, it feels mean to speak ill of a dead man. But no. There were discrepancies within the business, and they were increasing. I wasn't getting the answers I'd been asking for over a long period of time. I wanted to have it out face-to-face."

"And how did that meeting go?" asked Nicola.

Christine looked uncomfortable reporting all of this. "Not great. He was restless from the off, said he didn't have much time as he had to meet someone later."

"Did he mention a name?" asked Harry, pen poised over notebook.

"I wasn't there to go through his diary," replied Christine coolly. "My objective was to let him know some home truths and stress that he had a limited amount of time to get things in order or we'd look at replacing him. He was in rather a large form of denial about it. The whole thing became something of a shouting match, I'm afraid."

"And how did the shouting match resolve itself?" Nicola asked.

"With me giving him an ultimatum: sort yourself out or we throw you out."

"How did Mr. Tiernan take that?"

Christine Wilson looked up into the air, as if hoping that somehow the words she needed were hanging there and could be plucked. "He said it would make life very difficult for him. He said I didn't understand." She looked back to Nicola and Harry. "I told him it wasn't my job to understand his problems, it was my job to protect the brewery, its properties and its investments. He asked me who was looking after him."

That last sentence hung around for a moment. Nicola and Harry knew when to let the pause go on, to let a witness keep talking. Christine did keep talking.

She rubbed her ear. Nicola felt that she didn't realize she was doing it. Was it a tell? "I regret that now. He wasn't perfect, but which of us is? Especially the older we get. We all make mistakes. I like giving second chances to people. I believe they're less likely to mess up again: they know what's at stake. But I wish I'd been more supportive. I wish I'd listened more." Christine looked at them with what appeared to be anguish in her eyes. "I obviously didn't realize just how much trouble he was in."

CHAPTER SEVENTEEN

Rituals, leadership, power, fertility." As Nicola drove to the mortuary, Harry reeled off a number of theses on the meaning of deer in different cultures. "Possibility one: symbol of spiritual authority. Deer as god looking after her children. Devoted, caring, loving figure. Possibility two: deer as symbol of regeneration. Through death comes renewal. Possibility three: royalty. The deer is the head of the animal kingdom. Which could explain the chair he was on. The king on his throne. Is that mocking Jim Tiernan for something? The dead king?"

Nicola ground her teeth and clasped the steering wheel tighter, hoping he would shut up. He didn't.

"Deer is also the spirit animal of Gemini. Symbol of innocence, affection and fun, Geminis are outgoing and socially adept." Harry paused, brow furrowed. "I'm a Gemini. Anyway. Then there's the obvious connection to the name of the pub. The White Hart. A hart is the name for a stag. There's a deer and antlers on the pub sign. Could all this be about the pub? The building or the business? What if Jim is collateral damage in a fight about that place? Head of the White Hart, killed, deposed from his throne."

Nicola couldn't take it anymore. "Stop."

Out of the corner of her eye she watched as Harry lowered the phone he'd been reading his notes off.

"You're asking the wrong questions. Again. This is all theoretical bullshit. Theories won't find or convict a killer. Stop getting ahead of yourself. Think *practically*. What happened, *how* did it happen? Where did the killer get deer antlers from? How were they affixed? Where did the chair and the sack come from? What are all the possible routes from the White Hart to the spot where he was found? Get the answers to those, then we can talk about meaning and symbolism."

"Sure," came the quiet response from the passenger seat.

The remainder of the short journey passed in silence. Nicola felt bad about it, while also knowing she was right.

The pathologist, Adams, welcomed them to his "inner sanctum," as he called it. He poured them coffee, which Nicola quickly discovered was a thick, syrupy liquid which must have had five times the normal ratio of coffee to water.

"It's Peruvian." Adams beamed. "I brew it like they do there, got 'em to teach me." Nicola had been to Peru in her early twenties and this was not like any drink—and certainly no coffee—she had ever encountered there. It was as though Adams had confused coffee with gravy.

He was a cheery, small man with a comforting Dorset burr and seemed an unlikely pathologist by temperament: cheeky, impish and grinning. Nicola and Harry waited as he rummaged around for his notes, moving a Bluetooth speaker, two parking tickets and an empty Haribo packet. His side desk was the only part of the inner sanctum to display any mess. "Where are the notes? Sorry, you've caught me with me trousers down here."

"There speaks a man who works alone a lot of the time," said Nicola to Harry.

"How dare you, especially in front of the clients." Adams gestured to the two covered bodies. "Aha."

He turned back with notes in hand. He was an analog man, handwriting notes which he later transferred to the system.

"Tiernan. Poisoned. Big whack of morphine. Overwhelmed his system. Looks like one dose injected into his backside, via syringe."

He described the quantities and what it meant, but Nicola was still taking in the initial information as Adams bowled on. "Also, minor trauma to the head, but that would appear to be post-mortem. Possibly when the body was being moved, or having those antlers affixed." He stopped and looked at them quizzically. "What are you making of those antlers? Cos that's a new one."

Nicola ignored the question and returned to the new information Adams had just delivered. "The morphine—could it have been self-administered? An overdose?"

"Not impossible, but very unlikely, amount he had in him. It's not low-level medicinal painkiller levels. Also, weird positioning if it's self-administered. I'd say high probability, bordering on certainty, he didn't administer it. Far more likely someone poisoned him. Also: we found traces of human skin under his fingernails. We'll run them for tests and keep you up to date. But if they're from a struggle, we may have a DNA sample of the killer."

On the walk back to the car, the low buzz of Harry talking kept interfering with Nicola's cognitive processing. She half heard him saying he'd do a search on where you could get that amount of morphine from, locally. Maybe online, he thought, possibly hospital, could be pharmacy, guess doctors might have access to it, might keep some at care homes; also if you had someone in the house who was on a morphine drip, maybe in end-of-life care, and do vets use morphine on animals?

Standing by the car, she realized he'd stopped and was looking at her. "I feel like my talking annoys you," he said.

No shit.

"I'm also thinking. I just don't do it aloud," said Nicola. "That amount of morphine must mean it was pre-planned. This wasn't a struggle that went wrong and then the killer leaves the body elaborately staged to cover their tracks. Every element of this is deliberate and cold-blooded."

"Does it also tell us something about the killer?" Harry ventured carefully. Nicola knew he was now permanently alert to the possibility of her shutting him down. She hadn't meant for that to happen, but the tiredness was having an effect. "Maybe they didn't fancy their chances in any kind of physical struggle."

"Possibly," Nicola allowed—as Harry's phone buzzed.

"Oh God," he said, almost involuntarily, and turned away to answer it, almost cagily. Nicola found herself wondering who it was. Personal call, maybe? Did that explain his caginess? They hadn't really got into any personal stuff, not yet at least. Girlfriend or partner? He didn't wear a wedding ring, so—

She was pulled out of her own thoughts as he turned and looked straight at her, catching her looking at him.

"OK. We'll be right there," he said, ending the call and addressing Nicola immediately. "Farmer just found the body of a deer on his land. With no head."

CHAPTER EIGHTEEN

"Ever seen an animal without a head before, girl?"

Nicola stood looking down at the contorted limbs of a dead deer lying splayed at the top of a sloping hill beneath a tussle of brambles. She looked down toward the beach and the sea. The cold wind scraping against her cheek and scrabbling through her hair was the equivalent of a Red Bull. She could see Harry on the other side of the brambles, walking the line, looking up the hill. The coast road was forty yards away. A lone car whooshed past and then all was silence again.

Was it feasible that someone could, on their own, park up on the side of the coast road, carry the animal down and chuck it over the hedgerow into this field? The carcass was big and heavy—wouldn't it have taken two people to do that? Whatever the facts of it, they were unlikely to be observed, if timed right. The animal's body had all the signs of being unceremoniously tossed. Thrown, even.

One of Nicola's strengths, she had been told by colleagues over the years, was what they called her "absolute lack of squeam." They had marveled at her non-squeamishness when presented with gore, blood, injuries and all the sort of stuff lesser mortals would flinch at or look away from. She wore it as a badge of pride, especially at moments like this, when she had a big Dorset farmer peering down at her, keen to monitor her discomfort.

"I presume you don't have a wife, Mr. Deakins?"

Deakins looked confused. "What's that got to do with the price of fish?"

Nicola had a good sense for tricksy buggers and she had marked down Deakins as one from the moment they drove up, when he made them park in a particular spot, next to a knackered old Volvo estate, making her reverse into a tight corner. His Dorset accent came and went depending on what he was saying or what posture he was adopting, she noticed. She felt like he enjoyed playing the role of peasant farmer. But he was smarter, and possibly more affluent, than that. She had to let him know who was boss.

"What you see in front of you is a woman, Mr. Deakins. A girl is under sixteen. Unless of course you're being flattering about the youthful quality of my skin. Which, in this light, I doubt you are. And yes, I have seen animals without heads before. Plenty. I've seen humans without heads, too." She watched him blanch. *Didn't expect that, did you?* "Now. When did you find the deer?"

"Couple hours ago."

"And you're sure it was dumped here? Couldn't be just a wild deer, attacked by another animal? Like your dog."

Deakins looked to his collie. "This one? She ain't gonna take a deer's head off like that. She's too soppy. She wouldn't even catch it. Ten years ago she might've tried. But even then she'd've muffed it. And now, no. Besides"—he knelt down next to Nicola, pointing to the top of the neck—"that's no attack. Too clean, no roughness. Man-made, sawn off, that is. If it was an animal, there'd be remnants"—he pronounced it *remmernants*—"ragged bones and gristle and hide."

Nicola was looking closer. He was right. "Are we going to find your fingerprints or DNA on this animal, Mr. Deakins?"

Deakins shook his head. "Might get remnants"—*remmernants*—"of my stick but that's about it. Prodded it when I found it." He sighed loudly, which made Nicola look up. "This is to do with Tiernan, isn't it? Some bastard trying to fit me up." Deakins looked down to the sea, as if it held his thoughts. "First, the fire. Then this."

"You think the fire two nights ago was connected?" asked Harry.

Deakins nodded. "Didn't think anything of it when you was here. But I didn't know about Tiernan then, did I? Changes things, dunnit."

He looked at them defiantly, as if willing them to challenge him.

"Changes things how?" asked Harry.

"Don't pretend you don't know," retorted Deakins.

"*I* don't know," interjected Nicola. "Maybe you could enlighten me."

"So you can think the same as the rest of 'em?" said Deakins accusingly. "Why would I be doing that? Now, you gonna take this thing away?"

Nicola explained that they would, and that it would be forensically examined, and that they would also need his prints and a DNA swab to rule him out from having killed and dumped the deer, given it was found on his land. She also asked him where he'd been on Tuesday night.

He didn't blink. "In the White Hart. And then I was here. Alone."

"So why are you withholding information from us?"

"I'm not withholding anything," said Deakins. "All a matter of public record."

"What is?" persisted Nicola, her irritation poking through.

"Nobody here knows history these days, that's the problem," said Deakins. He's enjoying the power, thought Nicola. "Hundred years pass," Deakins went on flatly. "And same again. And you don't even know."

"What d'you mean, same again?" she asked.

"Three of 'em in the end. Bodies left down by the Fleet. Antlers stuck to their skulls. They never found who did it."

Nicola exchanged glances with Harry. "You're saying three people were murdered and were found with antlers attached to their skulls? When was this?"

Deakins sucked in the sea air. "Century back. 1925."

Nicola's mind was reeling as Deakins kept going. "I know what my grandfather would say if he were alive: *Devil never disappears; he only rests.*"

CHAPTER NINETEEN

Ayesha Barton opened the doors of the Fox and glanced up and down the street to see who might be watching. She ushered Nicola and Harry quickly inside.

In her early thirties, Ayesha Barton was composed and precise, around five foot six inches tall, with wide, deep brown eyes you could get lost in. Nicola noticed Harry surreptitiously run the rule over her in a way Nicola wasn't entirely comfortable with.

The Fox itself seemed a reflection of its landlady: smart, attractive and thoughtfully put together. It was unrecognizable inside now from the place it had been during Nicola's teens. The space was lighter, and with far less old dark wood than the White Hart: whitewashed wood paneling with coastal light blues and subtle use of beige in the soft furnishings. Classy coastal restaurant with a hint of modern spa. It was subtly divided into separate areas with different purposes and aesthetics—the flow of the space keen to whisk you from the bar into the food area, encouraging you to eat from the daily changing chalkboard menu. The prices were high for this area, thought Nicola. Her salary would not cover being a regular here: special occasions only. Ayesha's refit and reshaping had not come cheap, but it was obviously paying dividends. The contrast with the White Hart could not have been clearer.

"We're all in shock," she said, after thanking them for coming. "Anyone you speak to. Have there been any further developments?"

"What did you want to talk to us about?" asked Nicola politely, swerving Ayesha's question. They had come at Ayesha's request, straight from Deakins' farm, discussing his revelation of three similar murders a century ago. As she drove, Nicola instructed Harry to set Mel on research while they went to the Fox. The number of leads was growing fast, as was Nicola's concern about keeping track of them all, with limited resources.

"I wondered . . . should I be, could we, open up and do a sort of, I don't know . . . like a memorial or vigil for Jim? That's what I was thinking. Don't know. I felt I should check in with you."

"Thanks," said Nicola. "We wouldn't have any objection. When were you thinking of?"

"I mean, as soon as. Tonight? But I don't want to do anything that'll upset Patricia. And I didn't think it was right me just being in touch with her. How's she doing, d'you know?"

"We're due to see her this morning. We can ask her," said Nicola.

"That would be great," Ayesha replied. She hesitated. "And I guess, Irina, too?" Nicola left a space for Ayesha to expand on the question. Ayesha did indeed move to fill the quiet. "I wouldn't be able to predict how she'd respond." Another pause. "Obviously, the two pubs are in direct competition. She might think the White Hart should do it, but obviously her name isn't above the door, and—"

"The White Hart's a crime scene," said Nicola.

"Right," said Ayesha. "Oh God, of course. Well then, that makes even more sense. But still, maybe you can tell her, too. She must be . . ." Ayesha left the sentence unfinished.

"How long have you been in charge here?" asked Nicola.

"Four years now," said Ayesha. "I was quite a shock to the place initially. Dual heritage, biracial woman—we're not on every street here. I think they saw me as exotic. They know different now! Plus, as a single woman, you have to overcome a few raised eyebrows and rumor-mongering at the start. You smile at a customer and you're having an affair with them. I'm sure you've had similar in your line of work," she said, directing the last line at Nicola. "Different now I've got a ring on my finger," she added, twirling a subtle diamond ring at them.

"Congratulations," said Nicola. "What does your fiancé do?"

"Mick's a corporal in the army. Based out of the base at Fernley."

"Not too far, then," said Harry as he wrote in his notebook. Fernley sat about twenty miles from Fleetcombe.

"Exactly," said Ayesha. "When he's not there, he's here."

"Was he here or there, Tuesday night?" asked Harry without looking up.

Nicola noted Ayesha's surprise at that question. She liked the casual way Harry had asked it, and the fact he'd needed no prompting. *Tick*, she thought.

"He's been back in barracks since the weekend," said Ayesha, nodding.

Harry smiled at her and finished writing as Nicola went on to the next question.

"How much did you have to do with Mr. Tiernan?"

"Not much," said Ayesha, after what Nicola felt was a second's thought.

When nothing else was forthcoming, Nicola pressed Ayesha. "You're in the same business, though."

"*Rivals* for the same business," pointed out Ayesha. "He's never liked having competition. Before I came, the Fox wasn't a threat, or a place people came that often. I've put a lot of work into it. But you know, that has an effect. A village like this can't really accommodate two pubs. I said to him: you keep your regulars, the drinkers, I'll do food, bring other people into the area. I can't pretend he was ever happy about it. And Irina definitely isn't." She was quieter. "I told him, it's just business. No reason for us to be daggers drawn. But . . ."

Again, her sentence drifted off into an ellipsis. "Sorry, I'm unclear whether or not you got on," asked Nicola.

"Did we get on?" Ayesha looked offended. "What's that got to do with anything? If we didn't get on, then I might have killed him? Is that it?"

"No," smiled Nicola winningly. "That's not what I said." *Interesting*, she thought. *Hackles raised.* "When did you last see him?" she followed up.

Ayesha exhaled. *Almost theatrically*, thought Nicola.

"I mean, I don't know. I'd have to think. Maybe in the street, in passing? I'm not sure when. We're always working the same hours, when our pubs are open. Very rare we'd bump into each other. Mick probably saw him more than I did. He sometimes drank in there."

"And did they get on?"

Ayesha shrugged. "Sure." Then she added, "The way they're saying his body was left, do you know why they did that?" She looked from Nicola to Harry and then back to Nicola.

"It's early days. We're looking at everything," said Nicola. *Here, have a small platitude.*

"And can you confirm where you were on Tuesday evening, and that night?" asked Harry politely.

Ayesha looked surprised. "I was here, Tuesday evening, obviously. We were open. I have the bookings list and transactions for people who were in. I closed up as usual, and then overnight, I was just here."

"And your fiancé"—Harry flicked back through his book for the name—"Mick, was he with you?"

"He was in barracks, like I said." She smiled frostily, knowing Harry was trying to catch her out. "Is there anything else I can help with?"

Nicola smiled. "We'll let you know about this evening."

"Thanks."

As Ayesha opened the door, Nicola added, "If Patricia Tiernan gives it the go-ahead, we'll drop in ourselves. To reassure people."

Ayesha's smile didn't quite reach her eyes.

"Great!" she said.

In the car park there was a young girl, maybe nine or ten years old, leaning against the side of Nicola's car as they approached.

"Have you caught them yet?" asked the girl levelly.

Straight in, thought Nicola. "Not yet, but we will," she replied.

The girl walked up and down beside the car, mainly looking at the ground, and then stealing glances at them.

"What's your name? Should you not be in school?" asked Nicola.

The girl didn't reply. After a moment she said, "Is this your car?"

"It is," said Nicola.

The little girl looked delighted. "I guessed right. I saw you drive in, yesterday. I saw you from the slide on the playground."

Nicola looked over to the playground. It had a vantage point across a wide vista of the village. "I expect you see a lot from up there," said Nicola.

The girl looked back at Nicola, as if examining her. Nicola felt the girl wore the expression of an adult. "It's important you catch them," said the little girl with the older face.

Nicola stepped a bit closer to the girl and knelt. Quiet, calm, supportive.

"Where d'you live? Shall we give you a lift home? We could have a chat on the way."

The little girl shook her head. "They'd be angry."

Nicola could feel Harry having entered the same state of alert she had.

"Who would?"

The girl shrugged.

'Is there anything you want to—"

"Well, bye," interrupted the girl, and jumped over the low wall of the car park.

"Wait!" called Nicola.

But the girl was moving fast, off down the street, running. She darted down a side alley and was out of sight before either Nicola or Harry could follow.

CHAPTER TWENTY

"Are you new?"

Nicola looked at Patricia Tiernan, surprised. They were standing in Patricia's crisp, tidy front room. "Am I what?"

"I don't recognize you. I thought I knew most of the local police."

"Oh. I see. Sort of. Not new to the area. Or to the job. Born here. Moved back recently."

"Ah," nodded Patricia. "That'll be why."

Nicola had sent Harry from the White Hart to check on Mel and see what information they could find about similar murders in 1925. She had been given the nod by the family liaison officer that Patricia felt up to talking, so Nicola walked the seven minutes from the White Hart to Patricia's pretty, long and low whitewashed house.

On arrival, she had tried to ask Patricia how she was doing.

"I'm just tired," she replied, as if this covered everything.

Nicola sensed Patricia Tiernan was a person who both felt things deeply and thought talking about feelings was an indulgence. She decided to carefully ask questions which could only be answered with facts.

I'm nine years older than James. It's fair to say he was a happy accident by our parents."

Patricia stopped talking almost immediately. Nicola watched her studying the autumn light streaming in through the windows, suddenly unsure of herself. "I'm sorry," Patricia said, after a moment. "It's such a beautiful day outside and my brother is dead."

Nicola kept her voice soft, and her intent clear. "I'll keep this as brief as possible. I'd love to get a sense of your brother, and his life. You were both born in Bredy, correct?"

"Yes. Our father had a shop, which our mother worked in alongside him. Homewares. He would scour the country, and the continent, for anything under that banner. Great saucepans, or the best corkscrew, or foam pads that go under chairs." Patricia beamed when she spoke about their father. "Floor polishes, garden hoses that didn't tangle, butter dishes, cutlery, the best kettle of its kind. That's what made him happy. He loved traveling and finding something in Finland or Portugal, that one invention that hadn't yet come over here. The shop—all the shops in Bredy—have a strange shape; you go in, and they go back a long way, long and thin, because of the industry from years ago, the rope-making."

"I wondered whether you had a connection to that shop," said Nicola, smiling. "I had a Saturday job at the newsagent's across the road. I used to spend my lunch hour in there looking at all the stuff. Tiernan's was a local institution."

"Well, you never want to grow up in an institution," smiled Patricia. She was staring at Nicola as if she was a puzzle she could not yet solve. "You don't have an accent," she said distractedly.

"I've been working in Liverpool for the past fifteen years," Nicola explained.

Patricia nodded. "I *see*." Nicola took that as meaning it was a satisfactory explanation, and nudged her back on track. "So, James is born . . ."

Patricia looked at her as if she'd just woken up from a dream and didn't know what was going on, before realigning and carrying on. "Yes, and is adored. By all of us," smiled Patricia. "That boy could do no wrong."

"So you've always got on. You were close," asked Nicola.

"Well, not always," said Patricia, and Nicola sensed her making a decision. "I think I should be clear," she continued, "for all our sakes. What you need to understand about my brother is that he is a chancer. And I say that with great love and affection. His charm has been his strength. He scraped through exams without studying, then fell into a succession of jobs. The pub is the longest he's stuck at anything. What's that, four years? Which is what makes this all such a shock."

"What was he doing before the pub?"

"He was away for about nine years. Doing what, I'm not sure. This and that, he used to say. I know he traveled a lot—he'd got that bug from our father. He'd take Jim with him on his trips. Lord knows what they got up to. I'd call him and he'd say he was in London, but it was a foreign ringtone, you know, like if you ring someone in France. He'd turn up for Christmas, usually a day or two late, with piles of presents, bless him."

"And when he came back here to Dorset?" probed Nicola gently.

"He definitely had his tail between his legs. He got that pub because it was vacant and he knew one of the people from the brewery of old. He convinced them to let him give it a go. Give him his due, he brought it up to scratch. Worked like a devil, threw everything at it: food, raffles, bingo, quiz nights. I will say he was a different man when he came back. Less of a chancer, more of a grafter. But my God he looked older.

I said to him, 'What have you seen, since you've been away?' He just laughed and said he'd been round the block a few times."

That was Nicola's cue. "Patricia, our records indicate that Jim was in prison for nine months."

Patricia sighed and then nodded. "Yes. Fraud, I believe. Never the best with money. How he kept that pub going was always a bit of a mystery. I offered to have a look at the books, but he always refused. Which rather worried me."

"What is it you do?" asked Nicola.

"I was a data analyst for a consulting firm. Executive level. Had a team of three hundred beneath me, across the country." Nicola could sense that it had been a while since anyone had asked Patricia about this work and that she enjoyed the opportunity to talk about it. "I took voluntary redundancy four years ago. Company was taken over by a multinational. The culture was changing and I felt . . . underappreciated. The payoffs on offer meant I could buy this place, with an eye on living in this bit and using the other half for holiday rentals. But I've found I miss working. I tried a few part-time jobs, local shops, that sort of thing. Given it was once the family trade. But can't quite get the right fit."

"Was anything specific worrying Jim, or causing him concern recently, d'you know?"

"Not that he told me about," Patricia said. "Have you spoken to Irina? She would know."

That opened the doorway for Nicola. "What was Jim and Irina's relationship like?"

Patricia gazed out the window again. "Up and down." She looked back at Nicola. "Do you know she asked to stay here last night? It was quite a surprise."

"I did not know that," said Nicola neutrally, internally processing. "Why do you think she came to you?"

"I don't know," replied Patricia. "We haven't been on the best of terms for a while. But I think she needed somewhere she could feel safe. And being here perhaps holds those memories for her." She looked plaintively at Nicola. "But, and this is terrible, I can't help thinking, am I being played? If she had anything to do with his death, and then she comes here, banking on my sympathy . . . Nobody could be that cruel, could they? I don't think she's that type of person. But after she left this morning, my mind was all over the place with it. I'm in a muddle—I don't know what to think anymore."

Nicola said, "When did you first meet Irina?"

Patricia took a breath. "I agreed to host her, at the start of the war, under the Homes for Ukraine program. What was that, February '22? I thought I'd do my bit. We got on very well. I enjoyed having her here, it was nice to have company and it all seemed to work very efficiently. I thought we got on. I thought we told each other everything. Not that she had to—I'm not saying she owed me anything. But the thing is: she never told me about her and Jim. Neither of them did. I don't even know how it started. Obviously, he would come around, and we would all spend time together. But then, one day, she said she was moving out of here and in with Jim, and it was the first I knew of it. I felt a fool."

"Why a fool?" asked Nicola quietly. She found that word interesting.

"I was the last in the village to know. I felt like people were laughing at me behind my back for not realizing."

"So you didn't approve of their relationship?" Nicola kept gently probing.

"Oh, it's not down to me to *approve*, is it? They're both adults. I just don't like any form of deception. Just tell me. And also . . . I don't know, I always felt it would end in tears. I'm sure she had to put up with a lot. Two quite selfish people. I don't know what went on, what the truth was between them. But something never seemed right to me. I mean, I don't, deep down in my heart, think she could have anything to do with it. And I couldn't turn her away. We both loved him, after all."

"Can you tell me where you were on Tuesday night?" asked Nicola.

Patricia nodded. "I was in the pub. Just reading, and then Jim asked me to mind the bar while he went out. He was out a long time. Only came back near last orders."

"Did he say anything about what had happened?"

"Not to me. I think you can probably gather, I wasn't his confidante. But I can give you the address. I don't know the names, but I know the house. Everyone in the village does." The disapproving tone was not hard for Nicola to interpret. "You're going to find out Jim had a roving eye."

Nicola nodded and moved on. "When did you leave the pub?"

"When everyone else did. I'm not sure of the exact time, probably somewhere between half past eleven and midnight. I walked back alone, but I did pass Eddie Godfrey heading into his house. When I got in, I listened to the radio for a bit and went to bed."

"Nobody else was with you?"

"Correct." Her smile was brittle. "Nobody else ever is."

At Nicola's request, Patricia wrote out a list of all the people she could remember being in the pub on Tuesday night. It was ordered, efficient and helpful.

As Nicola was putting her coat on in the hall, Patricia looked remorseful.

"I'm sorry, I want to say something else about Irina. I feel I may have misrepresented her. I don't want to be unfair. I'm still in shock. I think she made him very happy." Then as Nicola was stepping out, Patricia looked her in the eye and added, "For the most part."

Patricia closed the door gently.

Nicola walked to her car, digesting the conversation. Irina clearly aroused strong feelings in both Ayesha Barton and Patricia Tiernan.

The question was: did that say more about Irina, or the people talking about her?

CHAPTER TWENTY-ONE

Having checked on (and tried to inject some urgency and enthusiasm into) Mel, at lunchtime, Harry went to Bredy library. It was his first visit since a school trip at the age of seven.

The absence of online information about a 1925 murder was frustrating: Wikipedia was silent on the matter, and Google searches yielded nothing, no matter what wording he tried. The online historical record, such as it was, had nothing to report about Dorset murders with similarities to the case they were investigating. Harry needed to have something to report to Nicola when she returned from talking to Patricia Tiernan. He needed to show his dynamism. Except his dynamism was rather more digital than analog.

He had asked Mel for suggestions on a subsequent approach. Mel stared balefully at Harry and said, "You make me feel a hundred years old."

You look it most days, thought Harry. Mel was mid-forties but in possession of the pallor of an octogenarian.

Mel looked back to his screen. "Check parish records of births and deaths. Local newspapers may not have been digitized, so you'll need physical archives. Bredy library or the local history museum. They have books. Do you know about these things called books? Or don't they discuss those on YouTube? Local historians might know more. This the most pressing thing, is it?"

There were many pressing things, some of which Harry had in progress, and others he would be doing this afternoon. He had already sussed that Mel's strength was analytical work. He wasn't fast, but he seemed rigorous: Mel did not want to be outside the building but, inside it, he would happily receive orders and instructions relating to information gathering and they would not be dropped. He was currently following up for Harry on all of Irina's possible routes through the Vale in the early hours of Wednesday morning—had her car been logged, could her story be corroborated?

However, Harry also wanted to know more about these 1925 murders, including whether they even happened. Deakins could be lying or playing games with them. He needed to know and had folded it into an expedition to get lunch, hoping it would be a quick process. It was not proving so.

The librarian in front of him was an older man in his sixties with long hair, parted in the middle and tied up in a ponytail at the back. When Harry explained what he wanted, the man went back to his supervisor, and Harry heard him say, "It's the bloody rozzers out front." Harry had not heard that word for a very long time.

He had been shown to the local interest section. He had gone through the small selection of books that pertained to the time and subject he specifically wanted to know about. When he asked about borrowing them, he was asked for his library card and had to admit he didn't think he had one. He was asked if he had ever had one. Harry confessed he'd visited as a schoolboy. The librarian looked Harry up on the system. He was still in possession of a junior lending card. It had never been converted to adult. Harry was asked if he'd like to convert that now, and was his address still the same. Harry asked if the rigmarole was necessary, he was the police, he was only going to go through the books once and return them, but the librarian said they couldn't make any exceptions, otherwise how would they ever know where any of the books were? Harry understood that. He also understood that the librarian didn't like rozzers and was making a point.

He asked for access to the local newspapers. The librarian told him they had been in the process of being digitized, but then the budgets were cut. They were all on microfiche, but the microfiche machine was broken, and they didn't yet have the budget to repair it. The local papers themselves might have books of their old editions, possibly. There was only one local paper at the time. The offices were now closed here, and the head office was seventy-two miles away.

Harry was at the door, ashamed of having been defeated by a library, when a younger female librarian sidled up to him, from the children's section. It was as if she wanted to make amends for her colleague's surliness. "What were you looking for?" she asked Harry.

After he had explained, she said, "You should talk to Pete Stanley." Harry looked blank. He had never heard of Pete Stanley. "He wrote a couple of books on all that stuff. We don't have his books, but we do have his details."

Peter Stanley's cottage was a fire hazard. Even in the thin, dark hall there were tenuous planks of bowing wood put to work as shelves, sitting unsurely against the wall. Harry did his best not to stand under them. The books were all shapes and sizes, and the small shafts of light that were permitted in through panes of the front door and narrow windows illuminated only dust and cobwebs.

The tiny cottage was incongruously jammed in a backstreet of

Bredy, between a number of long and low orange-brick town houses. It looked like a planning mistake.

Pete Stanley's notes were piled everywhere, handwritten and typed. They sat on tables, on writing desks (one each in the bedroom and the lounge), piled up in front of the old television, and hung precariously off shelves in front of books. Here was a man surrounded by thoughts—his own and others'.

It turned out Peter Stanley had written twenty-nine books, all centering around Dorset history, landscape and ("my most popular") pub walks. "They pay for the others," said Peter, disappointed in the taste of his readers. He was aggrieved when Harry brought up the fact that Peter's books were not in the local library. "I know. They have a vendetta against me," he said mournfully.

They settled into Peter's old and faded chairs, the dust kicking up into the shafts of light as Harry sank into the cushion.

"I wondered if you might find me," said Stanley. "I haven't slept since I heard," he added. His look was pained.

"Oh," said Harry, surprised. He brought his notebook out quicker than he had expected to. "Why's that?"

"I called your station, offering help. They treated me as if I were a crank. Which I suppose I am." He peered at Harry. "You're Trevor's boy, then. Didn't fancy a life in meat. Shame. Someone's got to carry on that line."

Harry didn't want to elucidate that he had always harbored higher ambitions than to be the town butcher. "What was it you were calling the station about?"

"I'm alarmed, of course," said Stanley. "The timing, the similarities, to 1925. The proximity. What do you know?"

"Not much," said Harry.

"Yes, the online world is not interested in the everyday events of our local past lives," mourned Stanley. "Too few clicks. Too little conflict. So much for knowledge. I expected it to be a library for the world, for all of time. And what do we have instead? Little more than a digital pole dance!"

"There are three possible explanations for what is currently happening," proclaimed Stanley with impressive certainty. "Either the killer has read about the events of 1925, possibly in my work, maybe in that of others', although I consider that less likely; or the killer has direct knowledge of the previous crimes; or the original murders and that of this current situation are actually proof of what people believed at the time: that the Devil stalked this coast. The folklore would have us believe it returns once a century—an inspection, if you like. The Devil's Time."

Harry tried to steer the conversation away from superstition. "There were three *murders*, correct?"

"Yes," blinked Stanley, maintaining the air of a teacher lecturing a recalcitrant student who hadn't been paying attention. "One every month, during that season. A dairymaid, a stable lad and a fisherman left propped up by the side of the road, with antlers bound to their heads. Sent shockwaves through the community. Seemingly no connection between any of them. But each time a death occurred, it was precipitated by a significant fire."

"I'm sorry, what?" burbled Harry as he scribbled away, adrenaline flooding his body.

"The night before every murder, a fire was lit which was visible for miles around, down on the coast. It came to foretell murder so definitively that non-work-related fires were banned for a good few years afterward. It scared the living daylights out of people."

The fire. The fire he'd been called to, when he got the call from Nicola.

Peter Stanley leaned forward.

"I don't want you to misunderstand, but I would be remiss not to inform you. The man who was eventually arrested, and hanged for the crimes—some say correctly, some say falsely—was a direct ancestor of the family who own the farm today."

"Which family is that?" Harry knew the answer before he asked.

"Name of Deakins."

CHAPTER TWENTY-TWO

"Where's Harry?"

Mel looked up from his screen and shrugged. "Westlife? Think he's on a lunch break."

"He's on a *what*?" Nicola hoped she'd misheard. She had returned swiftly to the station after talking to Patricia Tiernan, to find it full of boxed-up items and empty of fifty percent of her team.

Mel, eyes still on the screen, waved a hand around him. "This all came in."

As he said it, Reeta Patel came in from the back room. Mel hurriedly added, "Oh, and she's here," again without diverting his eyes from the screen.

"Didn't this place used to be a bank? Why've they shoved you here?" Reeta asked, looking around in disbelief.

"Proximity to the station next door," said Nicola. "There's a connecting alley. At least we've got space. If not much manpower."

Mel, despite not being part of the exchange, shook his head and muttered, "Whole force is falling apart."

"Good job the three of us are awesome then," said Nicola pointedly. She knew negativity was a virus that could spread through a team and an investigation quickly, and she would not allow it to happen here.

"He's not wrong," said Reeta as they walked to a corner of the space and a cheaply partitioned office Nicola had commandeered as her own. "It's like all the high-ups have had a mass nervous breakdown and are just doing mad things," she added, nodding at the piles of evidence boxes. "Fair bit to get through."

"I'm cataloging it all," said Mel, again without an invitation to participate.

"King of cataloging, our Mel," remarked Reeta to Nicola as she shut the door to the office. Nicola took this as confirmation that Mel didn't do much else.

As they sat, Reeta handed her an evidence bag containing a battered, thick A4 hardback volume. "Appointments diary recovered from by the till. Has all the bookings for the pub. Also seems to be a notepad for other things—names, phone numbers, the lot."

"Thank you," said Nicola, beginning to leaf through.

"There are a few boxes out there with years' worth of accounts and receipts. From a cursory glance, he seemed to keep everything, but not in much of an order."

Nicola nodded. She wanted Reeta to get to the question of where exactly she believed Jim Tiernan had been murdered and was hoping these important factual pleasantries were just the warm-up.

They were. "We're working on the premise that the victim was killed in his own bedroom and then moved to the site where his body was found. The clothes people described him wearing that evening were discarded close to the bed. The bed had been slept in on one side only. The pillow on that side had indentations and, obviously, his DNA and hair samples, as you'd expect. There was a duvet, thrown to one side, but no sheet on the bed. I don't know whether that was usual. What definitely *is* unusual is the absence of other clothes."

"How d'you mean?" asked Nicola.

"The White Hart was Jim Tiernan's main home, right? We didn't find any of his clothes there. The wardrobes and drawers were empty, like they'd been ransacked and left half open."

"Somebody stole all his clothes?" asked Nicola, incredulous.

Reeta shrugged. "Seems that way. But there's no evidence of a break-in anywhere across the property, or any forced doors or windows. We're continuing to carry out forensic examinations, but it's a big building with multiple areas, and we're limited in budget and time. If there's any area you want us to make a priority, just say."

Nicola counted off the issues racing through her mind as she took this all in. "So the killer, or killers, were able to gain access easily, would have to be strong enough to carry a body downstairs, and also have access to transport large enough to move a human body."

"Correct," said Reeta. "And this is before we get to what was done to the body. Killer would have had to source the antlers, plus the sack the victim was found in, have the means by which to affix the antlers to the head, which seems like it was a combination of epoxy and rope . . . oh, and cheers for the dead deer." She grimaced.

"You're welcome," grinned Nicola.

"I'll make sure you get more information soon as we work through it."

"Thank you, Reeta," said Nicola.

Reeta looked around and exhaled. "Are you getting enough support?"

"From you? Definitely," smiled Nicola.

"From high up," said Reeta.

For the first time since she had got here, Nicola felt that someone else within this force was actually looking out for her.

"It's early days," said Nicola diplomatically. She felt she could trust Reeta, but she had learned from past experience that it was wise to be more than certain before expressing disquiet about systems or senior officers to other colleagues. Her posting in Liverpool had been a snake pit of internal politics and she had spoken too freely and been punished for it. Despite the shortcomings of this new job, she was glad to be free of the febrile organizational jostling of her last place.

"OK," said Reeta. "We'll keep talking." She got up and looked around. "I quite like this place, in a sort of 'it's shit but better than plenty of other places they might've put you' kind of way."

She beamed and left. Nicola realized she was smiling, too. Every time she met Reeta, she ended up smiling. She turned her thoughts back to the question Reeta had left them with.

Where were Jim Tiernan's clothes? What happened to them?

Nicola checked her watch—more pressingly, where was Harry?—and began examining Jim Tiernan's appointments diary from the White Hart.

His diary noted that the day before he died he had been expecting a 9:30 a.m. visit from Christine Wilson, the head of the brewery. This confirmed Christine's statement to them. Then, under "11:30," it just said TFW. Nicola stared at the page—that must be the meeting Christine had mentioned Jim was going to afterward, but for now the meaning was opaque. There were no bookings for food at the White Hart that day. Quite the opposite. In what Nicola presumed was Jim's handwriting, JIM OUT TO LUNCH TODAY—BUSINESS MEETING. IRINA TO COVER had been scrawled in big capitals, and underlined.

To the side, linked to this in pencil, was written "Drayman's 1:30." Nicola thought it had been added later, or at the last minute. She was no cryptographer, but it looked rushed.

A quick amount of research told Nicola that Drayman's was likely to be the Drayman's Inn, about a forty-five-minute drive away, heading north and inland, over the border in Somerset. She called the pub but they had no record of a booking in Jim's name for that day, and it had been an uphill battle trying to describe Jim to confirm whether he'd actually been there.

Why would a pub landlord drive forty-five minutes to have lunch at another pub? Had he been meeting someone. If so, who—and why?

CHAPTER TWENTY-THREE

Eddie Godfrey wondered how many men of his age had sat alone in their vehicle, as he was sitting now, in an English lay-by, crying and howling.

Traffic whizzed past on the A35, oblivious to the delivery van parked halfway up a hill on the dual carriageway part of the A35, heading west. To his left, the landscape spread out magnificently, until it hit the sea in the far distance.

It was the physical symptoms which had made him pull over. His sight was blurring, and there was the equivalent of a pulsing, jagged vein in the top-left-hand corner of his vision. He wondered whether it could be the precursor to a migraine. He had never experienced a migraine before, but if it was going to come any time, he reasoned, it would probably come now.

He had placed his hand on his heart, once parked, as was his custom, then checked his pulse: both felt fast. He wasn't sure why he checked them like this; it wasn't as if he could do anything about it. It could be a panic attack. Eddie thought that "panic attack" was too mild an expression for what he was experiencing. His heart was racing. He felt short of breath. Neither of these things was unusual.

But today, in addition, his head had felt full to the point of bursting with conflicting thoughts and feelings and plans and revisions to plans and memories and multiple versions of answers to questions he expected to be asked soon.

Overruling everything was one governing thought: *Jim Tiernan is dead.*

His body had lain on this road.

A howl erupted from within Eddie. It had started deep within his chest and forced its way up his throat and out through his mouth. It was deep and heavily felt, and Eddie did not think it would ever stop.

The howl became a moan became a series of sobs, and then the crying and the howling became interchangeable, all one, filling the totality of Eddie Godfrey's van.

Throughout it all, Eddie knew stopping would make him late for every delivery the rest of the day. By now, he was beyond caring. He had bigger problems. He was so tired today. No, not just tired. Exhausted, in body and soul. Existentially knackered. Profoundly broken, by events. By life. And death.

Jim Tiernan's face, behind the bar at the White Hart, haunted him.

There were too many messages by the time he'd regained what would pass for his equilibrium today. His supervisor had sent him a very long voice note passing on the news that one of their business customers was escalating their complaint about deliveries not being received in full, and this being Eddie's fault. Eddie resisted the temptation to send a voice note back telling them to go fuck themselves. Instead, he called, said there must be a simple explanation, was sure it was just a misunderstanding or miscounting on the customer's part, but that he would check his records.

Eddie knew that his company gave lip service to the idea of customer satisfaction but in practice did little. Parcels and packages were frequently lost or damaged, or delivered to the wrong person or left in a place other than the place the customer had specified. All drivers knew how to protect themselves by posting the "sorry we missed you" slips through a door, or by concocting photos of parcels left and submitting them to management.

The message that caused him more anxiety was from a Detective Constable Harry Ward "just wanting a quick chat."

Eddie was frustrated that the young detective in front of him seemed unfazed by having to talk while Eddie unloaded boxes of artists' materials to a unit on a redbrick trading estate on the edge of Bredy. The buildings which decades back had housed industrial units were now split into smaller units inhabited by painters, sculptors, potters and the like.

As he walked, and the detective who introduced himself as Harry wrote, Eddie rattled through the list of people he remembered from the pub, his relationship with Jim ("He was a good bloke") and how they saw each other socially outside the pub ("though we both work hellish hours").

Eddie was trying to be cheery, trying to present as normal. Trying not to present as a man who had been crying in his van an hour earlier.

The detective smiled and asked more about Tuesday night, as Eddie rearranged the remaining parcels in the van. "What time did you arrive at the White Hart that night?"

"Would've been around half eight. Shift finishes at seven. Went home, got changed, bit of food, walked to the pub. Standard."

"Did you notice anything unusual during the evening? Either in the pub, or with Jim's behavior?"

Eddie shrugged the question off. "It was just a normal night."

He could see the detective was looking for more, and not getting it. "And what time did you leave?"

"When we got chucked out."

Harry asked, "Was anyone left in the pub other than Mr. Tiernan, at the end of the night?"

"Not as far as I remember. But it's not like I was checking. He was keen to get rid of us and get to bed. There was a handful of us walking back; we all peeled off to our own homes. Like I say, normal night at the pub. Can't believe it."

Harry asked, "Where were you between midnight and seven the next morning?"

"Dead to the world," said Eddie, and then hastily added, "asleep, I mean. God. Sorry. Asleep, in my house, there."

Jesus, Eddie.

"You didn't hear or see anything during that time?"

"I did not," said Eddie.

He watched the detective stop writing and peer into the back of the van.

Keep your nose out, PC Plod.

"D'you just use this for work?" asked the detective.

"Majority of the time—95 percent, 98 percent—yeah. But I mean, it's mine, I own it, got a good deal for it second-hand. It's not perfect, obviously, few things I need to get fixed, but yeah, work mainly. They want to own us, but they don't want to pay us, or give us any equipment. That's the gig economy, though, isn't it?"

Eddie realized that he had strayed way off the question there. He wondered if the detective would notice.

"So, it's also for personal use?" the detective persisted.

"I mean, occasionally."

"And when's the last time you used it for personal use—going somewhere, transporting something not to do with the work?"

Eddie blew out through his cheeks. "I mean, I'd have to think."

"That's OK," smiled the detective. And he waited.

"Oh, OK, um . . ." said Eddie, playing for time. "I brought a . . . table . . . back from Fernley earlier this week," he said. He watched the detective write that down.

"What sort of a table?" asked the detective.

Eddie stared back, trying to imagine a table. "Side table, for my mug of tea, next to the chair," he eventually replied, swallowing nervously.

"And that was the most recent non-work journey?"

"Yeah, and I keep a tight record of miles, and fuel, and all that. I mean, you have to, don't you?" *Shut up just shut up stop talking, Eddie.*

"How often do you clean it out?" asked the detective innocuously.

Eddie heard himself laugh. *Don't laugh—what you laughing for?*

He heard himself say, "Why d'you want to know?"

Eddie watched the detective stiffen a little. His tone became terser. The subtext was: *answer, please.*

"I'm investigating a murder, sir."

Eddie took a breath. He noticed the detective noticing that he'd taken a breath. *Why'd you take a breath like that, Eddie? Pull yourself together.* His heart was pounding now.

"Empty it, clean it, pretty much every day," said Eddie. "That's the routine. Unless I'm really knackered."

"So you last cleaned it, when?" asked the detective with a smile.

Eddie felt like he was being pulled somewhere he didn't want to go. "Tuesday? Wednesday?"

"Was it Tuesday or Wednesday?" pressed the detective.

Eddie leaned against the van. So tired. "What day is it today? Can

I be honest with you, Harry?" He made deliberate use of Harry's name there. "My head is scrambled. My mate's just died. I'm a bit at sixes and sevens. Definitely within the last couple of days." Eddie closed the van doors. "D'you mind if I get on? My supervisor is gonna be on at me if I get any further behind."

"Of course," said the young detective. "I've got your details for when I need to follow up."

They parted company. Eddie got back in his van and drove off. As he rounded the corner, he thought to himself: *what the hell did he mean by that?*

What had he let slip that might come back to haunt him?

CHAPTER TWENTY-FOUR

Frankie had observed Harry Ward as he approached the salon, late for their agreed statement-taking time, pacing up and down past the salon window, on the phone, seemingly being berated by someone—a boss, maybe? Frankie could hear him through the window saying, "What? Who said lunch break? I've been working the case! I'm just taking my final statement, now, then I'll be back." He'd checked his watch and said, "Yeah, outside the hairdresser's, half an hour?"

Frankie registered that their conversation had an end-time built in. Good to know. They watched Harry enter and look around, taking in the decor with a disbelieving smile on his face.

"This place has *changed*!" He looked at Frankie. "Last time I was here, this was like an old man's barbershop. Turn up, wait your turn, take the piss out of other people waiting, same trim for everyone and go home. I tried it once. Never again."

"Yeah, we've had a glow up," smiled Frankie.

"Shiny," nodded Harry, running a hand through his hair. "Looks like I should be coming here now."

Frankie grinned politely. "It's not exactly shabby, your trim. Not saying I can't do better, mind." Was that too familiar a thing to be saying to a detective? Frankie had no experience of this situation. This week kept throwing up new experiences which Frankie had never envisaged being part of.

"How long have you known Mr. Tiernan?"

Frankie shrugged. "Maybe two years. I was in the White Hart with a mate, we were talking with him at the bar, I told him what I did, and then he came in shortly after. He just became a regular. Came in first Wednesday of every month. Same slot. That's when I thought something might be wrong. When he didn't turn up. Especially as I'd seen him the night before."

"Was it just you in the pub on Tuesday?"

Frankie felt themself hesitate for a second. "No. Well, yes, to begin with. But then I was meeting someone."

"And who was that?" asked Harry, writing in his notebook.

"Sorry?"

Frankie watched Harry look up. They could tell Harry knew immediately that they were playing for time. Frankie did not have a poker face.

Harry repeated the question, phrasing it differently. "Who did you meet?"

Frankie looked straight ahead. "I'm blanking on the name, sorry. I think this has really freaked me out. It's hit hard, you know. Brain's all over the place."

Frankie worked their way through a quick-fire set of questions, giving short, straight answers, all the while wishing they'd not mentioned they were meeting someone, or pretended they didn't know their name. *What was it like that night in the pub? Can you name any of the other people who were there? How did Mr. Tiernan seem that night? What was his mood? Were there any people in there you hadn't seen before? Did anything out of the ordinary happen? No matter how unremarkable.* Frankie answered all these with ease. Harry carried on with "And what time did you leave to go home?"

Frankie thought this one was easy. "Maybe around ten thirty. Just before last orders. We saw Jim outside."

Frankie was alarmed to see Harry look up. "Mr. Tiernan was outside the pub, before last orders?"

Hadn't anyone else told him this?

"Yeah. He'd been out somewhere, to meet someone, or something. Not sure."

"You talked to him, outside?"

Frankie swallowed. "Yeah."

"How did he seem?"

"Out of sorts. I dunno what had happened just before. Not his usual cheery self."

"How d'you mean?" persisted Harry.

"Dunno," Frankie lied. "Just a bit off."

Frankie could see Harry becoming frustrated. "And how did you get home?"

"I drove."

"Alone?"

"Mmm-hmm." Frankie wasn't going to offer any more than that.

Harry circled back, persisting. Frankie realized this had been his plan. "Any joy on the name of the person you met?"

Frankie looked calmly at Harry. "No," they said.

A half beat of silence. It felt to both of them like an hour.

Harry tried again. "Do you have it on your phone, or a text? Was it someone you know, or were you meeting for the first time?" Frankie looked back, as if mute. "A friend, or a work colleague? Tinder date? No judgment here. I'm only after the facts. Even a first name will help."

"Oh, OK . . . yeah . . . maybe Dino?"

What the fuck, Frankie, what are you doing?

"We'll need their full name, how you know them, and a way to contact them."

Frankie felt a little sick.

And then the door dinged.

Frankie had never been more pleased to see a walk-in customer in their life.

"Take a seat, with you in one sec," said Frankie to the customer, before turning back to Harry. "I'm sorry," they said. "Can we maybe finish this another time?"

Harry looked at Frankie, kept their gaze. "Why don't I come back in tomorrow?"

Frankie wondered if the cold sweat they were feeling was apparent on their forehead. "Good. Sure."

They were about to part when Harry leaned close to Frankie, dropped his voice to a low volume and used his calmest, kindest tone. "Word of advice. You must tell me the truth. Because we'll know, in the end. We just want to eliminate you, and whoever you met, from our inquiries. That's the important thing. That's how you'll help us. Understand?"

Frankie nodded once more. Harry smiled politely at the customer on the way out. As he got into a car which pulled up outside, Frankie already feared that somewhere in that conversation they'd made a mistake.

The silence on the other end of the phone hummed with implicit irritation. Frankie hated silences during these calls.

After a while, they said, "Are you still there?"

There was a sigh. Exasperation, interpreted Frankie. They hoped it was not more than that.

"Have you got a pen?" asked the voice.

Frankie scrabbled around for one, near the till. *There should be one near the till. Where is it? Ah! Located.* "Yep," they replied.

"Take down this name and number. They'll say they were with you in the pub that night. If the police call them, they'll back you up."

Frankie wrote as he told them the name. There was a sinking feeling in Frankie's stomach. Dino, on the other end of the phone, was certain this was the solution, and he claimed to have experience of these situations. Frankie, who did not have the same level of experience, was not so certain it would work.

"Got that?" asked Dino.

"I have," said Frankie. There was a pause. "I'm not sure, though."

Dino's voice grew tighter. "I'm trying to help you out, Frankie."

Frankie understood the subtext of that. Dino ended the call without a goodbye.

The door opened, the bell tinged. Frankie turned to the next customer with a broad smile, plastering over the turmoil they felt in their guts.

CHAPTER TWENTY-FIVE

Nicola drove away from the coast, across the county line, deep into the hedgerow-lined lanes of Somerset. She drove fast along the single-track roads—they had to get to the Drayman's Inn, and then back in time for the memorial Ayesha Barton was hosting at the Fox that evening. She noticed Harry in the passenger seat hold on to the handle above his head as she braked and maneuvered the car into a passing space to allow an oncoming car to squeeze by.

"We don't take lunch breaks," she said, looking straight out through the windscreen, easing the car out of the passing space and acknowledging the other driver's gratitude with a raised hand.

"I know," came Harry's response from the passenger seat. "Who said I took a lunch break? Mel?" Before Nicola could reply, Harry continued, seemingly burning with controlled rage, "Because, with respect, he has no idea. He barely leaves that desk. I went to find out more about the murders in 1925, then I took statements from two more people who were in the White Hart on Tuesday night. Then I met you. I actually haven't had any lunch at all."

Nicola stole a glance at her detective constable. Maybe it was their proximity in the car, maybe it was the first time noticing his profile view, or even the passion in his voice, but she realized with a jolt quite how good-looking Harry Ward was.

She was kicking herself for taking Mel's statement at face value. No point hiding that. "My mistake," she said. "Accusation withdrawn," she added, looking over at Harry and smiling.

She saw him relax a little and smile back. Nice smile, she thought instinctively, and then was startled to find herself immediately wondering about his private life.

"SOCO think he was killed at the pub and the body moved from there," she told Harry, swiftly bringing all thoughts back onto work.

"Eddie Godfrey is a delivery driver, with a van big enough to move a body," Harry responded.

"Interesting. Alibi?"

"No. Pub, then home, then sleep. Alone."

Nicola nodded. "So, we're awaiting forensic confirmation on the headless deer, we want to talk to Ayesha Barton's fiancé, Mick, and to Irina Bortnick about her movements on the night of Jim's death. We now have Jim's phone, but it's a dumbphone, very old: apparently he hated mobiles and hardly ever used it. But I'm having Mel go through it anyway for numbers, calls and texts. What else?"

"I spoke to a hairdresser named Frankie who was in the pub that night. They met a man there, but they were reluctant to tell me the name. Tried to pretend they'd forgotten, but seemed like they were bullshitting. I'm giving them a few hours to come up with it."

Nicola nodded. "Good."

"Plus, the murders in 1925 were committed by a member of the Deakins family."

"Holy shit," said Nicola. "Did you not think to start with that?!"

"I also found out there were fires lit around the time of every murder back then," added Harry. "When you rang me about Jim Tiernan's death, I was at Deakins' farm, after complaints of a fire the previous night."

"Right," said Nicola, processing. Her mind was racing, internally configuring all these jigsaw pieces, seeing whether they'd fit together.

After she'd been thinking silently for a moment or two, she noticed Harry looking at her as if he was fit to burst and then he said, "I'm gonna work my arse off for you, boss. I know you might have doubts, cos I came through Professional Admission, but I'm not shit. I have experience of the real world and I'm good at this. And I'll only get better, working with you."

Nicola looked at Harry, surprised. "I don't think you're shit," she said.

"Thanks," said Harry.

Nicola thought it was a low bar for gratitude, given what she'd just said.

"So did you go from the butcher's to Professional Admission?" she asked.

"What?" Harry looked confused.

"Ward's, the butcher's, that's your family, right? You worked there and then came on to—"

Harry interrupted her. "I never worked there. I mean, Saturday boy, in my teens, yeah. But I went to uni in Nottingham, did a degree in sports science, worked in a few places around the Midlands after graduating, but just didn't like it. Didn't like the people, didn't see the point. So after a few years of that I decided I'd come back here and sign up for the Professional Admission Detective Scheme."

"Oh God, sorry." Nicola was actually looking embarrassed. "I thought you'd just worked in the shop in town."

"No!" Harry was outraged, but now they were both starting to laugh. "You *did* think I was shit! You thought I only knew about sausages!"

Nicola started to say, "Harry, I'm sorry," but was interrupted by a call coming in on her mobile, over the car speaker. She glanced at her phone in the dashboard cradle.

Mike.

Not now.

She fumbled with the Bluetooth controls on the steering wheel to decline the call. Instead, Mike's voice came through the car speakers.

"Nic?"

Shit.

"Hi! I'm driving. You're on speaker." Nicola smiled weakly at Harry, who courteously pulled out his own phone and started scrolling, as if to communicate: *I'm not paying any attention to this.*

"Just checking about tonight," came Mike's voice.

Fuck.

Nicola could feel her face reddening. She did not want to have this conversation on speakerphone, but she didn't know how to switch the call, and she was driving.

"Oh. God. Listen. There's a thing I have to be at. Work."

"Right," said Mike neutrally.

There was a silence on his end of the phone. Nicola winced. Harry kept scrolling.

"It's unavoidable," Nicola said, hearing the weakness in her voice.

"Mmmm-hmmm," said Mike.

There was more dead air on the phone line. Then:

"You forgot," said Mike.

Nicola squished her eyes shut, in reactive pain. Amidst the case, she *had forgotten.* It was really important that she did not forget things like this.

"No—" she protested, but Mike cut her off.

"This was kind of a red line, Nic."

Please don't be an arsehole about this. Not on speaker.

To cap it all, up ahead, the narrow country road was blocked. A large, vicious-looking piece of threshing equipment sat spilled across the width of the road. It had fallen off the back of a trailer, and several men were trying to get it back. There was no passing either side, so Nicola was forced to slow the car to a stop in front of it. She had forgotten the joys of being back in the countryside. This never happened in Bootle.

"I'm sorry, love," she said to Mike. "The day's just been—mad and—" She exhaled. "I, really, my mistake, I apologize."

Date night. Their pact, their agreement, in a whole suite of measures agreed when moving here. The pact stated that date nights were now sacrosanct and work was not allowed to take precedence. This was an early breach. She felt guilty and angry with herself. She also wanted to say: *I am investigating a fucking murder here! Do I not get a bit of leeway for that?*

Harry looked up, slightly apologetically, and said quietly, "I can cover tonight, if—"

Nicola cut him off. "It's fine—"

Then Mike could be heard asking, "Is there someone in the car with you?"

"Yeah, Harry, my DC." Nicola smiled at Harry. He smiled awkwardly back, looked down at his phone again in an effort to pretend he wasn't hearing any of it.

"You didn't say—"

There was yelling ahead: the men were singularly failing to navigate the threshing machine back onto its trailer. They stopped, reset and tried again.

"No, look, I'll be there—my bad, it's just it was this last-minute memorial for the pub landlord who got killed—"

"OK, fine," said Mike calmly. *Calmer since you know you're being listened to.* "I get it. Shall we do tomorrow? That work?"

"Yes," said Nicola, grateful they weren't going to play out their marriage further over speakerphone. "Let's do that. If you're sure."

"I'm sure. Good luck tonight. See you later. Bye, Harry," Mike added pointedly, and ended the call.

Nicola and Harry sat in silence, neither knowing quite what to say as they watched the spiky arms of the threshing machine finally being successfully heaved and cajoled back onto the trailer.

After a while, Nicola said, "Sorry about that," and gestured to her phone.

Harry waved her apology away. "No, no, not at all. All good."

The traffic was finally on the move.

The Drayman's Inn was the lone pub in a village called Frimpton, populated by honey-colored dwellings built from hamstone. The inn had a history to be proud of, having been the local hostelry since 1699. It boasted a thatched roof, flagstone floors, and a garden that stretched a long way out the back, with a canopied eating area which Nicola imagined would get a lot of use in the summer. The Drayman's now styled itself as a "restaurant with rooms" for those who wanted to enjoy the high standard of food and drink without having to drive back immediately from this out-of-the-way village.

The two detectives were greeted by Diane, the tightly smiling house manager, who looked back through the reservations system as the rest of the staff set the tables for dinner. There was no reservation for Tiernan on Tuesday 17th.

"Could he have been a walk-in?" asked Harry.

"I doubt it," said Diane. "We're booked up for lunch weeks in advance. I was working on Tuesday; I would have greeted him. I'm pretty sure there were no cancellations and we turned people away."

Nicola produced a picture of Jim Tiernan to show Diane.

"Oh! Him, yeah. He was definitely here that afternoon. I remember. Probably the booking was under the name of the woman he was with."

Nicola saw Harry, who had been looking round the dining room, swivel his head like an owl, and ask, "He was with a woman? Just the two of them?"

"Very much just the two of them," said Diane. Nicola had a sense Diane was enjoying the gossip. "They were like kids. Giggling, feeding each other. They couldn't wait to get up there."

"They took a room?" asked Nicola.

"They did. And then . . . they didn't even stay the night. Paid for the room for the whole night, left by quarter to five! We could've re-let it. Arrived and left in separate cars, not that I was looking. I shouldn't say it, but it was pretty obvious what they came for."

Nicola wondered if Diane remembered what room they were in. She did remember: it was room 3, their best one. The biggest bed—the best bed, at least.

Nicola then asked whether Diane had a record of what name the room was booked under.

Diane checked, and gave Nicola and Harry the name.

Jim Tiernan, the landlord of Fleetcombe's White Hart, had spent the afternoon before his death seemingly having sex with Ayesha Barton, the landlady of Fleetcombe's Fox.

CHAPTER TWENTY-SIX

Betrayal.

It was a hot topic, for Nicola. It was a word seared on her heart, now. A word she didn't just know the meaning of but one she *felt*. Viscerally.

She knew that for the rest of her life, whenever the subject came up, she would instantly remember where she was standing and how she felt when she was first told, in no uncertain terms, that she had been betrayed.

As she drove back toward Fleetcombe with Harry beside her, Nicola found herself trying to regulate her breathing. She knew her cheeks had flushed when the information about Jim Tiernan and Ayesha Barton had been revealed. Now, keeping her eyes on the traffic, she breathed slowly out through her mouth and in through her nose. And repeat. She was trying not to let tears poke through. Focus on what's in front. But it was hard. That sick feeling was pushing up from her gut once more.

That was what betrayal felt like.

And here she was, at the mercy of a torrent of feelings, on a B road in Dorset. The anger, the rage, the deathly sadness.

Take yourself out of it.

Nicola knew she had to control her emotions now, and later tonight.

She had to observe, not participate. She could not betray—*ha!*—what she knew. Wait for the right moment.

Deal with the case.

Had anyone else known about this assignation? Was this what Irina had been referring to when she'd said Jim could sometimes be a dick? Was her story that she'd gone driving a lie? Had Irina known about Jim's betrayal and confronted him, even killed him because of it? (But still, the antlers. The bloody antlers. Why the antlers? How would they fit with that?)

What a mess.

Betrayal was never clean.

Had it caused such a mess in Fleetcombe that it had led to the murder of Jim Tiernan?

She pulled into the car park of the Fox. It was dark and they were late. As she parked, she realized she had not said a single word to Harry on the drive back. As they got out of the car, Harry was looking at her, concerned. She wondered what her face had been doing.

"Everything OK?" he asked.

"Yep," said Nicola tersely. "Not a word to anyone about the Drayman's."

"Understood," said Harry.

"Watch everything," was her final instruction. She strode in.

The pub was packed. Ayesha Barton was clearly good at judging what people in Fleetcombe needed, thought Nicola as they walked in.

Especially Jim Tiernan, she found herself also thinking, uncharitably.

Not about you, Nicola.

There was a low hubbub of chat and the occasional respectful burble of laughter. There were pictures of Jim Tiernan on the bar and a couple of large, thick candles which had been lit and placed either side of the photos. Nicola felt the candles were a bit over the top.

As they walked in, scanning the crowd for Ayesha, Christine Wilson from the brewery walked past and stopped, surprised to see them.

"Oh hello," she said. "How are things going? Do you know any more? Now, wait, are you on or off duty?"

"We're just paying our respects," said Nicola. "What about you?"

Christine looked embarrassed. "We should have been doing this in one of ours. Ayesha rather caught us on the hop. This is what I mean: she's very dynamic, very proactive. And this is a very generous gesture. You can see the whole village is appreciative. I can't deny I'm borderline ashamed. None of *our* landlords thought about this. I mean, I know this is the other pub in the same village, but it's all about speed of thought, isn't it? Also"—she grabbed a mini Yorkshire pudding with a cube of roast beef in gravy inside it from a platter being offered around—"have you tried the food? She does such a good job."

She took the food and moved away effortlessly. There's a woman who has done a lot of social gatherings in her life, thought Nicola. A small mingle, a courteous exchange and move on. Nicola always found herself stuck with someone, unable to get away.

They made their way to the bar, where Nicola ordered two soft drinks for her and Harry. "Interesting she's here, given what was going on over there," muttered the barman, Len, to Nicola, nodding toward Christine Wilson. Len was in his sixties, with white mutton chops, a bold look in this day and age. He felt more White Hart than Fox, thought Nicola. Maybe the tourists like it; maybe they think this is how older men in Dorset look all the time.

"What situation was that?" asked Nicola, knowing full well that's what he wanted to hear back. She had been in this situation with men before, in and out of work. They knew the next seven sentences of what they were going to say and only required small prompts. Len had not asked who she was or how she knew Jim. Nicola was pretty sure he had no idea she was a detective. This wasn't intel, it was gossip, and she was here for it.

"We heard he was about to get thrown out. He owed them a lot of money. They'd found big holes in the accounts. She'd given him leeway, he'd taken it, then when it had got too big to be covered up, she gave him an ultimatum: pay up or get out."

"Really?"

Len nodded conspiratorially and leaned in closer. Bit too close, thought Nicola. "Her job's on the line. Imagine the humiliation. Their board of directors is going to get into it all. Except they probably won't now, because she can just say she knew nothing, and who is there to contradict her? Him getting killed is the best thing that could've happened for her. She can put it all on him, everyone carries on, they write off the debt. You local?"

It was Nicola's turn to lean in close to Len now. "I'm CID. Investigating Jim Tiernan's murder."

Len looked alarmed. "You're not!"

Nicola nodded.

"You could've said!"

"You could've asked," smiled back Nicola as she turned and handed Harry his drink.

The two detectives surveyed the crowd, sipping their drinks.

It took Nicola approximately three seconds to spot Deakins, sitting in a corner alone and taking it all in. No banjo, she noted. Everyone was giving him a wide berth. He caught Nicola's glance, and it seemed to throw him, seeing her. Just momentarily. Then he raised his pint at her.

She gave a cordial smile back and watched him neck a good third of the pint, keeping his eyes on her the whole time. She did not look away.

Harry, meanwhile, had caught sight of Frankie being waved over to a table by Eddie Godfrey. Frankie seemed to gratefully accept the invitation. Interesting, noted Harry. Those two seem to know each other. Drinking pals at the White Hart? He wouldn't have pegged them as natural friends: very different ages, and rather different personalities, from what Harry had experienced of them. He watched as Eddie leaned in and whispered something to Frankie—who nodded. They both had grim looks on their faces. Then Frankie looked up and saw Harry. Harry smiled, and Frankie returned it, unconvincingly. Eddie remained stony-faced.

Someone else joined them—a man in his thirties with short-cropped dark hair and blazing green eyes. He was leaning in talking, arms round both Eddie and Frankie. Familiar. He looked like he was saying something consoling. They nodded; Frankie touched his hand.

Harry wondered who this person was, just as Ayesha Barton appeared at their sides.

"You're here. I'm so glad you came. It's going to really reassure everyone. You've got drinks—have you had food? D'you need me to introduce you to anyone?"

"No, but I'd like a moment with you when it's convenient," said Nicola.

Ayesha looked thrown. "You mean tonight?"

Nicola stood firm. "I do. Were you closed this Tuesday lunchtime just gone?"

The unspoken words were *the lunchtime before Jim Tiernan was killed.*

Ayesha appeared frozen in time for a second—neither her face nor her body moved. "We were, yeah, that's right."

"Any particular reason?"

Ayesha took another moment to reply. "I was . . . under the weather." She recomposed herself. "Would you mind, could we . . . hold questions for later?"

"Sure," said Nicola. "We'll be here." She liked that it sounded vaguely threatening.

The two women smiled at each other, each trying to size the other up. Then, as if a switch had flipped within her, Ayesha called out to the man with the cropped dark hair and blazing green eyes.

"Mick, here a sec!"

The man who Harry had watched talking to Eddie and Frankie looked up and walked over, smiling. This was the famous fiancé, Mick. Nicola glanced at Harry. The evening was becoming more complicated.

"Hi," beamed Mick, making eye contact with Nicola and holding out a decisive hand to be shaken.

"This is—" Ayesha looked to Nicola as a prompt.

"Detective Sergeant Nicola Bridge. Detective Constable Harry Ward. We're investigating the murder of Jim Tiernan," said Nicola.

"Excuse me just one sec," said Ayesha, spotting an issue at the bar which needed attending to.

Mick blew out his cheeks. "He was a good feller, Jim," he said. "I had a lot of time for him." Was that a trace of a Geordie accent?

"Did you know him well?" asked Harry.

Mick nodded. "I drink in the White Hart whenever I'm around. I feel like a spare part in here. The missus has got it running like clockwork; if I try and help, I just get in the way and mess up the systems. Trust me, I've tried. Plus, it's work for her. We don't get to chat—I'm just sitting scratching me arse. If I go down the Hart, there's people to chat to, can sink a few pints. I can talk to Jim, and Eddie over there. Frankie, too. It's more my kind of gaff anyway." He nodded over at

Deakins. "Apart from that one. He can fuck off. No good at all. Where was I? Oh yeah. Don't tell Ayesha any of this. Kidding. She jokes I'm not classy enough to be allowed in here."

Nicola noted Mick's easygoing manner, seemingly happy to talk. An open book, that was the subtext of everything he was saying. She wondered: *does he know about Ayesha and Jim Tiernan? Did he know on Tuesday?*

Harry asked, "D'you mind me asking where you were on Tuesday night?"

"I was with Ayesha, here."

Nicola's ears pricked up. Ayesha had told them she was alone. She watched Harry stay ice cool, and ask, "All night?"

"Aye."

Before either could pursue it, Ayesha rushed back past, saying, "Here she is. OK, here she is," and headed for the archway into the dining room.

Standing there, cautiously, was Patricia Tiernan.

Most people present were good enough to keep talking and not stare as Patricia walked through. A few lowered their heads and gazed at their drink, but most smiled sympathetically, and although the conversational hubbub lessened slightly, silence did not envelop the room. Patricia looked exposed and lost. Nicola felt immediately sorry for her.

As Ayesha guided Patricia toward Harry, Nicola and Mick, Patricia was saying, "Is it all right? That I came? I thought it would be nice not to be alone. Nobody has to talk to me if they don't want to."

Ayesha replied, "What're you talking about? Of course we want to talk to you. I'm glad you're here. It's awful, what's happened. Awful, and shocking. I don't know how you're holding it together, I really don't. Let me get you a drink. The usual?"

Patricia nodded and smiled politely at Nicola, Harry and Mick. "Hello." She looked around. "He's got a good turnout, I'll say that. I think he'd be very pleased. Wrong pub, though, he'd be saying!"

They all smiled. Patricia's smile faded faster than anyone else's.

Ayesha pressed a glass into Patricia's hand before grabbing an empty wine glass from the side and tapping a spoon on it. The pub, now standing room only, quietened.

"Thank you. Hello, everyone. For those who don't know me, or haven't been in here for a few years, I'm Ayesha, I run the Fox. We wanted to take a moment tonight to come together, to mark Jim's death, to register our shock and sadness collectively. Jim was a valued member of the Fleetcombe community, and we are all still coming to terms with what's happened. We also should show our gratitude for the ongoing efforts of the local police, of whom DS Bridge and DC Ward are here tonight."

She gestured over to the detectives. As heads swiveled and eyes were trained on them, Nicola found herself irritated that Ayesha had picked them out. It felt like a power play. She would have preferred to stay anonymous. She and Harry just nodded respectfully as Ayesha said, "I'm sure we're all quietly praying that they find the person responsible very soon indeed."

"Most importantly," Ayesha continued, "we link arms to offer support to Jim's sister, Patricia. We are all here for you, Patricia. Whatever you need, whenever you need it." Patricia looked uncomfortable as Ayesha raised her glass. "I'd like to propose a toast. To absent friends. To Jim."

As people drank, Patricia turned to Nicola. "Irina said she might want to sleep on my sofa again tonight."

"Are you comfortable with that?" asked Nicola.

"I can't have her roaming the streets. And she says she can't stand to be anywhere near the pub." Patricia was looking around the room. "Do you think his killer is here?" she asked quietly.

"We're doing all we can to find them," said Nicola.

She could see it did not offer much reassurance to Patricia.

During the course of the evening, Harry managed to maneuver himself into a position where Frankie could not avoid speaking to him. When he spotted them on their own, he sauntered casually over.

He could see panic spread across Frankie's face as he arrived.

"Hi! Any joy with the full details for that guy?" Harry asked, all innocence.

"Yes," said Frankie.

Harry waited, happy to leave the gap.

"Theo Andrakis," said Frankie eventually.

Harry nodded. As he wrote the name down he said, "When we spoke, you said his name was maybe Dino."

He looked back up to see what he could only interpret as a panicky smile on Frankie's face.

"My mind's all frazzled. Dino, Theo—got muddled!"

"Right."

Frankie reached in their pocket for a scrap of paper. "That's his number, he can confirm it," they said.

Harry gave the number a cursory glance before pocketing it. "How long have you known this . . . Theo?"

"Not long," said Frankie. "Month or two, maybe."

"Where did you first meet?"

"He came in the salon?"

To Harry, that sounded more like a question than a statement. "OK. And how many times have you met since?"

Frankie's expression was gradually filling up with panic. "Maybe once or twice."

"Is it once, or is it twice?" Harry was being gentle, but his tone was firm.

"Twice, I think."

"Twice including Tuesday night at the White Hart?"

Agonizing pause. Harry watched Frankie wincing as they spoke. "No, twice before then."

"So, three times," said Harry.

"Yes," said Frankie, unconvincingly.

Harry looked at Frankie in silence. The pub gathering hummed in the background. Harry wondered whether Frankie would take the chance to alter their story once more. When that didn't happen, he just said, "OK, I'll give him a call. Thanks for the name. Have a good evening."

He walked away. As he did, he looked back to see he had immediately been replaced by Eddie Godfrey, who seemed as if he was quizzing Frankie on what had just happened. Frankie looked agitated as they spoke.

Harry moved to a quieter area of the pub and dialed the number he had just been given.

Nicola found Ayesha in the kitchen area, arranging more food on plates.

"I'll be out in a sec," said Ayesha.

"You and I need to have an honest conversation now," said Nicola quietly.

Ayesha stopped what she was doing and looked up. "About what?"

"Everything you left out when we first spoke," said Nicola pointedly.

Harry finished up his telephone call in the far corner of the dining area of the Fox. People hadn't really spilled this far back during the evening, preferring to cluster nearer the bar, no matter how crowded.

As he paced and spoke on the phone, Harry's eye landed on a distressed wooden bookcase built into the wall. It was filled with paperbacks and a nicely designed sign which read "The Fox Lending Library: all contributions welcome. Please return books when read, so others can enjoy!" It was stacked with books old and new, literary and otherwise, airport thrillers and the autobiographies of famous people. Harry could see five at least that he would happily flick through over a drink and some specialty wasabi mix. He hung up the phone, having got what he needed, and wondered why he'd never been in here before.

There were two more bookshelves on either side of the booth he was now next to, at eye height. One shelf was a collection of books targeted at a very specific clientele: pub jokes, anecdotes, shaggy-dog stories: compilations of humor in every form. Perfect for the lone drinker, or to liven up a tedious gathering.

The other shelf, closer to Harry, was a separate collection. As he peered closer, he could see that these were unified by a focus on local history. Dorset walks, coastal journeys, history of the area, plus a book on Dorset folklore, rituals and myths.

Interesting.

Harry casually pulled out the latter. On the cover: a selection of monuments . . .

And a stag with massive antlers.

Harry's breath caught for a second. He opened it up. Hardback, old but seemingly unread. He thumbed through to the contents.

There was a chapter called "The Myth of the Stag." He checked the page number, and flicked to it. He began to read—ten pages, interspersed with drawings and old photos of different types and sizes of antlers. And a section headed: "The Mystery of the Stag King."

Harry began to read—it concerned an unsolved murder from 1925.

Harry felt the hairs on his arms stand on end.

The page was folded down at the corner.

CHAPTER TWENTY-SEVEN

Please don't make me do this now," said Ayesha Barton, standing in the middle of the kitchen. "Not now, not here."

"You're withholding information from me," said Nicola, "and I do not have any more time to waste."

"You mean Tuesday," asked Ayesha. Nicola looked at her with a sharpness that could have curdled milk. Ayesha looked down and took a breath. "I saw Jim Tiernan the day before he died. In a . . . personal capacity."

"Explain what you mean by 'a personal capacity,' please," asked Nicola.

"We met for lunch," said Ayesha. "A non-work lunch."

"Just lunch?" asked Nicola, keeping her eyes locked on the landlady.

Ayesha was hypnotized now, like a mouse transfixed by a snake. She looked down, trying to break the spell. "And sex."

"Where?" asked Nicola curtly.

"The Drayman's Inn, in Somerset," said Ayesha.

"Why there?" Nicola asked.

"Far enough away that nobody would know us or see us; close enough that we could get to it within an hour."

"Was this the first time you and Jim Tiernan had sex?"

Ayesha looked genuinely terrified at hearing those words said aloud. "You cannot tell anyone else. This cannot go any further. If Mick finds out . . ." She worried at the ring on her finger. "It was the third time. The first was a month ago. We were sort of . . . on a high. On a high with each other." She looked around the kitchen. "I dunno what I've been doing. He's not even my type. I've always had a type. He was so not that type."

She thought about this silently for a moment as Nicola studied her, and then carried on. Now she could talk about it, a torrent had been unleashed.

"You know when you have this kind of magnetic pull toward someone, even though you know it's wrong, and it's going to cause you all sorts of problems, and it's a bad decision, and you know it's a bad decision before you make it, while you're making it and after you've made it . . . and yet you still don't care. You ever had that?"

Nicola replied coolly, "I understand that can happen."

"I get lonely. That's the thing about having a partner who's away. I'm sociable. I like company. Nobody understands what it's like, running a pub, apart from people who've run a pub. Especially in a tiny village like this. I bumped into Jim and we just got chatting. And he said something which really struck a chord with me, which was: everyone thinks we should be at each other's throats, but maybe we can help each other." She paused. "The first lunch, at the Drayman's, it was genuinely an innocent lunch, we meant to talk about business. And it just . . . escalated."

"Escalated into one of their rooms?" asked Nicola pointedly.

"Yeah," said Ayesha quietly.

"Who else knows about this?" asked Nicola.

"When you say this—"

"Any of it. Your relationship with Jim Tiernan—"

"I'd hardly call it a relationship," interjected Ayesha, with minor outrage.

"What then—a hobby?" shot back Nicola. She instantly knew the retort had been unfair.

Ayesha was quiet for a moment. Then she said, with a depth of feeling and melancholy: "An escape."

Nicola let that settle. "Did Jim confide in you about any worries or concerns he had? Was there anything worrying him that day? Is there anything else you may have omitted to mention that might shed any light on his death?"

Ayesha shook her head. "If there was anything else, I'd tell you. He was upbeat, he was full of energy, he . . ." She drifted off and looked ashamed, before correcting whatever it was she was about to say. "We had a great time, both of us, that afternoon."

Nicola asked, "Did you love him?"

Ayesha half gasped, half laughed, as if she couldn't believe Nicola would ask such a ludicrous question. "Did I *what*?" But then she hesitated, just for a second. "That's not what it was," said Ayesha.

After a moment staring at the food waiting to be served she added, "I think Irina found out, that afternoon."

Nicola was straight onto that. "You think or you know?"

"I know. Jim called me. They'd had a big argument when he got back. She'd disappeared. He said she was angrier than he'd ever seen her. I don't know how she knew. He told me we should keep a low profile. I was terrified Mick would find out." She looked at Nicola. "I still am."

"Have you had any contact with Irina since Jim's death?" asked Nicola.

Ayesha shook her head, looking worried. "I wondered if she might come tonight. But I understand why she hasn't." She paused before adding, "You know, there was a rumor going round at one stage that she wasn't actually Ukrainian. That she was maybe even from Russia and abusing the Homes for Ukraine thing. Do you think it could have been her?"

Nicola ignored Ayesha's question and continued with her own line. "Are you still maintaining you were here when Jim Tiernan was killed?" asked Nicola, with direct simplicity.

Ayesha stared at her. "What're you suggesting?! I was fucking him earlier in the day! Why would I kill him a few hours later?" Nicola noted that she had not explicitly suggested anything. She watched as, after the flash of anger, Ayesha composed herself. "Sorry. Sorry. It's all getting a bit much. Yes, I was here. Clearing up, getting ready for the next day, watched a bit of TV, was on my phone, then I went to bed, maybe half twelve, one."

"On your own?"

There was a silence as Ayesha stared daggers back at Nicola before answering, "On my own."

"Mick said he was here, with you."

"Did he? No. He's got his nights wrong," said Ayesha impatiently, before returning to her bigger concern. "I had no reason to kill Jim."

"Why didn't you tell us all of this at the start?" asked Nicola evenly.

Ayesha hesitated for a moment. "It was private. It was just . . . *mine.*"

Nicola felt a jolt through her system. She had an almost physical reaction to Ayesha saying that. She felt instinctively like she wanted to defend Mick. She knew where that was coming from, and she pushed it back down. "Not anymore. So, Mick doesn't know?"

Ayesha gave Nicola a look which Nicola felt bordered on a *fuck you.*

When Nicola left the kitchen and returned to the main area of the pub, she could see the evening was beginning to wind down. Deakins sat stoically silent. She watched Eddie and Frankie leave together, both offering polite smiles in her direction as they went. Elsewhere Mick was holding court with a group of blokes down the far end of the bar. They all laughed heartily and then looked round with an edge of guilt at having too much of a good time at such a solemn moment.

She saw Harry making his way over to her. As he came close, he seemed to be vibrating with excitement. He spoke sotto voce.

"Two things. First, just got email confirmation the deer in Deakins' field is a match for the antlers. Same animal. Second, little book corner over there, for the locals. I found a book on Dorset folklore, with details of the murders in 1925. And the page was folded down. Somebody's been reading it in here!"

He handed Nicola the book he'd been disguising under his jacket. "Page sixty-seven."

Nicola examined the book, and checked the page, the corner of which was folded down, as reported. She nodded and handed it back to Harry. "Have it checked for prints," she instructed. She knew the book was in a public arena, so anyone could have looked at it, but the book looked in good condition and mostly unread. It was worth a punt. "Good work," she added, and she thought she noticed Harry working hard to stop himself beaming with pride.

Nicola looked round the pub. Had someone here tonight read that chapter?

Mick walked past and she grabbed him. "You said you were here on Tuesday night, right?" There was a fraction of a beat where Mick looked uncertain, and Nicola followed up with, "Because Ayesha says you weren't."

Nicola watched either confusion or panic—hard to decipher which—flit across Mick's face. His tone had hardened. "Why would she say that?"

"Presumably because she's telling the truth to a police officer," smiled Nicola.

"Meaning I'm not?" said Mick.

Nicola was very still and very calm. "*Meaning* your statements aren't compatible. One of you must be mistaken. Tell you what: let me or my colleague know in the morning which it is."

She handed Mick a card. He looked at it and walked away, glancing back. As he did, out of the corner of her eye, Nicola watched Deakins drain his glass and leave. She hadn't seen anyone go near or talk to him all night. He stared at Nicola as he passed by without saying anything, only raising his chin an inch as he got close, in some form of acknowledgment.

Nicola tracked him exiting. Just as the pub door was swinging shut behind him she caught a glimpse of something.

The little girl was standing outside, across the road, watching. She caught Nicola's eye—and instantly started running off.

Nicola made quickly for the door.

She strode out of the pub at pace. In the distance, she could just see the figure of the little girl turning down one of the side roads.

She ran down the road and took the corner—being careful as she rounded it. She knew she had to be quiet and fast. If the girl spotted her, that would be the end of it. She already had respect for the girl's ability to disappear.

There was the girl up ahead, taking another turn and vanishing from sight. Nicola ran again, as quietly as she could, not wanting footsteps to tip the girl off.

She realized that if anyone saw her trailing this young child in the dark of the village night, they were very likely to call the police themselves. So she tried to look as innocuous and casual as she could, while also feeling filled with urgency. In the distance she heard a door slam.

She took the next corner. Three streets going off here. No sign of the girl. Shit. She'd lost her bearings. She was heading toward the edge of the village, where the houses faded away into open countryside. The houses here were less historic, more functional. The roofs were not thatched, the properties more modern, and not as affluent. These were the type of houses Nicola had grown up in, some six miles distant. She knew how the better-off residents of Fleetcombe would regard this part of the village. She also knew from firsthand experience how hard the people in these houses worked. This, not the rentable postcard-pretty properties, was where Nicola felt most normal people lived, and where she personally felt most at home.

She gambled on one street. Nope: a short cul-de-sac. Nothing to see here, unless the girl had already gone into one of these houses. She tried the next side street. This one was much longer. She walked down, looking into the houses: lights were on in some but not all.

There was another turning off to the right at the end. Nicola took it, and as she rounded the corner it instantly caught her eye.

In the top small window of a house forty yards down the street, a light was on. The rest of the house was dark. And in the window, on the ledge inside, sat a figure. Back resting against the side of the window inset. Legs drawn up to her chest, head resting on her knee as she looked out. The little girl, staring out into the night.

Nicola stepped into the shadows, away from the illumination of the nearest streetlamp. She wasn't sure why she did it, she just instinctively felt like she didn't want to be seen by the girl, at this moment. Nicola peered more closely. Definitely the same girl.

She would come back, in daylight. Whatever that little girl knew, Nicola would find out.

CHAPTER TWENTY-EIGHT

How was it possible to be this tired, and to wake so soon?

Three and a half hours' sleep and wham, Nicola was wide awake once more, adrenaline coursing through her body, her mind stubbornly refusing to rest.

No point feeling sorry for yourself, use the time, she told herself. So, she lay there, inspecting the ceiling, allowing the case to occupy every cascading thought.

First, order the facts. What did they now know? Jim Tiernan had started the day with Christine Wilson from the brewery. Tricky meeting. A note about TFW at eleven thirty was still unclear. Lunchtime saw him head to Somerset to meet Ayesha Barton. He was there until quarter to five, back at the White Hart for evening service. He must have had words with Irina immediately after getting back because he'd warned Ayesha. He'd worked in the pub that night. What then? He'd gone out, then returned. Had someone come to see him, after service? Ayesha? Mick? Did Irina return, angry?

Her mind segued straight into the questions. Was it likely that just one person killed Jim Tiernan, or could it have been more? Who had folded down the corner of the page relating to the 1925 murders in the book Harry had found at the Fox? A pub regular? Ayesha, or her fiancé, Mick? Both? One of them was already lying about whether Mick stayed at the Fox that night: why? Mel could get their mobile signals triangulated to see who was telling the truth.

Irina Bortnick had not been at the memorial for Jim. And she had been out driving the night of Jim's death: was she moving a body? She had access to the pub at all times. Nicola wondered if Irina and Mick knew each other. Mick said he drank in the White Hart. Could two wronged lovers have banded together?

And where did all this leave Deakins? Was his ancestor really responsible for similar murders a century back, or was that just a local rumor that became folklore? The headless deer had been found on his land. Had he left it there and called them to protest his innocence? Would his DNA be found on the deer?

One life, one man, many facets. It was like a sweater unraveling. Jim's death had pulled on one thread and now it was all slowly unwinding, revealing the mess of his life underneath.

That's what happens, reflected Nicola. You may think your life is tightly woven, but it just takes one tug for things to start falling apart.

She got up with the daylight and worked through emails and reports in the kitchen before anyone else came down. She made coffee and laid out breakfast things. *Like a normal family would*, she thought.

She wasn't sure she knew a normal family, but it was an idea she was aspiring to. Their family life had always lacked routine, too easily became chaotic and compromised. *We can't go on like this*, had been the refrain. And so they were trying not to. But Jim Tiernan, and whoever killed him, had put a potential stick in their spokes. *Only if you let it*, Nicola told herself.

She liked this new kitchen. It was light and airy and overlooked the small garden, which had now begun to offer up autumnal colors from the planting done by the previous owners. Nicola was already simultaneously grateful and worried about wrecking their good work in future by neglecting it. She realized she was feeling guilty about a thing that had not yet happened, and she had not yet failed at. This was, she noted yet again, her overdeveloped sense of responsibility. Mike, or Ethan, could take responsibility for the garden. It could be their project. Their problem if it withered. Not everything is on you, she reminded herself. She almost convinced herself.

"I hear you forgot date night."

Ethan had arrived in the kitchen, clad in T-shirt and boxers. He was fit and muscular, like his peers, thanks to a regular gym habit. Nicola could not get used to having a son who was basically a man. It made her feel so old. But also, it terrified her how fast time had spun past. She could remember that first morning, sitting cradling him in her arms. It seemed ludicrous that the tiny, fragile baby of that sun-tinted memory was now a hulking, opinionated near-man.

He was grinning at her. "First attempt, and you drop the ball, Mum."

"How do you know about date night?"

"I'm not deaf. I do understand what's going on in this house." He paused and added carefully, "I have for a while."

That last phrase, cautious. He was being sensitive, but wanted her to know, once again, that he was not stupid.

She didn't know how best to reply, so she nodded. Switch subject, she thought.

"How are things going? Made any more new friends?"

Ethan poured himself a coffee from the big pot she had made. "How d'you want me to answer that? Honestly, or in a way that won't make you feel worse than you already do?"

"Honestly," lied Nicola. "Obviously."

"Things are pretty shit. Most of my class are morons. The ones who aren't morons have known each other years and don't need a new friend. The work doesn't match up with what I was doing before. And my actual friends, in Liverpool, seem to be getting on fine without me."

"Maybe you shouldn't look at what they're posting for a bit," said Nicola helpfully. "So it doesn't feel like you're missing out."

"Yeah, but I *am* missing out. At least this way I can comment or like it and remind them I'm still alive."

"I'm sorry," said Nicola genuinely. "I hate it when you're not happy."

"Game's the game." Ethan shrugged. He said that a lot, and she wasn't really sure what it meant. Maybe it was a modern *c'est la vie*. Or *que sera sera*. She reminded herself to google it, the only way she could really keep up with half the phrases he brought into the house. "Date night tonight instead, then?"

Nicola nodded. Ethan toyed with some strawberries she'd put out, knowing how much he liked them. He didn't look at her.

"Will it work, all this, you and Dad? Long term?"

Now he looked up, having said it. She was struck by his expression: he looked eight years old again. *Is everything going to be OK, Mummy?*

I don't know. I don't know anything right now.

"I hope so." She smiled. It wasn't as definitive as he wanted, but it was the best she could offer him right now.

Ethan looked worried, and she watched him try to hide it for her benefit. She hated the complexity of these exchanges now. She wanted her son to have a simple life, as carefree as possible. But it had been trodden on, just as hers had. She wanted to turn time back, to before that happened. So they could be the people they were. It's not like they were perfect, or singing songs all day long, but they were less . . . *burdened*, by experience.

She felt the anger rising in the pit of her stomach again and tamped it down. Save it for another moment. For another person.

"Good morning! Ooh, coffee. And fruit. Amazing." Mike appeared and joined them.

He smiled. Nicola and Ethan smiled back.

Here we are, thought Nicola, *the normal family*.

CHAPTER TWENTY-NINE

Nicola left the family's coffee and fruit congregation to head to the White Hart to meet Irina Bortnick. But Irina did not arrive on time.

Nicola was doubly irritated to be kept waiting, checking her watch as she paced the deserted and silent main bar. She thought about the Fox last night, teeming with life, even in the shadow of tragedy. And now, here, the White Hart, bereft of its landlord.

A dead space.

She decided to make use of the time and scour the ground floor for anything she or others may have missed. She knew the forensic team had worked tirelessly upstairs, but she also knew they had been called away to another scene over seventy miles away, much to both Reeta's and Nicola's chagrin, once they'd completed the area around the bedroom. Nicola paced around the bar, looking under tables, down the backs of chairs, in corners, between booths and the walls. As she did so, she found herself thinking back to the conversation with Christine Wilson at the brewery and wondering: what were pubs for now, anyway? Why did people still come to these rooms? They were a gathering ground, a focal point, mostly for booze. But more than that: a pub was also a church of sorts, a social club, a release. A place to talk and reflect and socialize and debate and confess and dance and sing and yell and laugh till you cry.

And every pub was different: every pub was an idea, an identity. For Ayesha Barton, that was elegant food and drink for locals and tourists. For Jim Tiernan, something else. A drinking pub, an old-school local hub whose name connected back to history, to landscape, to an essence of old Dorsetness. Just as Jim Tiernan had tried to do, on his return to Fleetcombe.

She found herself walking behind the bar. Standing where Jim Tiernan stood. Seeing things from his point of view, across the room, thinking about the customers sitting at tables, and some sitting at the bar, talking nonsense, baring their souls.

Baring their souls.

A thought struck her—they'd been approaching this one way, trying to figure out Jim Tiernan's life and secrets. But what about the opposite angle? Couldn't a pub also be a place where secrets were confessed or blurted out? If the life of a pub reflected the life of its community, what had that made Jim Tiernan? A dispenser of wisdom? A desirable rogue? A priest of the confessional? What if Jim, the father confessor as appointed by Wilson's brewery, was a collector of secrets? A gatherer, keeper, a filer-away. What if somebody told him too much?

What if Jim Tiernan was murdered for something he knew, rather than something he'd done? A secret so deadly it was worth killing for.

Irina burst in, disrupting Nicola's train of thought, full of apologies. "I didn't charge my phone last night and I lost track of time."

"You stayed with Patricia last night?" said Nicola.

Irina nodded. "I don't want to be here. If they came for Jim, maybe they come for me."

"Do you think that's likely?"

"I didn't think on Monday he would be dead by Wednesday. What is likely? What does 'likely' mean to me anymore?"

"But you said to meet here."

"I don't want her listening. I don't trust her."

"Why not?" asked Nicola.

Irina shrugged. "Probably cos he told me she was a nosy fucking witch! She asks a lot of questions, too interested in other people's business. Because she has none of her own."

"Was that a problem for you with Jim?"

"Nothing's a problem with me," said Irina defiantly. "My problem is he's dead. It's like I've been hit in the head and the heart with a shovel. What do I do now?"

Nicola edged the conversation to where she wanted it to go. "You weren't at the memorial last night, at the Fox," she said.

"Correct," said Irina.

"Any reason?"

Irina stared at Nicola. "Why don't you say what you came here to say."

Nicola said, "We know where Jim was, the afternoon before he was killed."

"Good for you."

So she knew.

Nicola persisted. "Is that what you and he argued about?"

"That he was fucking the woman in the pub up the road?" Irina shot back. "Yeah. Would you argue with *your* partner about that?"

Don't get me started on arguments with my partner, thought Nicola, or we'll both be sobbing on the floor.

Oof. Is that how I feel?

Irina scrabbled for her vape and took a tug on it. Then she said quietly, "I told him, you have to be gentle with people's hearts. All the time, not just sometimes."

"Is it true there have been occasions in the past where you and Jim have fought physically?" asked Nicola. She wanted to test Christine Wilson's report of conflict between Irina and Jim.

"Sure," said Irina. "Not him hitting me, but twice I push him, one time he fell. Accident, nothing serious. People saw it, though. They called me Rocky for a week. I tried to be calmer. He's not so big. I'm pretty strong, I found out."

Irina was quiet for another moment, but Nicola felt she had more to say, like she was weighing up how much to volunteer, or perhaps searching for the right words in her second language.

"You think I killed him?" she asked Nicola directly.

"How we work," said Nicola in as calm and measured a fashion as she could muster, "is that until we can categorically eliminate a person from our inquiries, they remain a person of interest to us. And so far, we cannot rule you out."

"He fucks someone else, I'm angry, I kill him. That's what you think?"

"We can't rule you out, because you don't have an alibi for the rest of the night."

"I told you what I did. I went driving."

"By yourself. You didn't see or speak to anyone else all night?"

"I didn't want to speak to anyone else!" Irina took another tug on her vape. "You want to know why I drove? Why I didn't want to see anyone?"

"Of course," said Nicola.

"Because I was *scared*," said Irina, simply.

"Of what?" asked Nicola.

"Of not being allowed to be here anymore," replied Irina. "I already have one problem with a sponsor. When I left Patricia's house, when I moved in here, Jim became my sponsor, with Homes for Ukraine. We break up, where does that leave me? No home, no job, nobody cares. I have friends this has happened to, plenty of them. They fall out with their hosts, it's thank you goodbye don't come here don't call again.

And they have nothing. I know some, living on the streets. That's what I thought I had, when I found out where he had been . . . yes, I was angry, and we argued, but most of all . . . I could see a future where he is rid of me and I have nothing."

Irina looked down, scratching at one of her fingernails. "And you know what? I love it here. It's so beautiful. I felt safe here. First time since leaving Lviv, since losing my family."

Now she went quiet. Nicola once again allowed her the space.

"Second time in my life everything changed. First was a missile attack on our apartment. Our *apartment*. They said oh we just missed an infrastructure target. No. It was a war crime. I went to get bread and coffee for us all, when I came back . . ."

The sentence drifted off. Irina got up and walked to the bar. She started to make herself a coffee from the machine as she talked. "I ran then, too. From Lviv to here. I lost more than my father and my brother in the blast. I lost my life."

"I'm sorry," said Nicola.

"Since I left, more people killed, more friends lost. There is nothing for me to go back to. I found a new life here," said Irina. "But now, this week, everything changes again. Nobody is going to give a shit about me now. You just think, oh maybe she killed him. No. I went driving because I was scared everything was falling apart. Never mind he broke my heart, it was more than that. In that moment, I thought I had no future. No place to live, nobody with me or for me. I was alone."

Nicola watched Irina take a gulp from the black coffee and recoil at the heat. "Fucking machine, always makes it too hot." She blew on the cup and walked back over. "I left here that evening, I was in the shit. I came back the next morning, the shit was deeper. But it wasn't me." She sat down and stared at Nicola defiantly. "This answer your question?"

Nicola nodded. "Irina, can you help me with something? There are barely any clothes in Jim's cupboards and drawers. We're presuming he had more clothes than are left there now."

She noticed a new expression cross Irina's face. Was she looking . . . *sheepish*?

"Yeahhh," said Irina slowly. "That was me."

"That was you?"

Irina shrugged as if to say, *what did you expect me to do?*

"What did you do?" persisted Nicola.

Irina explained, in a tone that suggested it was obvious, "While he was serving, I took as many clothes of his as I could fit into my car, a little lighter fuel . . . and then, when it was dark, I put them in a big pile and I burned them. And you know, for a moment, I laughed my fucking ass off." She looked regretful. "Now, not so much. I can see . . . stupid thing to do."

Nicola was incredulous. "Not just stupid. You may have destroyed critical evidence."

"Stuff from his cupboards? Come on!" said Irina indignantly.

"What about from the bed? There was no sheet on the bed. Did you burn that, too?"

Irina seemed to possess a strong sense of disbelief that Nicola was focusing on this. "I don't know—maybe! Half the time he never put one on the bed anyway."

Nicola's frustration was rising, too. "And where did you burn it all?" asked Nicola.

Irina shrugged. "In the Vale. There was no one for miles. I made sure it didn't spread."

"Not down by the coast?" checked Nicola. She was thinking of where Deakins' farm was located, overlooking the sea.

"No! I told you, in the Vale! Nowhere near the coast."

"Would you be able to find where it was?"

Irina looked doubtful. "I don't know. I wasn't paying attention where. It all looks the same there, especially at night. Maybe we'll go look for a big pile of ashes."

Nicola stared at Irina, exasperated. Was she telling the truth? Or was this an elaborate lie designed to put her off the scent? "Did you come back later that night and see Jim?" she asked Irina directly.

"No. Did I kill him? No. Did I want to punish him? Yes. Did I want to kill him? No! Did I love and hate him at the same time? Yes. You don't kill a man for that. Would you?"

Nicola stayed silent. She did not wish to share that she had experienced plenty of variant feelings around love and hate in her life recently.

"You think, crazy woman, maybe killed him. No. Just clothes. Nothing else. Tell me he didn't deserve it. But why would I do that shit with a deer?" said Irina, as if what she'd done was now proven to be the reasonable path. "Are we done?"

Nicola sighed. "For now, I suppose. Have you given a swab to the team?"

Irina confirmed she had, and left the pub.

Before she left, Nicola was determined to continue her scour of the pub's ground floor for anything that could be of interest. She checked both sets of loos, the skittles alley, the back room where all the barrels were kept. Her last look-round was in the kitchen. In the far corner was a walk-in fridge. She opened that up. There were various remnants of food supplies, but the storage system looked chaotic and some things looked past their eat-by date by some distance. She knew from asking that Jim only had an extra member of staff at weekends, and the rest of the time attempted to run it by himself, with occasional moments of help from Irina. It seemed an incredibly tall order, and Nicola boggled at how hard Jim must've had to work to stay afloat.

As she went to leave the fridge, she saw it.

In the corner, behind the door, a smashed-up banjo was propped up against the wall. She knelt to look at it. The neck was snapped and a couple of the strings had also been broken. Their ends poked savagely into the air, ready to jab someone in the eye.

Why was this here?

Before she could even grapple with that question something else took her attention.

On the wall and floor, right in the corner, were traces of blood.

CHAPTER THIRTY

Detective Constable Mel Hardiman understood that people—colleagues, superiors, even family and friends—often dismissed him as moody or surly. Part of this was the way his face was built. He had come to understand this from quite early on in life. He had often been told to smile, or to cheer up, it might never happen! Mel had always found this difficult because, as far as he was concerned, he wasn't *not* cheery, or *not* smiling, but his visage was obviously communicating something more downbeat. One colleague had labeled him Morose Mel, early on, and it had followed him to the extent that he started to live down to it. If enough people keep saying you are something, you might as well be it.

Mel Hardiman was not morose. He was shy, and private, and his mind did not magnetize quickly toward quips and retorts. That often led people to assume he had no sense of humor. On the contrary, he *loved* humor—at home in the evenings, he would sit back and listen to old vinyl albums of Monty Python, Bob Newhart and (his personal favorite) Jasper Carrott. He spent his evenings smiling and laughing, and alone. In work, he always thought of the joke, or funny comment, thirty seconds too late. So he had stopped trying.

Over time he had found his niche, in police work. Detail. Cataloging, paperwork, spreadsheets. He loved to sift and analyze documents.

He could, and did, spend hours unmoving at his desk, slowly studying pieces of evidence for information which could be revealing. Mel Hardiman knew from experience that he and his skills were often underestimated, especially by new colleagues. He also had a confidence that, over time in any investigation, they would come to see the value of what he did. He thought often of the story of the tortoise and the hare. Mel was Team Tortoise.

He understood this was a fast-moving investigation with multiple suspects. He watched as Harry and Nicola whooshed in and out of the office, on a new tip-off or errand to interview someone. He regarded himself as the calm center, the eye of the storm. As well as carrying out the various tasks barked out by the other two—*look into this*, *get that analyzed*, *ask so-and-so about such-and-such*—he had set himself the task of focusing on several boxes containing multiple overstuffed lever arch files inside which sat bank statements, bills, invoices, receipts and accounts going back several years. Mel loved going through seemingly useless documents. He could do it all day—he would list it as his superpower. He viewed it as panning for gold. And this morning he presented the results of his panning: a ledger, buried—he thought deliberately buried—beneath old magazines and newspapers, at the bottom of one of the boxes.

"Interesting," said Nicola as Mel presented it to her and Harry.

Mel watched as she opened the scrappy, rough ledger, flicking through pages at random. There were names of businesses and amounts. Local businesses, including the brewery, were name-checked. There were transaction dates. There was a receipts/paperwork column listed on each page with sums of money. There were pluses and minuses next to each sum. There were other columns marked incoming and outgoing. There was a page further on which just said OWING and listed sums next to initials. Another page simply had the word "skim" alongside dates, over the past two years.

Nicola looked up at Mel. "I thought the accounts were all digital, and checked by the brewery."

"They are," said Mel.

Nicola looked to Mel, impressed, understanding what this was. "Jim Tiernan was running a second set of accounts which he kept hidden. Why?"

"Well," said Mel, "if you compare the two—the digital and the analog, the public and the hidden—alongside his bank statements, which I also dug out of the boxes, you'd say he was in a big mess. I went through line by line on all of them, trying to reconcile everything, and my head was spinning—personal and business money used interchangeably, bills not paid to full amounts, he seems to pick a number out of thin air and pay that amount, presumably hoping it'll be just enough to keep people off his back for a while, invoices and payments not aligning, petty cash being spent but seemingly no receipts . . . there's no way he was keeping afloat. In fact, I'd say he definitely wasn't."

"No wonder the brewery was worried. Especially if they knew he was no stranger to fraud," chipped in Harry. "Christine Wilson must've realized what was going on."

Mel found himself nodding.

"Good work, Mel," beamed Nicola. "Anything else?"

Mel had a list. "You had the forensics on the deer. I've given you the call and message logs for Jim Tiernan's dumbphone—very little on there of worth, but you have the log. You asked me to confirm Patricia Tiernan's vehicle ownership—a fifteen-year-old dark green Fiat 500. There are no ANPR cameras between the White Hart and the Vale that would have logged Irina Bortnick's car. The last triangulation of her mobile signal is at the White Hart, at 5:57 Tuesday evening, and then back on in the same location at 8:01 Wednesday morning. It was offline in the intervening hours. Also confirmed her nationality is categorically Ukrainian."

He thought that was it, then checked one other thing. "Family name for the address you asked me to check on the edge of Fleetcombe is Skillett. There've been three complaints for noise, one for antisocial behavior and two raids for drugs in the past year or so. Current intel is that mother Mandy, daughter Shannon both live there, with occasional male partner Kyle. Kyle's served time for stealing and selling prescription drugs. I've included his file in your briefing pack for today. Now, DC Ward asked me to cross-reference the research he'd done on the murders from 1925 with the public records, and it's confirmed that a member of the Deakins family was arrested and hanged for those murders. The request has gone in for testing of the blood in the walk-in fridge at the White Hart, and for the broken banjo. The interview room is ready and waiting next door for your first appointment with Frankie Winters."

He looked up. Harry and Nicola were staring at him. "Is something wrong?"

"No," said Nicola. "That's excellent."

"We aim to please," said Mel, miming doffing his cap at Nicola and then instantly regretting doing it. "It's quite a lot, though. Are we getting anyone else in to help?"

"No," said Nicola briskly. "Let's see what we get from Frankie Winters, but I also want to get out to the Deakins farm and the Skillett house, and later we have an appointment with Mick Donnelly at his barracks. Harry can give you a hand between these, but well done, Mel. Thank you."

As Nicola and Harry prepared for the arrival of Frankie Winters, Mel sat back at his desk with an unusual feeling. Her response had made him feel that he was a valued and important member of the team and that his work was of a surprisingly good standard. He felt—what was the word?—*appreciated*. It was a warm and gentle feeling and he had not felt it for a long time.

As he worked, he found himself whistling the theme to *Monty Python*.

CHAPTER THIRTY-ONE

Frankie Winters took a seat in the interview room, as directed by the female detective who had introduced herself as Nicola. Frankie recognized her from the drinks at the Fox. The detective exuded an air of calm and patience, coated in a "don't fuck with me" directness.

Frankie was not calm. Frankie was freaking out inside and trying to disguise it. Frankie had no sense how successful the disguise was. They had turned up at the agreed time, at the agreed place, the place where Frankie's dad once used to bank, to "clear up a few details," apparently.

Frankie agreed to fingerprints being taken. Everyone who was in the pub that night was being asked. Then they also agreed to a DNA swab. This was voluntary, they were told. The implication was: why would you not want to agree to it, if you haven't done anything wrong? Both detectives, the one who they'd chatted to initially and now this other seemingly more senior woman, were polite and respectful.

In the interview suite, Frankie watched as recording and filming devices were activated. They were reminded of their rights, and the fact that they had attended to make a voluntary statement. They were not under arrest, and the questions were in relation to the death of Jim Tiernan. Frankie was also asked which pronouns they preferred, and confirmed that they/them were their pronouns of choice. Amidst all the anxiety, Frankie felt briefly, gratefully, seen. And then wondered if that was part of the police's methods of making them relax and give too much away.

The two officers asked easy questions to begin with. Name, address, where did Frankie work, how long had they worked there. Then the questions began to zero in on Jim Tiernan. When had he first come into the salon? How regularly did he visit? When was his last visit?

They had covered all this before, thought Frankie. Luckily, Frankie had not previously told any lies about any of this, so they were unworried about answering again. Soon, the questions got to the day before Jim Tiernan was found.

"Did you see Jim Tiernan on the day of his death?" asked Nicola, the older detective.

"Yes, at the pub, in the evening."

"How did he seem that evening?"

Frankie shifted in their seat and looked at the younger detective, Harry. "I've already talked to you about this—"

"Just for the recording, please, Frankie," smiled Nicola.

Frankie obliged. "He was behind the bar. The pub was busy. He was fine. We said hello, I bought a drink, I didn't really have much banter with him or anything like that."

Frankie watched Detective Sergeant Nicola Bridge leaf through her notes, look across the table at Frankie. Frankie instinctively processed it as an "indulgent teacher" smile. It was designed to denote authority but also patience and support. Frankie worried that it was used to disarm, before sticking the evidential knife in.

Frankie was not stupid. They knew all the questions so far had been the easy ones, repetitions of previous conversations, the warm-up. The investigative equivalent of pre-drinks. Now Frankie felt they were being guided to the heart of what Nicola *actually* wanted to know.

Frankie watched her look up from her notes for a moment and pause deliberately. They saw Nicola make a sympathetic face. They were dreading the next question.

"Frankie, what was the name of the man you were with in the pub that night?"

Frankie swallowed and said with extreme clarity, "Theo Andrakis."

I sound like a train station announcer asking a passenger to report to the information desk. Far too deliberate, thought Frankie. And that was before the swallow, trying to clear the rock in their throat. *That rock would be the whopping great lie.*

Nicola nodded calmly. "Yes, that's the name and number you gave us. We spoke to Mr. Andrakis on the phone. He confirmed that you knew each other, and that he was in the pub with you that night."

Frankie exhaled as minimally as a human being could muster and felt their body relax a little. They saw Nicola, and silent Harry next to her, watch this happen, too. Frankie felt every gesture was under examination.

Nicola continued. "So, a couple of things, on that."

Frankie felt themself flinch. *A couple of things?*

"You said you met Mr. Andrakis first at the salon," said Nicola, studying her notes.

"Correct," said Frankie.

"He says you met socially."

Shit.

"Oh," said Frankie. "Really?"

"Yes," said Nicola. "He says subsequently he became a regular customer, and he gets his hair cut with you every month. He said he'd been in half a dozen times across the past six months."

"Oh," said Frankie. *"Oh"? Is that all you've got—"oh"?* "Did he?"

"He did," said Nicola. "He also said you'd been to the White Hart together a few times previously. That you were mates, but he was hoping it would become a bit more."

"Right," said Frankie, trying to stay calm while the panic-ignited fires of hell raged in their ribs.

What the hell has he said all that for? First rule of lying, Dino had said, keep it as simple as possible. So you can remember what you said. No unnecessary detail. Why hadn't he told his mate Theo this?

"That's quite a surprise to me," Frankie offered up.

Weak, Frankie.

Frankie looked from Nicola to Harry, then back to Nicola. Both detectives were staring straight back and holding Frankie's gaze. Time seemed to have slowed down. Frankie wondered if this moment would ever end. They felt as if Nicola, especially, wanted to ensure her gaze penetrated Frankie's soul.

"I thought it might be," said Nicola. "As you'd expect, we followed up on Mr. Andrakis. Do you know where he lives, Frankie?"

"I don't know where any of my clients live," said Frankie, in an attempt to be casual.

"But he's more of a social friend now, isn't he? That's what you both say, and you've been to the pub together. You haven't discussed where he lives?"

"No. We've not discussed that," said Frankie.

"He lives in Clapton, Frankie. Clapton, in London. That's where his driving license and vehicle tax and passport are registered to."

"OK."

Stay calm, don't show anything, give yourself time to think.

Fucking Dino!

"Why would someone who lives in Clapton come and have their hair cut regularly at your salon, Frankie? It's a three-and-a-half-hour drive. On a good day."

"I don't know," said Frankie truthfully.

"I just want you to remember that you're being recorded and that it's very important you tell us the truth."

Frankie shifted in their seat, realizing that Nicola's approach had shifted from indulgent teacher to disappointed teacher.

"Theo Andrakis wasn't with you in the pub, was he, Frankie?"

Frankie's mind was racing. None of it was useful. None of it helped them form a response.

"Shall I tell you how we know?" continued Nicola. "Because we have his car, and him visible, caught on a traffic camera entering the ULEZ zone in London on that evening, at the time you said he was in the pub with you."

Frankie bit their lip and, just as they were doing it, a thought zapped through their mind. *Don't bite your lip, it's a tell!*

Nicola stared Frankie straight in the eyes. "You don't know Theo Andrakis, do you, Frankie? You've never met him, have you?"

"I have," insisted Frankie.

"Describe him to us," said Nicola coolly.

Ah, this was the moment. The moment of complete humiliation. Frankie felt like they were sinking, being dragged beneath quicksand.

They had lost control over their life.

Frankie could not describe Theo Andrakis. Dino had sent through a photo, but Frankie had not paid immediate attention to it. All Frankie could think of, right now in this interview room where they had to tell the truth to the police, was the image of Dino. That was the only man they were able to describe right now. And they really must not describe him.

Frankie realized they were silent, and staring at the wall beyond the detectives. They heard Nicola's voice again. It had a kind tone, now. Wait, was it kind? Or was it pity?

"Frankie," said Nicola, "I would suggest you put a stop to any idea that you should lie to us. Do not tell us things that you know not to be true. Because the consequences are so profoundly serious. This is a murder investigation, and you are actively obstructing our ability to get to the truth. That can result in a serious charge. This is the moment where I suggest you stop and change your approach."

Frankie felt twelve years old. Their face felt cold. It was pricking with anxiety. This had never happened to Frankie before.

"Here's what I think," said Nicola. "I think you've been asked to do something, tell a small white lie, by someone. You've done it, but they haven't been thorough in their preparation. Now, can I tell you something? There is no such thing as a white lie where the police are concerned. There are only facts and falsehoods. You've told us a number of falsehoods, I think to protect either yourself or someone else. We've been able to disprove them. And that means you are in a difficult and serious situation.

"So, right now, you need to ask yourself whether you're going to keep lying for the person who's asked you to. You also need to ask yourself whether we can easily disprove whatever lie you tell next. Now, obviously, my opinion is: we will. Because we're good at our jobs, we're rigorous, and we're very angry that a man was murdered the other night. So, is there anything you'd like to retract, or alter, or tell us?"

Frankie felt more tired than they'd ever thought was possible.

They looked at the table, for a very long time. Then, they mustered the energy to speak.

"If I tell you," said Frankie, "I don't know what he'll do. I don't know what he's capable of." Dear God, they were scared now.

"What do you mean by that, Frankie? What who's capable of?"

Frankie remained silent and bit their lip some more.

On the back wall of the interview room, the light from the high window was spilling in and forming a slanted shape on the wall. Frankie tried to remember all the different shapes they'd been taught in school.

Rhombus.

Frankie nodded and transferred their gaze to Nicola.

"His name is Dino. I don't know his surname. He told me to give you the other name. Dino's my boss, I can't go against him. He knew Jim Tiernan. They were in prison together."

CHAPTER THIRTY-TWO

"There are moments—not often, but sometimes," said Nicola to Harry as they drove to Deakins' farm, "when you feel cases start to split open . . . like little first cracks on top of a massive dinosaur-sized egg. That may be one of them."

"Right," said Harry. He was enjoying Nicola's general upbeatness, if a bit nonplussed by his boss's imagery. "So—where's our thinking at now?"

"You tell me," said Nicola.

Oh God. She's testing me.

"Me?" replied Harry, startled. "You want to know what I think?"

"Yes, please, DC Ward," said Nicola, eyes on the road.

Shit. Come on, Harry. Sarge wants to know. Harry sat up straight, as if about to start a race. He felt like rubbing his face hard or splashing it with cold water.

"OK. Well, parking Frankie Winters for a moment . . . those who had motive, that we know of so far: Irina, she found out about his meeting with Ayesha. That triangle of her, Mick and Ayesha, they all feel like they could have motive and opportunity, given what went on that day."

"Agree, except it doesn't quite present as a crime of passion," said Nicola. "The way the body was left, not spur of the moment. But carry on."

"Opportunity, then—Eddie Godfrey, the delivery driver. He has a van big enough to move a body; unclear what his motive would be. He was in the pub that night, but no reports of any falling out between him and Jim. Could look into whether there's any money owed between them, given what Mel's discovered. Would he have had access to the pub that night? Maybe the doors were left open? Irina had a key, Tiernan's sister, Patricia, has a key, but you'd struggle to get a dead body into a Fiat 500, and again unclear what any motive would be." He paused to consider. "Plenty of people have opportunity, and no alibis, so we can't yet rule them out. And circling back to Frankie Winters, not sure they present as a killer, but maybe a witness, or maybe even involved in disposal of the body? They're definitely covering up something. Few things I want to follow up from their interview, after this."

"Good. And what about our friend here?" asked Nicola as she swung the car into the rough parking ground at the top of Deakins' farm.

"Three separate connections to the case," replied Harry, "all of them circumstantial. Four if you count him being in the pub that night. I feel like either he could be messing with us. Or it was him."

"Or both," smiled Nicola grimly as she brought the car to a halt.

The mist was still hovering over the fields as Nicola and Harry approached the farm building located on the edge of a line of trees. It looked out over the fields which sloped gently down to the shore. The sound of the waves drifted up. The farm occupied a prime location, thought Nicola. No wonder Deakins had been offered money by developers to sell up. Yet the farm building felt unloved: exposed and isolated, even at this time of day. Nicola shuddered to think how it would feel being out here alone at two in the morning. She always felt that the beauty of the landscape took on a lonelier, scarier hue when dark descended.

They had to bang several times on the battered farmhouse door before finally getting a response. Deakins opened the door.

He was holding a shotgun. He looked both detectives up and down. He said nothing.

"Mr. Deakins, mind if we come in?" asked Nicola.

Deakins stared at her coldly. "Don't want you here."

Nicola noted that Deakins was displaying a very different tone, and a different expression, from their most recent encounter over the body of the headless deer. The playful wind-up merchant was very much gone. His demeanor was colder, his eyes more vacant. His whole bearing was heavier, as if he was half absent.

"I don't want to be investigating the murder of an innocent man, but we all have to deal with it," said Nicola.

Deakins stared at her for a moment before silently trudging away from the door, leaving it open.

Inside, the farmhouse was cold, and without much in the way of decor or furniture. The floor was made entirely of cracked and broken large poinsettia-red tiles. The ceilings were low. Some of the beams appeared to be rotting.

It was more a working environment than anything homely. As she and Harry wandered through, following Deakins, Nicola took in all the tools that could be used as weapons strewn about the floor in piles or hanging off nails on the walls. Large saws, a drill, various hammers, mallets. There was also a large collection of buckets, fashioned out of every conceivable material a bucket could be made from, battered and splatter-stained brown and gray from decades of use. There were few creature comforts as far as Nicola could see. No television, no paintings, pictures or photos, few soft furnishings or covers. The house smelled musty and damp, with top notes of animal feed, wet dog (though there didn't seem to be any dogs present) and a brown sort of smell that Nicola knew wasn't quite strong manure but wafted across the nose like manure's younger sibling.

They found Deakins sitting in the kitchen, an area with its own charming fragrance of fried bacon and woodsmoke. The whole house reeked, in its panoply of thick aromas, of smoke. Was that just the ashy fire burning low in the grate, wondered Nicola, or an inhabitant who'd been lighting fires he shouldn't have? Deakins was lodged at a broken wooden table which boasted an old metal teapot, a chipped mug and an ashtray containing half a roll-up cigarette. Next to the ashtray was a large box of matches that looked a decade old. An old radio sat on the side, chuntering away at a volume which meant the words could barely be heard.

Fuck d'you want?" asked Deakins after eyeballing them for a good minute or so without saying anything. His voice was lower, and his eyes more bloodshot than Nicola remembered.

"Have you lost a banjo?" asked Nicola.

Deakins stared at her. It was the look of a man who wished harm on her, Nicola felt. She had often been on the receiving end of such looks, from men much scarier than Deakins.

Deakins smoked his roll-up and stayed silent.

Nicola took out her phone and showed him the picture of a smashed-up banjo she had found at the White Hart.

"Is this your banjo?"

Deakins squinted at it as Nicola added, "It was found in the kitchen at the White Hart."

Deakins stopped looking at the picture, shrugged and smoked. His eyes remained on the ashtray. Nicola persisted.

"Was there an argument or a fight at the end of Tuesday night at the White Hart, during which your banjo got damaged?"

Deakins exhaled smoke and looked to Harry. Nicola interpreted the glance at Harry as an attempt to communicate either *what's going on here?* or, more likely, *can't you control her?*

"We've got several witnesses who said they saw you playing that banjo that night in the pub. What happened to it, Mr. Deakins?"

After a moment, Deakins said, "He owes me money for that. Two hundred quid, that were worth. Even to get it repaired won't be cheap. How'm I s'posed to get that money now?"

Nicola said, "So you fought with him that night? Who broke the banjo? Was it Mr. Tiernan?"

Deakins kept eye contact with her and shook his head in the smallest of gestures, repeating it six or seven times, as if in disbelief.

"You don't know anything, do you? Same old story. I'd say this was what happened before. You want to pin this on me, like they pinned the last ones on my kin."

Nicola took the cue. "All right, then. The murders in 1925—one of your relatives was convicted of them, is that right?"

"My grandfather's brother. My great-uncle," Deakins said. "Weren't him, though. They like to say it were, but it weren't."

"What do you mean?"

"He was a simpleton, and he confessed. They never found who did the killings, so they lighted on him. They put some drink in him, got him to confess. And they hanged him for it, by all accounts. But it weren't him. Family said he was here all along. He never ventured far."

In the corner of the room, Harry wrote all of this down.

"I know how this goes," said Deakins. "You thinking it's in my blood? His ancestor hanged for the last 'un, we'll get him for this 'un. Body gets found, must be a Deakins done it."

"Why was there a fire lit on your land the night Jim Tiernan was killed, just as the books describe happening in 1925?"

"I wouldn't go believing books," said Deakins simply. "Do they say he was innocent?"

"Did you light a fire Tuesday night or Wednesday morning?"

"Told your boy already. No."

"How many times have you been barred from the White Hart pub, Mr. Deakins?"

"Not enough for killing a man."

"Why do you think there was a deer corpse in your field?"

"Ask who put it there. Put some heat on me, I'd say. Looks like it's working, dunnit."

"Who would want to do that? D'you have a lot of enemies, Mr. Deakins?"

"I 'spect so," said Deakins. "Don't keep a list, though."

"Do you drive?" asked Nicola.

"Course I bloody drive. Tractor and trailer, and that rust bucket out front."

"Has Jim Tiernan ever been in your car?"

"Why would he have?"

"Has he, or not?" Nicola was losing patience now, trying and failing to mask the tetchiness Deakins was provoking. "We are trying to eliminate you from this investigation. Why won't you help us?"

He leaned in toward her. "Why would I help the people who hanged an innocent member of my family? You know what that did to the rest of 'em? You know how that changed my family, my life? It broke 'em all, and we were never right after that. That's what I grew up knowing."

"Can you not see that there are a number of things which connect you to Jim Tiernan's death?" asked Nicola. She watched Deakins just shrug, infuriatingly. She kept going. "Do you live here alone?"

"Take a look," said Deakins flatly.

Nicola did exactly that, embarking on a quick tour round the single-story farmhouse. She looked in the lounge, such as it was, which appeared to have farm machinery parts on large, stained sheets, being worked on. The bedroom had a double bed and a single wardrobe. Another room was used for work gear, and a washing machine. There was a line of identical battered footwear by the door.

She thought: if you wanted to saw the antlers off a deer, and attach them to a corpse, this is the place to do it.

When she returned to the kitchen, Deakins said, "I'd say, whoever your lot didn't catch in the past, when they blamed my great uncle . . . most likely that person's bloodline's responsible now."

Nicola wondered if Deakins realized he was describing a theory which would suggest his own guilt.

"Do you have a license for that shotgun, Mr. Deakins?" asked Nicola, nodding toward the weapon lying on the table.

Deakins just stared at her without replying.

Outside, Nicola walked the boundaries of Deakins' farmland, leaving Harry to take more details from the farmer. As she walked the turf, she once again felt an unease, a desire not to be on this farm. She wasn't easily spooked, but she felt unwelcome here, like this patch of land did not want her. She assigned it to her ongoing lack of sleep. The case was getting to her, wriggling out from under her grasp. She noted the registration of Deakins' old Volvo. She peered in. It was unquestionably large enough to transport a body. If need be, they could return to test inside the car for Jim Tiernan's DNA.

As she and Harry left, Deakins stood sullenly, silently, in the doorway, holding the shotgun once more. He seemed a markedly lonelier, more bitter and wrung-out personality than the one they had encountered previously. The difference between how he presented each time was startling.

Which one was the real Deakins? And who had he been the night of Jim's death?

CHAPTER THIRTY-THREE

Harry returned to the office to work through matters arising from Frankie Winters' statement, while Nicola went to the Skillett house at the end of Lancing Drive.

She rapped at the front door. She had come alone, deliberately. She did not want to spook the girl.

The door was opened by a woman Nicola guessed was in her mid-thirties, not far from her own age. Nicola wondered for a second if they might have been at school together.

"Mandy Skillett?" she asked.

The woman was instantly confrontational. "What?"

Nicola flashed her warrant card. "I'm Detective Sergeant Nicola Bridge. I'm investigating the death of Jim Tiernan, the landlord of the White Hart pub."

"Good for you, love." Mandy went to close the door but Nicola put her hand on the door—she had to use a modicum of strength to stop it closing further.

Mandy gave Nicola a look which said, *what the fuck do you think you're doing, touching my door?* Nicola thought for a second Mandy might reach out and smack her. It wouldn't be the first time she'd been punched on the job.

"Five minutes. Set a timer if you like," said Nicola.

Mandy was weighing it up, trying to control her irritation. For a split second, Nicola looked beyond, to see a figure lurking in the kitchen doorway.

It was the girl she'd been looking for.

The girl locked eyes with Nicola. Very deliberately. Time slowed down.

The girl shook her head.

Her eyes beseeching Nicola: *don't do this. Not here. Not now.*

Don't come in. Please.

Nicola felt the shock, realized she may have misjudged—just as Mandy said, "Five minutes. And I *will* put a bloody timer on." She released her grip on the door, relenting, stepping aside.

The little girl looked terrified. Nicola hovered, momentarily unsure.

"Well, come on, if you're coming. And take your shoes off, I've just hoovered."

Nicola stepped inside.

Is it just you in the house, or is there anyone else?"

Nicola was perched on the edge of the sofa. The house was dark inside, the sofa a scratchy fabric. The room was long and narrow. A large TV sat at one end.

"Me and my daughter." Mandy Skillett's eyes were wider than was natural, and she was staring at Nicola, wired.

"Is she in?"

Mandy stared at Nicola. "Fuck sake." She yelled, "SHANNON! GET IN HERE!" and then looked back defiantly at Nicola. "That's a minute gone." She showed her the screen of her phone on which she had set a timer going, as promised.

The girl—Shannon—entered the room by the door at the back, sheepishly.

"This woman's the police. All right?"

Shannon nodded meekly. Looked at Nicola. Mandy placed her hands on Shannon's shoulders. Nicola wasn't sure, but she thought perhaps Shannon recoiled at the touch.

"We wanted to reassure everyone that we don't believe there's any danger to the public, or to the wider community," Nicola said.

The woman smiled. "How d'you know that then?"

Nicola stopped mid-breath. "Well, it's our assessment—"

The woman talked across her. "But you ain't caught 'em, have you, so how do you know? We could all be in danger. Could be a serial killer. Until you get your job done properly, we won't know, will we?"

Shannon had not moved. The woman still had her hands on the girl's shoulders.

"Do either of you have any information you think might be relevant to Mr. Tiernan's death?"

"It's not a surprise, is it?" said Mandy Skillett.

"Why's that?" replied Nicola, coolly.

"He should keep his nose out of other people's business," Mandy snapped back. The girl looked at her mother, and then sneaked a look at Nicola. Nicola felt the girl beseeching her mother not to keep talking. "He brings her"—here, Mandy tapped Shannon's shoulders heavily—"home, telling me she shouldn't be out, that she'd been in the pub, that it was late. Fuck has it got to do with him?"

Nicola nodded and noted. "This was on Tuesday night."

"She can be out; it's not up to him. You can't control her, though—Christ knows I've tried. I told him, you wanna have a go, be my fucking guest. And I told him to fuck off." She turned to Shannon. "And now you bring the police here. Happy?"

Shannon looked down.

"Shannon? You were in the White Hart on Tuesday night?" Shannon did not look up. Nicola persisted, carefully. "Is there anything you can tell me about that night? Anything you might have seen?" she asked, looking directly at the girl.

Shannon slowly shook her head, refusing to make eye contact with Nicola.

Mandy checked her phone. "One minute left. What else?" she demanded. "While you still got time?"

Nicola pulled out a card. "Can I leave this with you? If there's anything you hear, or think of, or are worried about and want to talk to me or another officer about, just call this number. Or Crimestoppers, that's also on there. Anything you say would be completely anonymous, and—"

Mandy refused the card. "We won't be doing that."

The timer went off.

Nicola looked at Shannon. Her downward eyeline hadn't shifted.

"Go on then, fuck off," said Mandy.

"Shannon?" asked Nicola. "Is there anything at all—"

Mandy strode forward, right in Nicola's face. "Oy oy," she said threateningly. "You don't talk to my girl without my permission. And you do not have my permission."

Within a few seconds, Nicola had been steered back onto the street and had a door slammed in her face.

As the door was closing, she saw Shannon looking out of the lounge window at her.

Then the girl was pulled back in, and away.

She watched the policewoman leave the house through the window.

She was disappointed in her.

Had she not seen the signal?

She couldn't have been much clearer. Not without risk.

How could the woman have been so stupid? Adults were stupid. Stupid and dangerous. This would only make things worse, now.

She knew what was coming next. She would stay out for as long as she could.

CHAPTER THIRTY-FOUR

Driving back to Bredy, mulling on her day, Nicola took a call, which led to a memory, which ignited a hunch. In order to follow it, she took a detour into the hair salon where Frankie Winters worked. The sole barber, a bumfluff-bearded bloke in his late twenties, wielding a shaver on a lad in his late teens, looked up at Nicola, as if she'd walked into the wrong place. "You all right there, love?"

How has "love" still not gone out of fashion here?

Nicola took in the surroundings. It wasn't the brightest or the flashiest or the most expensive salon, just laser-targeted at the clientele who were waiting, faces in phones. Nicola thought that if any one of them were asked in ten minutes' time whether anyone had come through the door recently, they'd all say no.

Nicola smiled charmingly. "Yeah. My son's coming in later. Can I pre-pay for him? On a card or phone?"

The barber nodded at a logoed sign. "Cash only," he said.

Nicola nodded. Cash. Always cash. She'd seen this before.

One of the phoneheads looked blankly up at her as if to say, *when did you come in?*

Nicola chanced her luck. "Your manager about? What's his name, Dino, um . . ."

Frankie had said that a Dino owned the salon, but Harry had called while she was driving to explain that his research into its ownership had not revealed anyone called Dino. In fact, this little salon was owned by a holding company which in turn was owned by a different company, a shell company about which information was even harder to track down. Small little salon in a small market town—why would it need such an opaque ownership structure?

Her gambit to provoke a surname didn't fly. "Why d'you need his name?" asked the barber suspiciously.

Nicola was tired of the pretense so flashed her warrant card and introduced herself. The barber looked alarmed and became much more obliging as Nicola asked again for the manager's name.

"Never met him. All the HR stuff is done by text."

"You've never met your boss?"

The barber shrugged. "I've only been here a month. I think he works out of the other salon, at Ebbsley, is it?"

"How d'you get paid?" asked Nicola. "Is that cash as well?"

The barber's client, who must have been all of fifteen, piped up with "I think you need a lawyer, mate."

The barber looked uncertain. "Really?"

The fifteen-year-old hotshot lawyer wannabe carried on. "Don't say nothing, or you'll regret it later."

Now the barber looked properly worried. "But I haven't done anything."

"Yeah, but you know what this lot are like. Five-0, innit."

"Oy you," Nicola interjected. "This is Dorset, not Detroit. I know your mum. Pipe down."

Nicola did not know the lad's mum, but Bredy was small enough that she thought the lad would probably believe her. The number of times Nicola had been admonished by that phrase when growing up had left it scarred on her brain. She had not used it against gangmasters in Liverpool.

The kid looked at her. "I'm allowed to speak. You got a warrant?"

Nicola was getting irritated now. "Oh, do me a favor."

"This don't smell right to me, call your lawyer," said the kid in the chair.

Nicola knew when a room wasn't going to yield anything further. "Thanks for your help, boys," she said, heading for the door. She turned back and said to the young lad, "And it's a solicitor, not a lawyer, he'd need."

As she closed the door behind her, she heard one of the phoneheads say, "Pigs, man," and suck his teeth.

They grow up so fast, she thought.

Refusing to let her hunch be defeated by a bearded barber, Nicola drove swiftly to Ebbsley, a smaller town seventeen miles away. She soon located the salon. It was closed and boarded up. Interesting.

She picked up some gum at the newsagent's next door, all smiles. "What happened to the salon?" she asked innocently.

"Front, wannit," said the disinterested girl in her late teens behind the counter.

"Front for what?" asked Nicola.

"Money-laundering. All cash. Shut down before they got busted, that's what I heard. Month back, maybe."

Nicola nodded and paid for her gum. Inside, her brain was fizzing. She chanced something.

"They get Dino?"

The girl shook her head. "He hadn't been around. I miss Dino. He was always very nice to me, to be fair."

"Yeah," agreed Nicola. "He was the tall one, right? Blond hair? Quite fancied him."

The girl laughed. "No! Dino's like dumpy—short. And bald. Looks like a bullet. Dunno who you're thinking of."

Nicola pretended to be kicking herself. "God, yeah. Him. Yeah, he seemed all right, didn't he? You never know, do you?"

The girl agreed that you never did know and Nicola could not get back to the station quick enough.

Back at the office, she relayed the information to Mel and Harry. The listing for the defunct Ebbsley salon also hinted at an obscure ownership structure, seemingly unconnected to the Bredy salon. Mel had been checking for any charges, or any further details relating to the Ebbsley salon but had come up with a blank so far. It looked like the girl in the shop was right: they got out before being busted.

Harry's mind was already racing ahead. "Could this connect to Jim Tiernan's other set of accounts? Jim and Dino know each other from prison; they've kept in contact," he theorized. "Dino already has something going with the salon."

"We know Jim was having trouble with his finances," Nicola added. "Did he agree to run money through the pub and lose track? Is that where his debts come from?"

"Maybe they have an agreement. It goes wrong one way or another. The two fall out. Jim Tiernan owes money. The row escalates, Jim gets killed for it."

Nicola nodded. "Or even a grudge from their time in prison."

"Either way," said Harry, "it puts this guy Dino in the frame as a person of interest."

"Mucho interesto," agreed Nicola.

There was a pause between her and Harry before she said, "Sorry. I don't know why I do that."

She did know why she did that. She and Mike had been on holiday to Spain when they were first married and they had thought it hilarious to add "o" to English words and phrases to make them sound Spanish-ish. It had become embedded in their marriage and now, she realized, in her work and social life, too. It had sounded all right at home, once upon a time, and now it sounded absolutely terrible at work.

Mel's computer pinged and Nicola felt a surge of irritation. She had already asked him to *please* turn off notification sounds, but before she could remind him of this, Mel was looking up, excited.

"Initial analysis of the blood traces found at the White Hart. It's not human blood. It's from an animal."

Nicola and Harry looked at each other, and Harry verbalized what all three of them were thinking: "Could it be from a deer?"

"They can't tell, not that specifically. But it's not from Jim," said Mel. His eyes went to the clock on the wall. "Aren't you supposed to be out at Fernley barracks?" he said.

"Shit!" exclaimed Nicola and Harry simultaneously before grabbing their coats and scooting out the door.

CHAPTER THIRTY-FIVE

Nicola and Harry found themselves on a slight high in the car, as if the discoveries around Dino had energized them both, along with the entire investigation. They had been in need of something like this. Even so, Harry tried to exercise caution as they drove through the thick pine woodland which surrounded Fernley barracks.

"It could be from meat," said Harry.

"Could be," said Nicola, "but it didn't look like that." She checked the time. "We should get to Fernley half an hour later than we said. Will you message him? Where's the day gone?"

"On making progress," said Harry. "But promise me one thing," he added.

"What's that?" asked Nicola.

"You won't forget date night again tonight."

There was a silence in the car as Nicola looked, astonished, at Harry.

Harry realized he was grinning still, but as the seconds ticked past he suddenly thought he had not only overstepped the mark but made the biggest mistake of his fledgling police career.

Then Nicola said, "You cheeky fucker!"

And they both burst out laughing.

"Sorry, I'm sorry!" said Harry apologetically.

"Fucking speakerphone, yesterday," said Nicola. "Mortified! Not used to the buttons on this thing. I was hoping you hadn't heard. You did a good job of pretending you hadn't."

"I didn't hear," laughed Harry. "Didn't hear anything. Dates, no dates, nothing, nothing to do with me whatsoever. Sanctity of the vehicle; it goes no further. So long as I can occasionally rip the piss," he said hopefully.

"Not sanctioned!" said Nicola, still smiling. "What about you, is there a special man or woman?"

"Not at the moment," said Harry. "On the lookout if you know of anyone."

"I'll have a think," said Nicola.

"Listen," said Harry. "For what it's worth, I think it's great you guys do that. How long you been married?"

"Ninety-seven years," said Nicola.

Harry smiled, but he felt the mood had changed. He wasn't sure why.

The conversation subsided into a lull. Yet throughout the rest of the journey, Harry felt it was not quite finished. He felt Nicola wanted to say more.

They met Mick Donnelly in a neutral, small white space with frosted windows, within the reception building at the barracks. The sound of training maneuvers floated in from the swathes of land in the distance. Voices, cracks of gunfire, the sound of vehicles.

Corporal Mick Donnelly was pacing the room when they came in. He was dressed in his uniform this time. He had a lot to get off his mind. The pleasantries were brief and he got down to business, leading the conversation.

"First off, I did get my days wrong. I wasn't at the Fox on Tuesday, I was there Sunday to Monday. On Tuesday I was out with some of the lads from here—it was one of the lads' birthdays, last night before we were back on duty, we all went out in Bournemouth. Pub, dinner, club, stayed over at a B&B. We didn't get in till stupid o'clock, maybe four or five in the morning. Off our faces. We were all together. I've got a list of three of their names, they can vouch for me."

Convenient, thought Nicola. Get the lads to cover for you. She was already thinking she would want to see CCTV of them entering or exiting a club, or out in Bournemouth, to really back up this story.

He handed over the piece of paper. He kept pacing. There was more to unload. Mick looked at them nervously.

"I need to tell you about the pheasants."

The Sunday before Jim Tiernan's death there had been a conversation between Jim, Mick and Eddie Godfrey at the bar in the White Hart about doing some shooting.

They had been wanting to give this a go for a while now, and Mick had overheard chat earlier that afternoon between a couple of old fellers that a load of pheasants had escaped from a local estate, two miles inland, and were causing havoc on the lanes nearby. Absolutely stupid birds, said Mick, ever tried not to run one over? They'd been laid down by some poshos in one of the big houses, but something had gone a bit wrong, and now pheasants were all over the National Trust woods, adjacent to the estate, which were all public, and full of birds bred to be shot. If the three men got down there maybe early the next morning, they'd get to shoot pheasants, like the rich. When were they ever going to get the chance to do that otherwise?

Mick had organized the guns, pulling a favor from a bloke he knew who also ran a shooting range just past Fernley. The trio had met up at sparrowfart Monday morning. Sun was rising, woods were misty, and they had tots of whisky, just like the nobs do. Mick had read up on systems of beaters and shooters and they divided up and took turns accordingly. They'd shot a few birds, but they knew their time would be limited, because strictly speaking they shouldn't be shooting on public grounds.

"No shit," said Nicola disapprovingly.

"Also, we thought, once the lot next door start hearing shots, they'll probably come and investigate, so we knew we didn't have loads of time."

So, they had collected up their birds. But as they were heading back to the car they had spotted a male deer up ahead. They had paused, watching it, being quiet so as not to disturb it.

And then, as they watched, one of them took a shot—and killed it.

Who shot the deer?" asked Nicola.

"I don't think I should say," said Mick, adding hastily as he read Nicola's expression, "because you can't just kill deer, can you? They're like property of the Crown, aren't they? They all belong to the king."

Nicola looked at him. "That's swans."

Mick looked genuinely confused. "Oh. Shit. Is it?"

"Yes," said Nicola.

"I thought it was deer," insisted Mick.

"No. Deer are wild animals."

"Right. I didn't know. In which case, it was me." He looked beseechingly at them. "I thought I'd get thrown out of the army if I'd shot property of the king."

Nicola brought him back on track.

They had carried the deer between them back to Eddie's van and jammed it in the back with a fair bit of effort. "I drove the van back because Eddie had one too many tots of whisky."

Nicola and Harry exchanged glances. Eddie Godfrey's van. "And what happened to the deer?" asked Nicola.

"Jim took it, shoved it in his walk-in fridge. He said he was gonna cut it all up himself, said he'd seen a YouTube video on butchering carcases, and then he'd have better, fresher venison even than Ayesha's gaff." Mick hesitated. "But then . . ."

He stopped. Nicola fixed him with her hardest stare.

"Keep going," she instructed.

"I went in and nicked it the next morning. For a laugh, like. Also, I had a feller who was going to give me a bit of cash for it. I could see Jim's car was gone, and I knew he left the back door open for the cleaners. So I robbed it, as a joke. To wind him up, like. Got my mate to cut off the head and give us it back. And then I put just the head back in Jim's freezer. As a laugh. Like in *The Godfather*, with the horse's head. That was Tuesday afternoon."

While your fiancée was having sex with Jim, thought Nicola.

Mick grinned. "Then that evening I get a call from Jim: 'someone's fucking taken the deer and left the head! Was that you?' I was like no, why? And he's going: 'it's freaking me out, I dunno what's happened, I've been robbed, maybe it was Irina, I'll have to ask her,' and I'm pissing myself laughing."

Nicola and Harry were not laughing.

"What happened to the deer?" asked Nicola.

Mick looked down. "After I heard about Jim, I called my mate and said, 'Get rid.' I thought he'd incinerate it or something. I didn't think he'd leave it headless in a bloody field!"

"Did Eddie Godfrey know about any of this?" asked Harry.

Mick nodded. "I told him about the head, yeah. He thought it was funny."

"And did you not think, did none of you think," asked Nicola with a high degree of exasperation, "to mention it to us, given that Jim Tiernan was found with deer antlers attached to his head?"

"I thought it was illegal. I didn't want to get in trouble."

Harry was checking his notes. "So to be clear, who knew there was a deer's head in the fridge at the White Hart?"

Mick shrugged. "I guess me, Eddie and Jim. Probably Irina, if he told her. Oh, and my mate who cut off the deer's head."

He paused. "I might've mentioned something to Ayesha that day, I don't know."

Then, for a moment, like he'd just been tripped up or triggered by his own last words, Mick stood very still, as if he'd disappeared into himself. Nicola and Harry stayed silent, observing.

Then Mick quietly said, "She's told me what went on with her and Jim. I didn't know then." There was a long silence. "I'd fucking kill him if he weren't already dead."

Nicola watched him carefully. He was telling them he hadn't known about Ayesha and Jim. Was that true?

"For the avoidance of doubt, Corporal Donnelly," said Nicola, "did you have any involvement in Jim Tiernan's death, or deer antlers being affixed to his body after his death?"

"No, absolutely not. Nothing whatsoever. I did not."

As they walked back to the car, Harry said to Nicola, "At least it confirms the blood traces you found at the White Hart." Nicola did not respond immediately so Harry kept talking. "His story lines up. Question is, do we believe it? Is it convenient he says he didn't know about Jim and Ayesha until after Jim was dead?"

"Check his alibis for that night," said Nicola. She was testing the angles: mentally working through, but not yet sharing aloud, a version of events where Ayesha Barton and Mick Donnelly had conspired in Jim Tiernan's death. Did that track, she wondered? They only had Ayesha's word for precisely what had gone on in the room at the Drayman's. But what would they gain? How calculating was either Mick or Ayesha? What did Jim Tiernan have that they wanted? Did they want the White Hart closed for good? Ayesha said she and Jim didn't get on when Ayesha first arrived in Fleetcombe. Could something have happened which resulted in a long-held and deadly grudge?

That could wait. The practical action was the most important.

Eddie Godfrey was present for all this. Eddie Godfrey had transported the deer in his van. Eddie Godfrey had not mentioned any of this.

What else was Eddie Godfrey hiding?

She checked the car clock. Heading into evening. "I know it's late, but we should go and talk to Eddie Godfrey when we're back in Bredy."

She realized Harry was fidgeting a bit, looking at her.

"What's the matter?" she asked tetchily.

"Um, it's none of my business, but . . . date night?"

Nicola looked at the clock again and exclaimed, "Shit!"

CHAPTER THIRTY-SIX

Nicola and Mike were honking with laughter, and not just because of the margaritas. They were having a great time.

The restaurant was a start-up. The young couple who ran it had previously worked out of a food truck which could be found at Bredy's Saturday market. They had now taken over one of the many empty shops to be found on the high street. "Cuban and Central American street-food fusion" was how they labeled it. The space had been stripped back to bare walls, with rustic tables, low light, lots of banners, prints and artifacts evoking a Central American vibe.

Tonight, it was quiet and their server was not a natural fit. He was in his forties and Nicola and Mike felt he had not been out of Dorset. He told them even when taking their drinks order that tonight was his first night, and it seemed from some of his comments that he was suspicious of the whole enterprise, really. "It's all very 'exotic,' isn't it?" he had said, deploying his fingers to put air quotes around the word, his tone leaving no doubt that "exotic" was a byword for "over-fancy" or "delusional."

Date night had started well, even if Nicola had made it by the skin of her teeth. They had arrived separately and, when she turned up, she saw that Mike had made an effort. Freshly shaven, smelling good (was that a new scent?), and wearing a stylish, expensive-looking shirt she didn't recognize. He was already seated at the far end of the venue and raised a hand to gain her attention. From a distance, she thought, if I didn't know him, I'd want to know more about him. He's my type.

She liked that feeling, and she tried to suppress the undertow of pain that accompanied it.

He stood up and they kissed before she sat down. She nodded at the shirt.

"Is that new?" she asked.

"Does it look daft?" he asked. "I bought it for tonight."

"No! It's great, very nice," said Nicola, instantly regretting that she had not made more of an effort. She had applied makeup in the vanity mirror of her car, in the car park round the corner. The car would for the next day or so smell of the perfume she had over-liberally applied before racing out. She was often playing catch-up in their life, and this had apparently been part of the problem.

A small part of the problem. Not the biggest.

Drinks ordered, she asked him about work. "Tell me all about the people, the station, I want to know everything." She made sure she was attentive.

Mike regaled her with jaunty descriptions of his new colleagues, their quirks and personalities, their dynamics and rivalries, the set-up of the fire station, the equipment, the bosses, the good things, the challenges. Mike was a gregarious raconteur, always the center of attention down the pub, holding court with a great story or joke. It was part of what had attracted her to him in the first place. He could make people laugh, and was a great laugher himself. She found that sexy, even now. It was what she looked for and it was what she had found with Mike. A night with her husband was always a good time. Tonight was no different.

She found herself watching herself, realizing she was both present, listening to him, and also detached enough to be observing, as if looking down on them both from the ceiling. She was working hard, wanting him to know that she was here. Similarly, he was at his entertaining best—good stories, good jokes, loads of energy.

This feels like a great first date, she thought.

In the middle of the evening, she said, "Hey, did you get any calls about a fire in the Vale on Tuesday night, going into Wednesday morning? Like a bin fire or a wildfire that had got out of control?"

The atmosphere shifted around the table immediately.

"What you doing?" asked Mike. He was still smiling, but the smile had tightened.

Nicola panicked. "Fuck, sorry, yeah. Sorry."

They had rules. No talking about cases, or police work, or the detail of Mike's work. They were allowed to talk about colleagues, general banter, general how was your day, but anything specific about work was not allowed.

"No worries," said Mike, and the smile warmed up again. "Now, I've been thinking about holidays. We could go on holiday. We haven't had a holiday in forever."

Nicola looked worried. "Can we afford it?" The move, and the new house, had rinsed them.

"I think so," said Mike. "I think it'd be good, for all of us."

"With Ethan?" asked Nicola.

"If he wants to, yeah!"

They talked further and Mike showed her some pictures of a couple of places in Spain he'd found and costed. They looked fabulous. This was a plan for the future. A future together. Nicola resisted the urge to say that a holiday felt a long way away right now, a few days deep into a murder investigation.

She excused herself and asked the waiter where the loo was. On her way she thought to herself, this is turning out to be a great evening. Date nights are a good idea. She and her funny, charismatic, hunky husband had gossiped, chatted and laughed. They had tried each other's food, tasted each other's drinks. Why hadn't they put a system like this in place before?

Because they hadn't been in crisis like this before.

As she closed the door to the loo and sat down, she felt a wave of unbearable sadness wash over her. These date nights were little more than a thin coat of paint over a past that had almost destroyed them.

She had been gaslit. There was no doubt, looking back.

The suspicions had been there for a while. A new firefighter called Kirsty had joined Mike's station. He had mentioned her glowingly enough times for her to be on Nicola's radar. When they eventually met and Nicola could put a face to the name her first thought was: *oh my God, you are exactly his type.*

It was a running joke of Nicola and Mike's relationship that she was not his type but they were the perfect couple despite that. When they first met, they'd found it funny that if he had to describe his perfect woman it wouldn't be her. *Good job I came along*, Nicola would say as they lay in bed together, *you don't know what's best for you. Or who.*

Kirsty, an athletic redhead who Mike said gave all the lads a run for their money, was Mike's type as he had described it in years past. And now they were in close proximity, on every shift. Nicola had joked about it after meeting Kirsty. Mike had brushed it off: *I found my perfect woman.*

Being Mike's perfect woman had not been enough.

Nicola was not naive. She and Mike were the classic blue-light romance, turning up at the same scenes together often enough in Liverpool that it felt like fate was pushing them together. When he asked her out she wasn't sure but was persuaded by another colleague who fancied him. Nicola still believed the colleague had encouraged her to go so that it would fail, and then the colleague would be next on Mike's list. It had not turned out that way. It had turned into marriage and a beautiful son. It had turned into many years of busy, happy family building.

Many years before the deceptions began.

It took her too long to notice. But they began with changes so small, they barely seemed noteworthy.

He began being out longer than his shift patterns. She knew his shift patterns. She knew there was overtime, there were emergencies, there was cover. He had also disabled location services on their family Find My iPhone account. It was the first big flag which really cut through for her—*why do that?*—but he said he didn't want Ethan to worry about where fires were, or how long he was attending them for. It seemed a weak reason at the time, and she didn't really understand it. But she did not make the connection.

She did not make the connection, she would later tell herself, because she was a terrible detective of her own life.

But was that true? She knew how to interpret evidence. She knew how to track facts. She understood human psychology and emotions. She understood how these things mapped onto each other. She had confronted the perpetrator and was told that it was all nonsense. That there was no trail. That she was delusional. That just because she suspected people in her professional life, she didn't have to bring that approach home.

Mike had said those things directly to her. In the heat of the moment, yes. In their kitchen. With a straight face, and a burning air of injustice in his beautiful, trustworthy hazel eyes.

She had accepted his protestations. For too long. She began to lose confidence in work, in her professional instincts. If she could be wrong at home, could she be wrong at work? She thought she was going mad. She had to know the truth.

In the end, it took a simple solo stakeout. She hired a car Mike would not recognize, and waited, parked outside Kirsty's city-center flat, for three nights in a row. On the second, she thought her paranoia had reached levels that would have her signed off from work.

On the third, she saw her husband exit Kirsty's apartment, wrap his arms around her body, pull her to him and give her a long and lingering goodbye kiss. Their body language was post-coital, she thought.

Nicola, feeling like she was dying, sat in her car looking ahead for two hours after Mike had left and Kirsty had gone back inside.

A bomb had gone off in their family life. How they addressed it, whether they split or stayed together, how it affected Ethan, took months to figure out. Could Nicola forgive him? For the longest time she did not know herself.

In the hot and bitter arguments that followed, Mike told Nicola that she, Nicola, had been having an affair for years. It was just with her job. She had not been there for him, or for Ethan, he had told her. He had done all the heavy lifting in their family. The criminals of Liverpool had got all her attention. So, was it any wonder?

She hated him for saying that. Because somewhere within it was a kernel of truth. One she had not spotted until it was pointed out to her, until it was too late. But the victim blaming came thick and fast at one point: Nicola worked too hard. She was never there. When she was there she was exhausted or preoccupied. He had attempted to talk to her about it many times before Kirsty. He had suggested couples counseling.

Yes, she had been absent. She had been consumed by her work. She had looked at the Workaholics Anonymous website and done their questionnaire and got fourteen out of the twenty possible signs. She hadn't thought that was too bad, until she read at the bottom of the page that if you got more than three you were probably a workaholic.

OK, I'm a workaholic—try doing this job without being one. What am I meant to do? These are people's lives. These are serious crimes. Am I just meant to clock off at five thirty on the dot? Am I meant to not think about it? Not to care?

It was not a job, it was a vocation. They both knew that. It was part of the deal. She had never hidden anything. But then the deal was apparently not the deal. She held the guilt for it, despite him having done The Thing. She resented and was furious that she held the guilt. How dare he. And also, why wouldn't he? The two thoughts raged against each other within her, every day and night.

In their eventual couples therapy, when deciding whether or not to remain together, Mike's behavior had been classified as a "cry for help."

Nicola had been forced into a choice: which did she value more—her work or her family? There was no choice. She could sacrifice a husband, just. She would not sacrifice her son. The adoration there was mutual, and Ethan was not ready yet. He was not yet cooked. Another year or two, through A levels, off to university, out of the house, maybe then it would be a different story, but not yet. *Staying together for the kid.*

She had gone through a number of models: a sabbatical from her work in Liverpool. Being at home, being present. It didn't feel right, even if Mike walked away from his job and found something else. After weeks of pain, of late-night and early-morning rage-fueled crying, of endless group WhatsApping with mates, with colleagues, of what she should do, she came up with this plan.

She would fight for her marriage, and she would sacrifice for her family.

They would leave the northwest and get far away from the site of Mike's indiscretion, and any further temptation. He would look for a new post. He would have to go where she chose.

She chose her childhood home of West Dorset. It would be so much quieter, so much less challenging than the job she was in. She—they—could rebuild. She found, through various conversations and back channels, a force willing—no, desperate!—to bring her in. Now she understood why: they would have had no chance of recruiting someone of her experience or quality if she hadn't been in these circumstances.

Ethan was alternately furious and sanguine. He would be dragged from all his friends. He devised suggestions for living with friends while he finished school. But he also, really strongly, did not want to be a child of divorce. He had too many friends who were. He encouraged them to stay together. And in the end, he admitted that if he had to make a sacrifice, then he would. And he did. For her. She loved her son endlessly for that.

You OK?" Mike asked as she sat back at the table.

"Yep!" said Nicola, all smiles. She knew she had been gone for a while but wasn't going to acknowledge it. He would probably suspect it was work. It wasn't. She had been staring into space, wondering if any of this would work. She wished she could see the future. Were nights like this just a charade?

But she had promised to give herself fully to the process of reconciliation. *He's allowed a chance and he's working hard at it.* She told herself, if this was the first date with a new man, she would be keen to see him again. She told herself that people were allowed to make mistakes.

Which nudged her mind back to the case. Ayesha Barton and Jim Tiernan. Was that just a mistake? Affecting both Irina Bortnick and Mick Donnelly.

"I've paid. Shall we go?" smiled Mike.

They walked home, arm in arm, like romantic couples do. The two margaritas had softened both of them up. They played each other a new track on their phones—which was this date night's task: bring a new piece of music the other person probably hadn't heard. It was less romantic than an old-school mixtape, but it was fun.

At home, Mike hovered on the landing.

"You wanna come in?" asked Nicola.

Date night did not have to automatically end in sex. It hadn't done previously. But tonight, Nicola decided she wanted it to.

As they lay there entwined afterward, Mike's head nestled into her neck, he said very quietly as he fell toward sleep, "I'm sorry."

Not an apology for the sex (that had been Not Bad At All, Thanks), but for the more profound crisis he had brought about in all their lives. Whispered, as he drifted off.

Nicola felt a rage progress up her body.

Fuck you, she thought. *(Oh, I just did.)*

Did he think that was what she wanted to hear?

Mate, that won't even scratch the surface.

As she lay there afterward, with Mike asleep next to her, Nicola experienced a twin state: desirous love twinned with an icy corner of her heart which still wanted to maim her husband.

Is that what someone had felt about Jim Tiernan? Maybe Ayesha? Or Irina?

Stop thinking about the case. Go to sleep.

She tried to clear her mind.

It drifted onto Harry Ward. She remembered his expression when he was on the phone earlier talking to Deakins, rather than what she had assumed was his girlfriend. He had no girlfriend. Maybe he'd been out on a date tonight, too. Maybe he'd even pulled. Maybe he was having sex right now. And if he was, she wondered if—

Jesus, Nicola, stop! she admonished herself sternly. He was almost a decade younger than her. He was a colleague, a subordinate. Stop!

She instinctively raised her hand to cover her mouth in surprise at the thought. Then, very quietly, she suppressed a laugh. She lay there for a moment, her body shaking at the illicit thought that had bubbled up, unbidden.

As Nicola eventually drifted toward sleep, less than two miles away another fire was being lit.

CHAPTER THIRTY-SEVEN

Nicola woke with a start. It was still dark. Her phone was buzzing with a call from Harry Ward.

"Another fire, near Deakins' farm. Fire brigade have been called, I'm on the way there now."

"I'll meet you there." Nicola scrambled out of bed, grabbing clothes. She noted Mike was no longer in the bed.

She had a look in the spare room—he was gone, the bed unslept in.

The night was clear and cold as Nicola drove along the coast road with the window down, past the entrance to Deakins' farm, toward the fields up ahead illuminated by the lights of a fire engine. The hills and cliffs around were dark shadows against the blue-black of the night sky.

She could not escape the pounding feeling of dread that news of another fire had provoked in her. Surely this case was not going to follow the pattern of the 1925 murders? Another fire couldn't be the herald of another murder . . . could it?

She left her car in the coast road lay-by next to the field, noting it was an easy drop-off point for anyone wishing to unload materials to burn.

She arrived at the site as the fire crew were finishing up. The fire itself looked like it had been small but significant, laid for visibility, not for damage. As Nicola walked toward it, Mike was on the other side, supervising the end of the fire crew's work. Their eyes caught each other across the remaining smoke. He smiled at her; she returned it. She had a flashback to the old days, meeting at crime scenes.

Her line of sight to her husband was interrupted by Harry Ward. She almost blushed at the reminder of her earlier thought.

"I've had a chat to the fire crew," said Harry. "They're saying it was mostly bits of old wood and a box of firelighters. There isn't any wind, so it didn't spread. Apparently, the way it was laid meant it stayed contained. Oh, I think I met your husband? Mike?" Before Nicola could reply, Harry's gaze shifted. "Shit, here we go."

Nicola followed Harry's gaze.

Deakins was walking over to them from the direction of his farmhouse, yelling at them.

"Check my hands, check my clothes, you can even check my hair—you won't get nothing! Weren't me, y'hear? Tell you what *was* me, though: phone call reporting a fire. So don't come to me with no theories tomorrow, all right? Just get speaking to that feller next along. I told you he was doing this."

"Thanks for the context, Mr. Deakins," said Nicola politely.

Deakins stopped and turned back. "Problem for you, though, now," he said, staring at Nicola, "if they're following the pattern, you'll have another body to find, come sun-up."

"Good night, Mr. Deakins," said Nicola firmly.

As Deakins walked away, Harry said quietly, "Can't pretend the same thought hadn't occurred to me."

"Our job is to keep a calm head," admonished Nicola, not admitting that she had gone through the same thought process. "Whatever the reason behind this fire, we don't let it throw us. And we mustn't let it frighten the local community. People are scared enough right now." She looked up the pathway. "Simple access here, easy not to be seen, no camera coverage for miles, deserted at night. You can see why they chose this site."

"So do we think it's the same person both times?" asked Harry.

"Let's wait for the full fire report and compare it to the previous one before we jump to conclusions," said Nicola.

Harry nodded and began to move away, suddenly interested in his phone—Nicola wondered why but then realized that Mike was coming over to join her.

"Bit like old times," grinned Mike. "Nice . . . date night," he added pointedly. *He doesn't mean date night, he means the sex after date night.*

"It was fun," smiled Nicola noncommittally.

Mike was looking at Harry, still studying his phone nearby. He lowered his voice to Nicola. "You didn't tell me your partner was that good-looking," he said, teasing.

"Is he?" asked Nicola, in all innocence.

Mike gave her a look as if to say *you know he is.*

She was trying to sort through her thoughts and feelings about her husband *of all people* talking about the attractiveness of a work colleague, when Mike added:

"Oh, by the way, I asked about a fire in the Vale—and yes, there was a shout around 2 a.m. Wednesday morning. Woman from the White Hart, burning a load of clothes. They think she was a bit pissed. She got a telling-off. Wait, duty calls—"

Mike was being called away by one of his officers, but Nicola barely paid attention. One of Mike's fire crew had just provided an alibi for Irina Bortnick.

"Holy shit . . ."

Harry's words had floated over on the September breeze. He was already walking over, handing her his phone to show her an email that had come in overnight. Nicola read it and looked at Harry.

"Holy shit is right," she said.

The lab had got a match for the traces of DNA found under the fingernails of Jim Tiernan.

Frankie Winters.

They stood in silence for a moment, before Harry could no longer resist the urge to say:

"*Mucho* interesto."

CHAPTER THIRTY-EIGHT

It felt different this time, thought Frankie. The atmosphere, the faces of the detectives. Even the recording machine in the interview suite seemed more ominous.

They had answered an insistent banging on the front door of their flat shortly after 8 a.m., "inviting" them to attend the station. And here they were.

In truth, Frankie had been waiting for this to happen since giving them Dino's name, and a DNA swab. They were cornered and knew it. Quite *how* cornered, well, they were about to discover.

The female detective, Detective Sergeant Nicola Bridge, reminded Frankie that they had attended voluntarily and were not currently under arrest.

Currently.

They could choose to have a representative present should they wish.

Frankie wasn't sure anymore what their wish was. They shook their head, for now.

DS Bridge leaned forward and spoke in a quiet, steady and calm voice.

"Traces of your DNA have been found under the fingernails of Jim Tiernan. Can you explain how that happened?"

Those who've survived car crashes talk of everything happening in slow motion. Time, in this moment, slowed down for Frankie.

They knew exactly why their DNA was under Jim Tiernan's fingernails.

But was answering truthfully the right thing to do?

Frankie felt there was no choice anymore. They were caught in a whirlpool of other people's actions.

Jim Tiernan was incandescent with rage. He was not thinking straight, thought Frankie. This was not the man who came into the salon and chatted amicably once a month.

Jim had been walking back to his pub as Frankie and Dino were leaving. Frankie had been doing as they were told. That was the brief for the night: follow instructions, agree, don't do anything clever.

Dino had said to Jim, "You can run but you can't hide. I told you. Time's up."

Jim had run at Dino, trying to take him down. The two men started scrapping.

Frankie tried to break it up. In the melee, they had ended up being pinned to the wall of the pub by one of Jim's hands while he tried to fend Dino off with the other. Jim obviously thought Frankie was on Dino's side. Frankie was on no side.

"D'you know what this guy did?" Jim was yelling at Frankie, before turning to Dino. "Was that you? With the deer's head?"

Frankie tried to push Jim's grip away from their clavicle. Jim was strong. What the fuck was he doing? Frankie scratched his hand and arm and pushed back at Jim, who yelled in pain—

Dino barged the landlord against the wall and held him there. Jim was now out of breath. Dino was in the stronger position. Frankie was free.

"I want what you owe, tomorrow," said Dino calmly. "And if that's not possible, then we both know what will have to happen, Mr. White Hart."

Jim was trying to get his breath back. He looked at Frankie. "D'you know who you're working for? D'you know what he does? He wants me to run money through here, like he does through your salon."

Frankie did not want to hear this. Frankie did not want to know this. They could see Dino's irritation.

Dino said, "What is the matter with you? Are you some sort of child? Did you think I was lending you 50k out of the goodness of my heart? Nothing's free, pal! So, if you don't want to work together, you have to pay the money back. And if you can't pay the money back . . . maybe I'll have Frankie here do a swift scissor in the back of the neck, first thing tomorrow, just when you're at your most comfortable and vulnerable. Yes, I do know when your appointment is. Or maybe I'll have someone nip back into your little pub later tonight and disabuse you of the idea that you're some sort of king round here."

Before he went inside, Jim looked, bewildered, at Frankie. "You see what he is?"

Frankie wanted to tell Jim that they were just doing as they were told. They'd been instructed to have a drink with their boss. They realized now that Dino was simply using them as a prop, an accompaniment. Dino had wanted to come and remind Jim of whatever power Dino held over him, remind him, apparently, that his time was up. Frankie did not want to be any part of it. Frankie did not know the history of what was happening here. Frankie did not think Jim would believe that.

But Frankie never had the chance to explain or tell Jim Tiernan anything ever again.

How was Dino after Jim went back inside?" asked Nicola.

"He seemed pleased, like he'd enjoyed it—you know, the adrenaline. It was like he'd got what he came for. He was sort of . . . it's hard to describe . . . excited, maybe?" said Frankie.

"Had you seen him like that before?"

"Not to that extent," said Frankie. "I mean, he seems to like a bit of a dust-up. If something goes wrong in the salon, or a customer gets arsey, and Dino's there, he seems to get a kick out of making things as confrontational as possible."

"Did you think he was going to attack Jim, that night?" asked the younger detective.

Frankie thought about it. "I don't know. I still don't know. The squaring up, the yelling, that's where he sort of stops. But then . . ."

Frankie paused, held back what they were about to say.

"But then, what?" nudged Nicola.

"I feel like he probably has people who do that sort of thing for him. If it becomes necessary. I don't mean I've seen it, but I've heard him, on the phone, once or twice. I don't know it for sure . . . but I dunno . . . maybe?"

"What happened that night after Jim went back inside?"

"Dino dropped me back at my flat. That was it. Then I came into work early the next day and . . . I found out about Jim, when he didn't turn up."

"What did Dino say when he spoke to you, after you'd heard Jim Tiernan had died?"

"He just said I didn't need to tell anyone about what had happened."

For the next hour, the detectives peppered Frankie with more questions: had Frankie ever seen Dino with Jim before this? How long had

Frankie worked for Dino? How much day-to-day involvement did Dino have with the business? What times on what days was he in the salon? Was Frankie only ever paid cash? Had Frankie ever seen Dino be violent with anyone else? Did Frankie know any of Dino's other associates? Did Frankie know why Dino's other salon had closed down? Where did Dino live?

Frankie told them what they knew, which was very little.

"I just need the job. I like the work, I love my job, I love my clients, I just want to do that," they told the detectives.

"Do you think Dino killed Jim?" asked the younger detective.

Frankie thought for a long time. "I don't know," they replied in the end. "Maybe?" And then they added, "You cannot tell him I said that."

There was one final question. "Is there a time when Dino comes in, regularly, to collect the cash?" Nicola asked.

Frankie was tired now. Defenses were down.

They said, "Fifteen minutes before closing, every day."

Nicola nodded. "OK," she said. "Thank you for coming in, Frankie. Thank you for talking to us."

Yeah, thought Frankie. *Like I had a choice.*

Frankie stumbled out of the station into the morning sunlight. They phoned in sick to work. They could not face the possibility of being in the salon. They were also smart enough to know that the likelihood of the police dropping by at the end of the day to confront Dino was high. Frankie did not want to be there when that happened.

They went home. Went to bed. Did not sleep.

Frankie knew one thing: the police were going to talk to Dino. And Dino was going to know who had spoken to them.

If Dino was questioned and released, Frankie knew who he would come to see first.

Should they run? Should they leave Bredy?

Had Frankie made the biggest mistake of their life by telling the police their boss might be a murderer?

CHAPTER THIRTY-NINE

Jim Tiernan owed Dino Jones fifty grand, was refusing to launder money through the pub, and Dino had run out of patience. He wanted his money back," said Harry.

He and Nicola were huddled by the kettle in their office's makeshift break room, theorizing.

Nicola nodded. "Would explain Jim's dual set of accounts, would explain why he was skimming, in an attempt to find the money to pay Dino back. But he couldn't do it."

The phone rang on Mel's desk and both Nicola and Harry looked over, jumpy. All morning they had been on high alert, triggered by the fire last night. Would it prove to be the precursor to another body? Nicola had even gone so far as to ask Mel to check on admissions to local hospitals within the past twenty-four hours, or reports of disturbances locally, in case it related to the fire and their case. Mel had looked at her and said, "Feeling jittery, Sarge?" which hadn't helped matters. Nothing had been reported.

She checked her watch. It was past lunchtime. She had not eaten breakfast, partly nerves, partly rushing out to question Frankie. She needed air, to clear her head and think, and she needed food.

"I'm gonna get a sandwich."

The girl was waiting in front of the station entrance as Nicola walked out.

Shannon.

She strode over to the waiting girl.

"How did you get here?" asked Nicola, shocked.

Shannon nodded to a bike discarded nearby.

"It's a three-mile bike ride from your house. Does your mum know you're here?"

Shannon shook her head. As she did, Nicola noticed a wound on her face. The lip had been split. She knelt and held Shannon's chin gently in one hand. Shannon didn't resist or recoil. She looked Nicola deep in the eye. The girl had fierce green eyes.

"What happened to you?" asked Nicola.

"You shouldn't have come," said Shannon sulkily. "You shouldn't have come to the house, and you shouldn't have asked to come in."

"I wanted to talk to you," Nicola said, guilt washing over her. Had her visit caused Shannon to be harmed? "Shannon, did your mum do this to you?"

"I'm fine," said the girl dismissively.

"You're not. Whoever did this needs to be spoken to."

"It doesn't matter," insisted Shannon.

"It *does* matter," said Nicola firmly. "Nobody has the right to injure you like that."

"You don't know what happened," said Shannon defiantly. She said nothing for a few seconds, and then, softer, said, "Anyway, she doesn't mean to. She just has bursts. It's hard for her. It's only me and her. And I'm annoying."

"Is that what she tells you?" asked Nicola.

Shannon did not reply. Nicola took a deep breath.

"I'm sorry if my visiting caused your mum to get upset. You have not done anything wrong. You know that, don't you?"

Shannon didn't move. Just stood there looking at Nicola, saying nothing.

"But I think you might know something about what happened to Jim Tiernan, the man who ran the White Hart pub. Would I be right in thinking that?"

There was an agonizing pause. It was starting to spot with rain. Nicola looked up at the sky.

"Should we go in there?" She nodded at the deserted café across the road. "They do a good hot chocolate."

Shannon nodded.

Nicola watched as Shannon attacked the hot chocolate. She had beamed as the tall glass, brimming majestically with the sweet liquid and topped off, or overflowing, with a pile of whipped cream and marshmallows, was brought over, with a long teaspoon jiggling against the saucer it sat on. A tower of delight.

Nicola was weighing up what to do. She had to get Shannon's confidence. But in terms of process, any conversation they were to have about the case would need to be recorded, with a chaperone present, if it were to be admissible as evidence. Nicola felt she was a long way away from getting Shannon to participate in something like that. She had to win her trust first. But it was a delicate balance. Conversations with a minor were fraught for police officers, and Nicola knew she was tiptoeing through a minefield, just by having this conversation alone. The prize, though, on the other side of the minefield, was information that seemingly nobody else possessed.

Shannon winced as she drained the hot chocolate. The glass stung her injured lip.

"You all right?" asked Nicola.

The girl nodded.

"Shannon, how would you feel about talking to somebody from social services about what's happening at home?"

"No, thanks." The answer was said lightly, the brush-off definitive.

"They can help ensure you're safe."

"I can look after myself."

"You shouldn't have to. There are systems in place to support children like you."

"Can you really protect me?" Shannon asked.

"Yes," said Nicola.

"I know what happened. But they don't know I know."

Nicola's heart rate quickened. "Who's 'they,' Shannon?"

Shannon looked into space. Then fixed Nicola with a plaintive expression. "I don't want to die," she said.

"You're not going to die," Nicola reassured her quietly. She put her hand across the table and placed it on Shannon's. Shannon looked at it as if it were an alien object, as if no one had ever done that before and she was unsure how to react.

"If they know about me, they'll kill me, too."

"I won't let that happen," said Nicola. "Tell me what happened."

Shannon was quiet for a moment. Then she said:

"Sometimes I sleep in cars."

CHAPTER FORTY

Earlier

She crept downstairs, holding her trainers so as not to make any noise. She could not be heard going out. She had already been brought back once tonight and caught hell for it. She would have to be even quieter leaving this time.

Shannon looked through the gap between the door and the wall, where the hinges were, into the front room. Her mum was not there. She did the same in the kitchen. No sign. She must be upstairs. She must have made it to bed.

She was presumably still with The Man.

Shannon had not seen The Man before. But she did not like being in the house when there was a new The Man. There were too many ways in which things could become unpredictable. She had found from experience it was safer not to be around. The Man might be nice, he might give her money or sweets or a cigarette, or weed (which she would throw into the bin in the playground), depending on The Man. But he might not be as nice to her mum. And when The Man is not nice to her mum, her mum is not nice to Shannon.

She pulled her hooded coat from the hook, the small black rucksack from the corner and, still clasping her trainers, opened the front door slowly and quietly. She braced—the first quiet *sssccht* of air being shifted and the door detaching from its seal sounded thunderous to her. But it was a long way from her mother's bedroom and the door would be closed. Plus, the kitchen and front room bore the debris of drinking. Shannon was banking on her mum being in a deep sleep.

She opened the door just far enough to slide through—she enjoyed being small and slight at moments like this—and stepped out into the night.

Her bare feet touched the wet, dark paving stones outside. She enjoyed the shock of it. The feeling of escape. Of freedom.

She looked around to be sure no one was watching. The street was deserted. All the lights in all the other houses were off. It was long past midnight.

Shannon pulled the door shut, with the handle still bent. Once the door was as firmly back in place as it could be, she slowly raised the handle so that it locked silently.

She looked around. There was a damp mist hovering around the yellow streetlights. The night was full of moisture. She liked autumn, preferred it to summer.

She pulled her trainers on, leaning against the wall of her house. She slipped into the thick coat and pulled the hood up. Zipped it all up, encasing herself. It was like being hugged.

Shannon walked purposefully, lightly, down the street. A tiny, slight figure in a winter coat and trainers, dwarfed by the lampposts and houses and trees.

She made her way to where she thought she might have some luck.

At this time of night, Shannon always headed for the car park on the edge of the village.

It was next to the playground where Shannon spent much of her time. She would watch the stream of cars and vans and motor homes and caravans and motorbikes come in and out. She would watch people leave them for the night.

In the summer she had noticed a few camper vans setting up for the night in the car park, despite the clear warnings that overnight camping was prohibited and this car park was for village residents only. She had once watched a couple who seemed quite old—maybe even sixty, which was an unimaginable age to Shannon—set up an awning over their motor home, bring out a barbecue and start grilling. They were drinking wine, too. The man draped a large beach towel over the sign warning off overnight campers, as if, by doing that, they couldn't be punished for breaking the rules.

On any given night, there could be thirty or forty vehicles parked in here. And after 10 p.m., there was nobody about. Fleetcombe was a village which went to bed early.

It was way past ten o'clock now. She knew it was after midnight, but she didn't know how much. Everywhere was quiet. The night was damp, though. The mildest of rain spots fluttered through the air. Mizzle, she'd heard it called. It made the roads and pavements shiny. The windscreens of the vehicles were all dotted with tiny droplets.

The little girl in the big coat and trainers surveyed the opportunities for tonight.

Not everyone left their car unlocked in this car park. Not even the majority did. But Shannon was always surprised—and happy—to discover that a few—*enough*—did. She wondered if they just forgot, or didn't care, or thought it was safe.

Her routine was simple. She started on the car nearest to the entrance. And she worked her way up and down the line, from one to the next. She tried all the car doors, and the boot of every car to see if it had been left unlocked. She was methodical: most had central locking, but not all. She had learned from experience not to take anything for granted.

If any door opened, she had a quick peek inside: did the back seat look comfy? Was there room to stretch out? If it was one of those big cars where the boot and the back were the same, could she lie across there? Did the car smell bad? Lots of cars smelled bad. Some smelled bad-bad, some just had those little air-conditioner things that made her wrinkle her nose and sneeze.

If a car was unlocked, she noted it, and kept going. Unless it was obviously perfect. She had time, and she did not sleep much anyway. She enjoyed the game. And any car she did not sleep in this time, she could remember for next time. She sometimes returned to the same ones again and again (she developed knowledge of people who often left their cars there for a few days, people who parked there Sunday night and didn't return until Friday evening). But she also liked trying new ones. There might always be a better car to sleep in until the sun rose.

She was lucky that the first glimpse of light always woke her. For the most part, it enabled her to sneak out before anyone arrived.

The best part of the car park, the one with the big prize, was toward the back. This was where the bigger vehicles were. The vans and motor caravans. Not many of them were ever unlocked. But sometimes, just sometimes, they were.

This was one of those sometimes.

And this sometime would be the last time Shannon ever played this game.

She was getting tired and a little bored as she edged round the far side of the car park to the bigger vehicles. She tried the front door of a van which had some comfy-looking seats inside. Locked. Shame.

She tried the tried the handle of the sliding door behind the driver's door. It slid open a short way! Shannon beamed. She looked around to check again that she hadn't been seen. No one, anywhere in sight. She peered inside.

There were three mini-seats forming one long seat, almost like a cushioned bench, directly behind the driver's seat. There was a nice amount of space between these seats and the front seats. She'd be able to put her stuff on the floor down there. Behind those seats was a wire grille, separating the back seats from the rear storage area.

Behind the partition it seemed like it was easily big enough and wide enough for her to lie down, and roll around in, with room to spare. Shannon couldn't see what was in there, because it was dark and the grille obscured it.

She went round and tried the rear doors. Locked.

She returned to the back passenger sliding door. The seats there were good enough for her. She could lie across those without her feet or head banging the doors either side. It did not smell bad in here. It smelled quite clean. She didn't mind the smell of the seats either.

Shannon got in and slid the door shut from inside.

Then she panicked and opened it again, to check that she could. Yes, that worked. Phew. She imagined herself as a cartoon character wiping a flood of sweat off her forehead at that moment. That made her smile.

She looked out the front window. A sea of cars ahead. The van she was in was parked right on the corner, where the light from the rest of the car park didn't quite reach. It would be hard for anyone early in the morning to look in and see her. They probably wouldn't come this far anyway.

She always had to think ahead. She had learned that. If you didn't think ahead, sometimes it ended up hurting. She had become an expert in what people might do, or think, or punish you for. Stuff you didn't even realize you were doing wrong was often wrong, according to adults, later.

She sat on the seat nearest to the door and opened up her rucksack. She pulled out the soft, fluffy charcoal-gray blanket she had been given for Christmas a few years ago. It always reminded her that they had had nice Christmases once. She laid it out over herself as she stretched out across the length of the three seats. She found a position where the red seat belt holders didn't poke into her. It was a trick she had developed from doing this quite a lot: you had to lie toward the edge of the seats, even if it meant you risked falling off.

She pulled the tiny, cracked old phone out of her hoodie pocket. She set the alarm for 6:15 a.m. Six felt too early, but people started being on the move from six thirty, so this felt safe.

Lying down, she pulled the rucksack over, zipped it up, slid the phone into an outside pocket and pushed the rucksack under the seat she had her head on. She registered where everything was, running through it, in case she had to make a quick exit in the morning.

As Shannon lay there, she wondered what other children her age were doing right now. They were all probably asleep in beds, with nightlights nearby, parents down the hall. They would never have thought about doing this. They wouldn't know anything about car parks, about what you needed to stay warm when you were sleeping in a stranger's van. They probably wouldn't ever need to have that idea. They would wake up to the smell of breakfast: chocolate cereal, or eggs, or bacon, or pancakes, or all of it and orange juice. They might have a dog or a cat.

Shannon had none of those things, nor any prospect of them ever coming into her life. She felt suddenly and irretrievably sad, like she was falling down a deep well. But then she stopped herself thinking like that, applying a mental slap to her own mind—*stop it*. She turned onto her side: she knew how to adapt, how to survive. She knew how to keep herself safe. If there was a nuclear bomb, or zombies became real, Shannon backed herself to survive. All those other pampered babies would be in trouble then. Shannon would win.

With that comforting thought, she pulled the hood further over her head, and the charcoal blanket up over her face. She smelled it. It smelled like her, and she was the best comfort she had in moments like these. Shannon smiled and closed her eyes. She felt incredibly tired.

Within forty-seven seconds, she was asleep.

It was the slam that awoke her.

Her eyes flashed open in panic.

It was nearby. That noise had been close. Hadn't it?

She could hear footsteps outside the van. They were walking round from the rear of the vehicle.

Somebody had opened and closed the back doors.

She peered through the gap to the front seats and out through the windscreen. It was still dark. Middle-of-the-night dark. How long had she been asleep? Hours? Minutes?

The footsteps were coming round to the driver's side. This must be the owner. They were going to go somewhere. A shadow fell across the window into the back seat as a figure passed.

Shannon knew she had no time to get out—she only knew that the door by her head was unlocked: that was the one she'd come in through. But that was the one where the person was currently hovering.

She could try getting out through the door by her feet, on the other side of the van, but she didn't know for sure whether it was open. If it wasn't, and she tried to make an escape that way, she'd draw attention to herself and there would be trouble.

She didn't think she could run fast enough, with her rucksack, to definitely escape an adult coming after her. So she could not chance getting out the side door while they were there.

These thoughts raced through her head in a matter of seconds.

She made a decision. Still covered in the blanket, and with her hood up, she gently lowered herself onto the floor in the footwell behind the driver's seat, and in front of the line of rear seats. It was dark down here, and sheltered.

Then she bunched herself up behind the driver's seat, curled up in a ball, pulling the charcoal blanket over her. If the driver got in, they would not be able to see her. She shoved her rucksack under the rear seat behind the driver, too.

It was a squash and a squeeze, like in the story her reception teacher used to read to the class, back in the days when Shannon went to class. She was once again thankful to be slight and small.

The person outside got in and sat in the driver's seat. They started the van immediately.

Shannon had no sense of them, or who they were. She knew that even trying to take a peek would be dangerous.

Suddenly, the van was moving, bumping over the gravel of the car park, and then out onto the smoother road. Shannon thought they had turned right out of the car park. She was trying to track the journey, so she could retrace it and get home again.

She started to think ahead. Maybe if the van stopped at traffic lights, she could jump out and run. So long as they hadn't gone too far.

She wondered where the person was going, and what time it was, and why they had to go somewhere this time of night. Her mum had worked night shifts at the all-night supermarket once; maybe that's where this person was going. That would be all right, Shannon knew her way home from there. It would be a long walk, but she could do it.

In truth, though Shannon was running through all the possible scenarios, she knew she couldn't act on a lot of them, because she could not move. She was paralyzed by fear. She was terrified of being discovered. She was worried what might happen if she was found, and what the person who found her would do. She knew that there were many bad people out there who did bad things to children. Had she ended up here with one of them? Would she regret this for the rest of her life? Would she be held hostage? Would she be hit, or worse?

She told herself, in a stern instruction, not to cry. Not to sniffle. Not even to breathe loudly. She blinked away the first hint of tears. That would not help. She knew that from experience. Pull yourself together, that was her mum's favorite phrase. She was going to do that now. She was going to pull herself together.

As she sat there, and the van went over a speed bump, she heard something move around in the back. It clattered.

They did not go far.

The van stopped. The driver got out.

Shannon's heart soared: a chance for escape—

Schunk. The sound of the van's central locking.

The driver had left, and locked the van. Shannon was locked in.

Unless. Unless.

Maybe the door Shannon had got in through was faulty. She could try it and get out.

But, but. What if an alarm went off? What if she was caught?

Shannon remained wedged into the footwell, covered in her blanket. She did not know this van. If she opened the door, she might set off an alarm. The driver might be nearby anyway; she didn't dare look. She didn't know where they were. And she was so low down, when she looked up all she could see out of the windows was the black of the nighttime sky.

Should she risk it? Should she try? It had been a minute or two. Maybe the driver wasn't coming back. Maybe they had just wanted to move their van for the morning.

She was about to risk it when she heard the back doors open again.

She could hear someone's heavy breathing.

Then a thump. Something heavy being dropped down.

The van shook and Shannon thought the driver had climbed in. They were doing something in the back.

What was going on?

Shannon remained unmoving, terrified of being found, for what seemed like ages. Then it felt like the driver got out of the back.

The back doors slammed. Shannon could hear the driver walk round.

For a moment, she realized the driver could be about to open the door where she was sitting. She held her breath.

The door she was leaning against . . . did not open.

The driver's door opened. The driver got in.

As they did, Shannon caught the briefest glance.

It made her even more terrified.

The driver was wearing a scary suit.

Shannon had once accidentally watched ten minutes of a program about a nuclear power station disaster which her mum was watching. It was so scary she had to leave the room. Her mum had laughed, and said, "It's not real. I mean, it's based on a real thing, but it's not real."

In that program, men had got garden sprayers and were spraying things around. They wore the same protective suits as the driver now, with a hood over the head.

Why would they do that?

Shannon didn't dare contort herself to look round anymore. She was properly scared now. She thought she had been scared before in her life, and she had. But this felt different. It felt more threatening than any of the other times. It felt worse than the knowledge she was about to be hit by her mum.

It felt like she might be about to die.

The van's engine restarted. She was trapped again.

She had not made the most of a chance to escape.

She didn't know how long it was before the van stopped again, but it felt like forever. When it stopped, and the driver got out, she realized she had been sort of holding her breath for a very long time. She breathed out, as quietly as she could.

She was getting tired and was worried she might fall asleep. What if she was discovered?

Should she move? She couldn't hear any footsteps or movement. She wondered where the driver was.

She heard the back doors open again, and someone got into the van. She wanted to know what was happening. That might give her a clue to where she was, in case she was able to run, and run home from here. Home was often the place she was desperate to get away from. Now, for the first time in a long time, it felt like the place she wanted to run back toward.

She waited for a little while. Dragging sounds in the back of the van had continued but now died down. It had been a while. She had to look. She couldn't bear not knowing.

She moved the dark blanket from around her carefully, balling it up under the rear seats so it couldn't be spotted and she could retrieve it easily if she had to dart back down.

Keeping her hood up, she snuck up onto the rear seats, being careful not to let any part of her body be seen. Could she peer through the grille? The dragging sounds had stopped. It had gone very quiet.

Maybe the driver wasn't anywhere nearby. Shannon listened, so hard. She had got good at listening during her short life. Listening meant detecting incoming jeopardy. Listening could save you a lot of pain, if you acted on it. It enabled you to get out of harm's way, or not be found.

It also was a curse sometimes. When you knew what was coming, and you knew there was no way out. Sometimes it's better not to hear, better not to know.

She wanted to know what *this* was, though.

Shannon moved her body so she could gradually raise her head above the line of the back seats, to look through the grille and out through the back of the van. She was banking on the darkness of her hood preventing her from drawing attention. She only needed to get her eyes above the seat line.

She moved very slowly, very cautiously, until she could see.

It took her a while to process what she was looking at.

Both the back doors of the van were open. They offered a window onto the world beyond. It was black, thick with night. They were not near any buildings. She thought she could glimpse a bit of road, illuminated red by the rear lights of the van that still seemed to be on.

She saw the driver—a hooded figure in a protective suit. They were wearing gloves. What were they doing? Why were they wearing that weird suit?

But taking up the majority of the view from where she was looking was a figure. A person. Or maybe a statue. A doll. A—what was the word?—shop dummy. Mannequin! She'd heard that word used once in a story, and she'd liked it. Mann-uh-kin. She'd sounded it out.

Through the open back doors she saw that the statue was in a sitting position on a wooden seat, a little further down what she thought was a road. All Shannon could see was its silhouette. It was facing away from her.

But the silhouette scared her.

It was a human shape.

Except its head. Its head had antlers on.

The driver was standing in front of the dummy, looking at it. Like the driver was assessing it, working out whether it was right.

Something bad was happening. Something so bad it was beyond what she understood.

Suddenly, the driver's head snapped away from looking at the dummy and looked sharply back at the van. Like they knew they were being watched—

Shannon darted back down, her head pressed against the back of the seat.

Her heart was thumping against her chest in a way she'd never known before. She could feel it against her ribs.

She thought she was going to be sick.

She was frozen. She could not move. She wanted to move. Her body was not doing what she wanted it to.

She listened. Had the driver seen her? Were they coming back?

Could she hear footsteps? Big, heavy footsteps.

In her mind, the driver was tall and big and could floor her with a swipe of his arm, like Dave, one of her mum's old boyfriends, had.

I need to be back down on the floor, please can I get back down on the floor?

She could think it, but she didn't seem to be able to do it.

She had been in positions of fear before and she had managed to move. She summoned that memory and willed her body to move, even though it was telling her it couldn't.

Please . . . she asked of it. *Please.*

Slowly, it did. Desperate not to make any noise.

Is he coming?

She slid, as slowly and quietly as she could, into the hiding space she had been in before. She pulled the charcoal blanket back over her. It covered her head.

All was darkness.

She tried not to breathe, or sob. Or make any sound.

She had no idea where the driver was. She didn't want to know.

She just wanted the night to be over.

She wanted to be out of this van.

She didn't want to know anything more about anything.

She just wanted to be a child, like the other children.

She felt hot tears roll silently, slowly, down her cheeks. She didn't even want to move to brush them off. She wanted to feel them so that she could learn this lesson.

Why did you get in here? Why have you been doing this?

Because you're stupid, Shannon. That thing Mum says, that thing everyone thinks, that you're weird and strange and stupid, is true.

So whatever happens to you, you deserve it.

She was braced for the door to open. She was leaning against it, so she would fall out, and she would hurt herself, and that was no more than she deserved.

She waited for it.

She didn't know how much time went by.

The door did not open.

It may have been seconds, it may have been minutes.

SLAM. It made her jump. The back doors were shut, one two *bang*.

She heard the footsteps.

She held her breath. She burrowed into her hiding place.

She wanted to disappear and could not disappear.

Now she was going to be discovered.

Her door still did not open. She still did not fall out.

Eventually, the driver's door opened. The driver got back in, out of breath, and started the van. There was something in the way the driver was breathing, fast and heavy, and the way they were revving the engine; Shannon felt they were panicking.

They were on the move again, lurching off.

Hope flooded Shannon's limbs. Was there a chance she *wouldn't* be found?

There was a chance the driver would not notice the stowaway in his van.

But where were they going now?

The journey back seemed bumpier, faster, the braking more sudden. The driver's breath at times quickened.

After a while, the van turned and Shannon could hear crunching gravel.

Had they come back to where they started?

The driver got out quickly.

They didn't see me.

They didn't find me.

Shannon wanted to cry, a different sort of crying now. Relief. *Relief.*

She could hear the footsteps getting further away on the gravel. *Go, keep going*, she thought.

Then they stopped.

Shannon's heart raced.

They're coming back.

Click!

The central locking was activated.

Shannon was locked in again.

Panic rose in her once more.

This never-ending night would become morning. And she would be discovered.

And then what?

They would ask her what she had seen.

She listened to the footsteps go and disappear.

She waited for what seemed like hours. It was around five minutes.

She knew because she counted. *One elephant, two elephant.*

She got to three hundred elephants.

Nothing else, no sounds, no movement from anywhere nearby.

She took off the blanket. She turned and raised herself slowly up.

She looked out of the window.

They were back in the car park where they had started. Back at Fleetcombe.

She was near home.

There was no one else around.

She looked out the front windscreen. She scooted over to the other side and looked out the window there. No one.

She looked at the time on the car's clock: 02:17.

She wondered if her mum had noticed she wasn't at home.

Why would she?

Shannon considered her options. She could stay here until the morning, and risk being discovered. She did not know when the driver would be back.

Or she could make a run for it. Set the alarm off. Draw attention.

She did not know how soon someone would come to attend to the alarm. She did not know where the driver lived. Maybe it was close. Maybe overlooking the car park. Or maybe it was further away, on the other side of the village.

She felt like she would have to risk it.

She would run. She was ready to run.

Maybe this van was different. Different vans had different systems.

Shannon moved back across to the door where she had got in what seemed like hours ago, looking for a safe night's rest.

It had been neither safe nor restful.

She didn't want to have a night like this again, ever.

She had shoved the blanket back into the rucksack. She had put the rucksack on her back.

She took a deep breath.

She pulled the handle.

She attempted to open the door—the lock clicked, the door slid open and Shannon spilled out.

There was no alarm.

For a second, she stood there, staring at the van, wondering why it was making no noise, why she had been allowed out. And then her mind kicked in—

RUN!

She slammed the door and ran.

The car park was silent.

No car alarm rang out.

Except in Shannon's head.

As she ran, all she could see in her mind was that figure in a scary suit standing next to a mannequin with antlers on it.

Deep down, she knew that it was not a mannequin. It was far, far scarier than that.

Shannon kept running.

CHAPTER FORTY-ONE

Shannon put her little finger into the empty hot chocolate, trying to mop up the last bits of froth, sucked on her finger and looked up at Nicola.

"It wasn't a lorry. But it wasn't a car. It was sort of in-between."

Nicola nodded. She thought she knew the type of vehicle Shannon was talking about. "Can you remember what color it was, Shannon?"

"It was gray," the girl said without hesitation, "or maybe silver."

"Was it shiny or dull, the color?"

"Shiny," said Shannon. "Not dull. More silvery than gray-y."

Nicola scribbled all this down. Her notebook was nearly full.

"You've done brilliantly, talking me through this, Shannon."

"I didn't see the face. It would have been better if I'd seen the face, wouldn't it?"

Nicola reassured her: everything she'd described was incredibly important and useful. Shannon didn't quite look convinced.

"What happens now?" asked Shannon. "Can you catch them now?"

"I'm going to take everything you've told me and share it with my colleagues, and we're going to put it together with all the other evidence we've collected from other places. Solving a crime is like doing a massive jigsaw puzzle, often without half the pieces. But what you've given us is a huge part of the jigsaw. And probably a really important piece. Not just a bit of sky, or anything like that." Nicola smiled at Shannon.

Shannon didn't smile back. Nicola thought that perhaps she had not done many jigsaws.

"And then what?" asked Shannon.

Nicola took a deep breath. "Would you be able to come in and say all this again, but this time being recorded?"

"What sort of recorded?"

"It would be on a video camera, and there would be another adult present, to ensure everything was aboveboard, and that you hadn't been forced into saying any of this."

Shannon looked confused. "But I've just told you what happened."

"Yes, but this is only a conversation. As police, we need an official record."

"Why isn't this an official record? You're a police person."

"I know, it's confusing. But there is a process we have to go through. It's called safeguarding. It's there for your own protection."

"I have to say all of that again?"

"Yes, please. We'd make it very easy, and as quick as possible."

"But you'd record it. So anyone could see it."

"We'd record it, but nobody would be able to access it without us approving it."

"What if my mum saw it?"

"She wouldn't."

"How do you know?"

"What do you think? Could we do all that tomorrow?"

Shannon shrugged. It wasn't a yes, but it wasn't a no. Nicola persisted.

"Do you want to come here, at a specific time, or would you like me to come and pick you up?"

Shannon looked alarmed. "You can't pick me up."

"So will you come here, or to the police station?"

"I don't want to come to the police station."

"Shall I meet you here then?"

Shannon shrugged again.

Nicola was worried. Shannon was not on board with this plan. Maybe she was tired. It had been a long time talking, and she had had to relive an extraordinary set of events.

Shannon pushed the saucer, glass and teaspoon away. She was done. "I have to go home now."

"Would you like me to drive you?"

Shannon shook her head.

"Are you sure?"

"I'll be OK."

"Shall we meet here at one o'clock tomorrow?"

Shannon shrugged again.

They walked to the door. Nicola pulled the door open. Cold air blasted in. She gestured for Shannon to go first.

Shannon hesitated for a second. Looked up at the adult by her side. "If they knew I knew, if they knew I had told you, they would want to kill me, too. Wouldn't they?"

Nicola put a hand on Shannon's shoulder. "I won't let that happen."

Shannon looked back at Nicola with a "don't be ridiculous" expression. "But you don't know who it is. So, you can't stop them, can you? Unless you catch them. And you haven't."

And she went off, heading for her bike without a goodbye.

Haven't *yet*, Nicola wanted to call after Shannon. But we will.

Then she thought: *who are you trying to convince—the girl, or yourself*?

Nicola thought again of last night's fire, still terrified by what news the day could yet bring.

CHAPTER FORTY-TWO

"Will she come in and talk on tape?" asked Harry after Nicola had relayed Shannon's story to him.

"I hope so," replied Nicola. She didn't want to admit her doubts.

"If she doesn't, nothing she's told you would be admissible," said Harry.

"Aware of that, thanks."

"You could've called me, if there'd been two of us—"

"Don't lecture me on process, Harry. I'm aware. She wanted to talk. I couldn't get her to wait."

Harry nodded, admonished. He tried to make up for what he felt was an overstep. "You know it matches the description of Eddie Godfrey's van."

Nicola replied, "Yes. But before we jump to any conclusions, let's see how many are in that car park."

Harry was about to say the same thing. "I'll go to the car park this evening to check. I'll cross-check with all the vehicles owned by anyone we have as a person of interest."

"Good." Nicola checked her watch. "Before you do," she said, "Operation Dino."

Nicola and Harry were sitting in her car, tucked away out of view but with a good angle on the salon, when they got their first surprise.

A vehicle pulled up directly outside the salon.

"Looks like this might be him," said Harry. "Bang on time."

"Fuck . . ." said Nicola.

They both looked at the vehicle: a silver van, which matched the description Shannon had given Nicola earlier.

Before they could take in the full implications, a man got out of the back side door of the van. He fitted exactly the profile vouched for by the girl in the Ebbsley newsagent: bald, short, and would answer to the description of "bullet."

Nicola and Harry moved simultaneously, getting out of her car and striding quickly across the road just as Dino was approaching the door to the salon.

"Dino!" Nicola called, and watched him stop at the door and look round, confused to hear his name called out that way here; irritated. "Can we have a word?"

"Who are you?" The balance between confusion and irritation was written all over Dino's face. Inside the salon, the last customer and the fluff-bearded barber were both gawping.

Nicola and Harry flashed their warrant cards. "Police. We'd like to speak to you in connection with the death of Jim Tiernan," recited Harry.

"You want to what?" said Dino, stepping away from the door and toward them, as if he was about to slap them for their audacity.

"We'd like to talk to you at the station. You can come with us voluntarily, or we can arrest you here and take you in," said Nicola.

She watched Dino standing there, in expensive jeans, a black, torso-hugging top and black trainers, sizing the situation up before shrugging. "You don't need to do that. Happy to come. I'd like my solicitor, though."

He looked to the driver of the silver van, who was sitting with the window down. The driver nodded: instruction received.

Nicola walked around the van. "This yours?" she asked Dino.

"Belongs to the business," said Dino.

Nicola nodded, writing the number plate down. She opened the door Dino had just come out of and looked in. It was pristine: two rows of seats, a grille, room for goods in the back. She would have loved to test the alarm on this side door, but there would be time enough for that. She slammed it, and smiled at Dino, who was looking at her, bemused.

"Our car's over here. The station's just round the corner," said Nicola.

"Oh, I know where you are," smiled the bullet-headed man. He nodded at his driver and went along with Nicola and Harry.

Dino's aftershave arrived in their car before he did. Nicola complimented him on it. He told her they sold it in the salon and he could get her a discount if she was nice to him.

After that, Dino did not say anything. He sat back, relaxed, quiet, looking out the window, his arms placed in his lap.

He gave his details at the beginning of the interview. His full name was Dean Jones. Dean-o, thought Nicola. Originally from Ystradglynlais in Wales. He had a driver's license on him to confirm his ID. While Dino had a cup of tea and awaited the arrival of his solicitor, Mel handed over the file of research he had diligently prepared on him and his associated businesses. Nicola smiled at Mel with gratitude, and he walked off whistling.

Dino's well-suited solicitor was at his side. They clearly knew each other of old. Nicola felt this wasn't their first time in a police interview together.

"What's the nature of your business locally, Mr. Jones?"

"I own the salon round the corner," came the reply.

"How long have you had that salon?" asked Nicola.

Dino shrugged. "Year or two."

"How many other salons do you own?"

"Eight or nine in total," said Dino.

"Including a salon in Ebbsley, until recently?"

Dino became very still, looking at her. He was assessing her, she thought. "You been doing your research then."

Yes, I have. "Was there a particular reason it closed?"

Dino looked at his purple-socked solicitor, who made a tiny negative gesture with his head.

"No comment."

Nicola smiled. "How do you know James Tiernan?"

"We were banged up at the same time," said Dino.

Nicola smiled patiently again. "Wandsworth. Correct?"

"Correct."

"Did you have a good relationship with him?"

"We worked in the kitchen together. We helped each other a bit, when necessary."

"Did you stay in touch on release?"

Dino looked at Nicola. "It's not like going to Spain. You're not sharing holiday photos and meeting up."

Nicola smiled again and took her time looking down at her notes. She could feel that her smile was rattling Dino. He obviously didn't know many people who smiled at him. "When was the next time you saw Mr. Tiernan?"

"About a year and a half ago. He was having his hair cut when I dropped into the salon."

"Was Mr. Tiernan pleased to see you?"

"How could he not be?" smiled Dino. "We chatted, said we'd see each other around. No plans."

"And when did you subsequently see Mr. Tiernan after that?"

Dino shrugged. "Don't think I did."

Nicola produced a piece of paper and slid it across the table, naming the document for the recording in progress. She watched Dino look puzzled. "This is a copy of a page from Mr. Tiernan's business diary, dated February 7 this year. If you look at 10 a.m., you'll see he's written next to it: 'Dino, re: finance, here.'"

Dino looked at it. "OK."

"So, you remember the meeting now?"

"I have a lot of meetings."

"Did you attend that meeting, Mr. Jones?"

"I think I did, yeah."

"In this particular one, what aspect of finance were you discussing?"

Dino took a breath in, and then exhaled, like an aggressive mindful meditator. "He was finding it difficult running the pub, and we discussed ways it could be easier, as well as his personal finances."

"How were his personal finances?"

"Not great. He's a spender, that boy. And bookkeeping wasn't his strength either. He said the brewery were getting antsy. He told me, not long after he took over, he'd staged a break-in so he could siphon off the money he said had been stolen to pay off his own debts. Not exactly the best start to running a boozer, is it?"

Nicola put the revelation about the break-in to one side for now.

Whether or not it was true (and she suspected it might be), she knew Dino was trying to put her off her line of thought. He wouldn't manage that so easily.

She pressed on. "And at that meeting, were you able to help?"

"I just talked him through ways he could simplify things, and told him to make sure someone else was doing the books—get someone in, make it all watertight."

"Did he ask you for any money, Mr. Jones?"

There was a pause, after which Dino said, "I don't remember."

"Did you lend him any money?"

He looked straight at Nicola and said, in the same tone, "I don't remember."

The solicitor now piped up, his purple socks showing as he crossed his legs impatiently and his pinstripe trousers rode up. "Where's this going, Detective Sergeant?"

Nicola pulled out another document, and once again named its classification for the recording. "This is a page from Mr. Tiernan's financial books dated April this year. As you can see, he mentions in the column marked 'amounts owing,' a £50,000 debt to Mr. Jones."

Nicola sat back as Dino and his solicitor leaned forward simultaneously to examine the new document. She saw the solicitor glance at Dino. Dino didn't acknowledge the look.

He said, "I did loan him fifty grand, yes."

"Did he pay it back?"

"Not yet," said Dino caustically.

"When was it supposed to be repaid?" asked Nicola. "Had you set a deadline?"

"I was relaxed about it," replied Dino dismissively.

"I wish I could be relaxed about fifty grand," smiled Nicola. "Don't you, Harry?"

"I do, Sarge," agreed Harry.

"Maybe you're in the wrong game," said Dino pointedly to Harry.

Harry held Dino's glance with a smile. "Or maybe you are."

Nicola loved that Dino looked irked at that.

"How did you give Mr. Tiernan this loan?" she asked.

Dino shrugged. "Don't remember."

"Because," said Nicola, "we couldn't find any payment from you to him, or from your business to his, in either his personal or his business accounts."

Silence.

"Probably cash, then," said Dino.

"You're very much a cash man, aren't you, Mr. Jones?" said Nicola, brandishing a smile that now had added steel.

"Dunno what you mean," said Dino, all innocence.

"Your salon only takes cash, doesn't it? Is there a reason for that?" asked Nicola.

Dino shrugged. "Convenience."

Nicola nodded. "Really? When the whole world is moving to cashless and contactless? You're just an old-fashioned guy, is that it?" She waited for a response, but none came. "Convenient for you. Some would say convenient to hide money coming in and out. Easier to falsify records."

Purple Socks piped up. "I hope you're not accusing my client of anything untoward, because you would need to show some proof."

"The salon in Ebbsley closed down under allegations of money-laundering, didn't it, Mr. Jones?"

"Nothing proven," said Dino.

"Because as soon as you got whiff of any investigation, you closed the salon down, didn't you?"

"You've got a suspicious mind. It wasn't washing its face. Not worth my while," said Dino.

"Did you try and induce Mr. Tiernan to launder money through the White Hart, Mr. Jones?"

"I did not," said Dino.

"Were you angry with Mr. Tiernan for not paying you back the £50,000 he owed you?"

"Not at all," said Dino.

"You were in the White Hart, seeing Mr. Tiernan, the night before he was found dead."

"I met an employee for a drink."

"Did you go there to put the frighteners on Jim, for your money? To threaten him? Or to strong-arm him to launder money for you?"

"Just went for a drink. Not a crime," said Dino, his tone remaining the same.

"We have a witness," said Nicola, "who heard Mr. Tiernan say you had lent him the fifty grand on the understanding he would launder money for you, through the White Hart."

Dino didn't flinch. "Bullshit. People make up a lot of stuff."

"They also heard you threaten to have someone break into the pub later that night."

"Oh, come on, love," said Dino, testily. "Who's telling you this shit? Gimme a name."

Nicola looked at him. They both knew he had suspicions over who it was. She was not going to confirm it yet. Nicola was concerned for Frankie. "Are you denying that conversation took place, Mr. Jones?"

"Course I am! I just went out for a drink. I mean, there was banter, but someone's got the wrong end of the stick there."

Nicola changed tack. "Where were you between the hours of midnight and 6 a.m. the following day, Mr. Jones?"

"In bed, asleep."

"Alone?"

"With my wife. You can ask her," said Dino. "You can check my phone, we've got a doorbell camera at home; it'll show my car parked there all night."

Bollocks, thought Nicola. "Thanks, we'll check all those," she said.

"Good," smiled Dino. "One bit of hearsay, late at night. Not strong, is it? Not given I've got a cast-iron alibi. That all you working from?"

Nicola had no response.

Purple Socks looked to the two officers. "I think, unless you wish to take this any further with a charge, we can call it a day."

Nicola and Harry convened by the coffee machine.

"Confirm his alibi, check the van details. If we get Shannon on the record tomorrow, we could bring the van in, give it the once-over. They have history, and there are unpaid loans, he has motive and he definitely has opportunity." She pressed the button for an extra strong shot. "He thinks he's got the better of us, Harry. I'm not having it."

Dino had wriggled away from them, for now, and she was furious.

CHAPTER FORTY-THREE

As evening faded to night, Harry worked his way doggedly around Fleetcombe car park. It took him sixty-seven minutes to note every make, model and license plate number.

As he progressed round the car park, however, his heart was slowly sinking. He could not see the vehicle he was looking for. Where was Eddie Godfrey's van? he wondered. Did he even park here? Could it have been Dino's van that Shannon had described?

Harry got back into his own car and was about to press the start button when he noticed a pair of headlights turning in. He looked through the windscreen. The headlights dazzled him for a moment and then, as they turned, he was able to see the vehicle arriving.

It was driving to the far edge of the car park, where Shannon had described finding the open door.

It was a gray-silver van—matching Shannon's description of half-car, half-van with a sliding side door. It parked right on the edge of the car park, as Shannon had apparently described.

A figure got out and used the central locking—the vehicle's indicators flashed.

The person walked away from the van, toward Harry. Eddie Godfrey walked past Harry's car without noticing him there, and on in the direction of his own house.

Harry waited until Eddie was out of sight. Then he sprang out of the car and strode over to Eddie's vehicle. He had seen him deploy the central locking and walk away. Shannon had described a fault with it.

Harry walked round to the driver's side. He put his hand on the door handle for the rear seats. He pulled on it.

The door slid open.

The alarm did not go off.

The lock on this door was faulty.

Exactly as Shannon described.

Harry called Nicola.

CHAPTER FORTY-FOUR

The bang on the door at 5:47 a.m. sucked Eddie Godfrey from his dream and back into his bedroom with a jolt. He sat up, panicky. His heart pounding. What was going on?

The banging got louder.

He fumbled out of bed, pulling on jogging trousers and a top from the pile of clothes that had accumulated over the past few days.

He stumbled through the flat, almost falling over his shoes from the night before.

"All right, all right!" he yelled.

He opened the door. A man and a woman. Blearily, he took them in. He recognized them. Where from? Wait, behind them, two uniformed police officers.

"Edward Godfrey?" asked the woman.

"Yeah," said Eddie, confused. He'd spoken to her before; she knew his name, she didn't have to ask.

"Could you come with us, please. We'd like to talk to you in connection with the death of James Tiernan."

"What? Why?"

"We'll explain everything at the station."

"The station? Do I have to?"

"Yes."

"What if I don't want to?"

That didn't go down well.

As Eddie was escorted to the police car, the people in the upstairs flat had their faces pressed to the window. Across the way, four different houses had their doors open, with people either peering out or standing in dressing gowns and slippers. Watching his every move.

Eddie thought, *walk of shame.*

One of the police people pushed his head down to stop him banging it as he got in.

As he sat in and they drove off, he thought, *this is going to be all over Facebook*, just in time for people to read it over their breakfast.

He should call work. They would be expecting him. If he wasn't loaded up and out delivering by 7 a.m., he was going to be out of a job.

They drove past the Fleetcombe car park on the way to the station.

As Eddie looked, he saw there were two police cars blocking the entrance, and crime scene tape up all around. At the back of the car park there was a tent. The tent seemed to be up around his van.

"What's happening there?" he asked.

He caught the eye of the woman detective—she seemed to be the one in charge—via the rearview mirror as she glanced behind him.

"Your vehicle has been impounded and we're conducting a forensic examination."

Eddie looked alarmed. "What for?"

He watched the woman's eyes flick back from him onto the road ahead. She did not answer the question.

Eddie was running short of breath.

"I need to let work know I won't be in." He looked at the clock on the car display. "I should be starting in about forty-five minutes."

"You can make a call at the station," explained the lad in the passenger seat.

Eddie said plaintively, "I've had no breakfast." There was a silence. "Will I get some breakfast?"

He caught the woman looking at him in the rearview again. As he caught her glance, he expected her eyes to flick back to the road. This time they didn't. She kept looking at him, like her eyes were seeing into his deepest secrets.

Eddie was worried that he was going to have a heart attack.

Can you just tell me, what exactly am I doing here?" asked Eddie. He sat on one side of the table, Harry and Nicola on the other. A duty solicitor had been assigned, to Eddie's consternation, and was sitting in the corner. Eddie had been swabbed and fingerprinted.

"Is this your vehicle?" asked Harry, showing Eddie a picture.

"Yes, why?" asked Eddie.

"Do you normally park it in Fleetcombe car park overnight?" asked Harry.

"I do, yes, why?" asked Eddie, again.

Nicola intervened, stern. "You need to answer questions, and not ask them, Mr. Godfrey."

"Oh, OK, all right," said Eddie.

"What time did you leave the White Hart pub on the night of Tuesday 17?" asked Nicola.

"When it closed, whatever time that was. Half eleven, maybe a bit earlier? I don't really remember. We were all a bit shaken."

Both Harry and Nicola looked up at Eddie. Eddie wondered what he'd said wrong.

Harry asked, "Bit shaken by . . . ?"

Eddie proceeded slowly. "There was a bit of a barney at the end."

"Outside the pub?" asked Nicola. Had Eddie seen Dino and Frankie with Jim?

"No, no, inside," said Eddie. "Although we'd heard some raised voices outside a bit earlier, I think it was with that Frankie, from the barbers'? They were with someone; I don't know what was going on, you'd have to ask them. No, I'm talking about when Jim came back in. He was red-faced and in a right mood. And he took exception to Deakins playing his banjo—he'd been playing it for a while but it was like Jim just needed to take something out on someone—and then Deakins ignored him, refused to stop playing. Jim got irate, his sister was behind the bar, trying to calm things down, Jim was having none of it, and then I got involved and he had a go at me and he was shoving me—it got a bit pushy—then Jim just snatches Deakins' banjo out of his hands and smashes it on the bar! And he was like, you can all fuck off! So then Deakins was complaining, and Patricia was trying to calm things down, so she got everybody a free round, told Jim to cool off. Which he did. It was a storm in a teacup, really. He was very apologetic, Deakins wasn't happy, Jim said he'd pay for it, or Patricia did, I dunno, but then we all had chasers. It sort of all happened in a flurry."

There was quiet for a moment after Eddie finished recounting this.

He was by no means clairvoyant, but he could sense irritation from across the table, and yes, here it came.

"Why didn't you tell me all this when we first spoke?" asked Harry.

"You didn't ask," retorted Eddie instinctively, and then immediately regretted it.

"Are you kidding me?" bristled Harry. "I asked you for anything that happened in the pub that night or anything that could be relevant. You didn't tell me anything about hearing a fight outside or the way Jim came in."

"It was only a couple of minutes across the whole evening," said Eddie defensively.

The younger detective looked mightily pissed off, and Eddie felt like his duty solicitor was looking at him askance, possibly wondering what she'd got herself into.

"Did you walk home at the end of the night?" asked Nicola.

"Yeah," said Eddie.

"Alone?" asked Nicola.

"Don't think so. I mean, if it was chucking-out time, usually one or two other people walk back the same way. I have a vague memory of that."

"OK . . . but you remember arriving home? You remember getting in the house."

Eddie shrugged. "Ish."

Nicola shot back: "'Ish' is not an answer, Mr. Godfrey."

"Sorry," said Eddie, and Harry noticed a couple of beads of sweat on his temple. "I remember having problems with my front door. Maybe I dropped my keys trying to get them in the lock? I can remember sitting on the ground with my back against the door. Then I remember being on the sofa, I think I had a massive Berocca and some paracetamol to stop me having a hangover, in fact, I definitely did cos I remember—sorry—peeing orange the next morning, but anyway I fell asleep on the sofa, telly on, in my clothes, and then, it's the next morning, 6 a.m., phone alarm going off, woke up. Oh—I'd dropped my wallet the night before, trying to get in, it was like in the front garden right by the door, I saw it when I went out to work."

"Thanks for the detail about the Berocca," said Nicola witheringly. "Does anyone else have keys to your vehicle, Eddie?"

"No."

"Has your vehicle ever been stolen?"

"No," said Eddie.

"Have you ever lent it to anyone? Does anyone else ever drive it?" asked Nicola.

"No. Nothing like that. It's only me."

"Then how do you explain the sighting of your vehicle, close to the place where Mr. Tiernan's body was found, on the night of his murder?"

"No. I mean, it wasn't there."

"Can I remind you you're under caution."

Eddie rallied a little, more combative. "I was at home all night. I'm the only one who has the keys. I'm the only one who drives it. And I'm telling you, it can't have been there."

Nicola raised an eyebrow at him. "We're going to take a little break," she said.

The two detectives repaired next door to Nicola's office. She gestured to Harry to close the door, just as Mel was arriving with his open laptop in his hands and an expression like a child who'd done such a good drawing they felt it needed to go up on the fridge straightaway. He got to the door just as Harry was closing it. He made a noise that indicated he'd like the door not to be closed in his face, but Nicola held her hand up and said, "Wait two minutes, please, Mel." His face fell and he waited outside.

Nicola took a deep breath. "He's on shaky ground. But on the sighting of his van, it's his word versus the word of a child. And we don't have her on record."

Harry said, "I didn't want to say that. But yeah. Tricky."

Mel was visible, hopping from one foot to the other outside the window, so Nicola waved him in. He looked excitable. "ANPR has come back on your suspect's vehicle."

"Which suspect?" asked Harry. Mel had been instructed to run plates for both Dino's and Eddie's vans.

"The one you're currently interviewing."

Nicola sat up slightly. "And?"

Now Mel had the air of a conjuror pulling a rabbit from a hat. "It *was* detected on the A35 at one forty-six a.m. It was coming in the other way, not from Fleetcombe. I widened the search area because I realized we were only looking at one route—the logical route, mind, coming from Fleetcombe. But I thought I'd check the other direction, on the off chance. And there it was, photographed less than half a mile from the location where the body was found, heading in that direction."

Nicola looked to Harry. "Come *on*! Show me. Show me now." If she could've fist-pumped without looking like an idiot, she would've done. "Can we see the driver?"

Mel shook his head as he brought the laptop over.

He showed them the image. Eddie Godfrey's van; driver indistinguishable. "Resolution's not strong enough, middle of the night."

"Oh Mel, I could kiss you!" said Nicola, and noted Mel's alarmed expression. "Don't worry, I'm not going to."

"Good," said Mel, and then added hastily, "with all due respect."

Nicola looked at Harry. "Eddie just told us his van was in the car park and he was at home. This proves at least half of that statement is a lie."

Harry grinned. "Shall we go back and quiz him on the rest?"

CHAPTER FORTY-FIVE

They returned to questioning Eddie Godfrey. Nicola wasted no time in laying out a screengrab from the Automatic Number Plate Recognition camera on the desk in front of Eddie.

"Can you tell me what this is?"

Eddie pulled it toward him. Peered at it. Looked up at Nicola and Harry. Looked back down at the picture. He seemed confused by why they were asking him. It was obvious.

"It's my van."

Nicola nodded. "That picture was taken by a traffic camera at one forty-six on the morning Jim Tiernan's body was found on the A35. The camera was located approximately half a mile from the site where Mr. Tiernan's body was left."

Eddie looked up. Shock was too small a word for the expression on his face.

"Don't lie," said Eddie.

"I'm not the one lying, Mr. Godfrey. Can you tell us how your vehicle was captured on camera at that time, in that place, when you claim no one else drives it, and you also claim to have been asleep on your sofa?"

Eddie was becoming angry now, his expression more desperate. "I don't *claim* to be, I *was* asleep on my sofa! This is false, you've made this up, you're trying to fit me up!"

Eddie's solicitor put a hand on his client's arm to calm him, but he shook it off. "They're stitching me up! They're framing me!"

"And this picture is of you, disposing of Jim Tiernan's body. Everything else you've told us has been made up after the fact."

"No!" exploded Eddie. He rubbed his temple as he stared at the photograph. "Even if that is my van, that's not me driving!"

"Who *is* driving then?" asked Nicola.

"How the hell should I know?" Eddie was running his hands through his hair now.

"Why didn't you tell us about the deer, Eddie?"

Eddie's face betrayed his increasing worry. "Um . . . how d'you mean?"

"The deer Mick Donnelly shot. The deer that was brought back to Bredy. The deer whose antlers were found attached to Jim Tiernan's head. Is it ringing any bells?"

"How do you know about that?" Eddie asked, alarmed, and then regretted the quick reply.

Oh, he fidgeted in his seat now. Harry and Nicola both watched him glance at his solicitor, back to them, then down at his hands. "OK," he said eventually. "But that was Mick. He shot it. He did everything. He took back the carcass but left the head as a joke on Jim. Just because it was in my van, it doesn't mean . . ." His voice was fading, he was straining to complete a sentence. ". . . what you think it means."

Nicola continued, calm and in control. "We are forensically examining your vehicle for any traces of material that link to the murder of Jim Tiernan. As you can see from that photo, we have reason to believe it was used to transport his body. If there is even the tiniest particle of evidence in your vehicle, our team will find it. I promise. Now, please, whatever you know, whatever you're not telling us, speak up now."

Eddie looked exhausted. "You won't find anything, because I had nothing to do with it."

Nicola wondered if he knew his voice sounded full of doubt.

It's not much of a defense, is it? *It wasn't me*. And no alibi," said Harry.

Nicola just grunted an affirmative, while checking her watch, preoccupied. She looked up at Harry. "She should have been here by now."

Shannon had not turned up of her own volition. An hour past the appointed time, there was still no sign and, leaving Eddie to stew further, Nicola decided to head for Shannon's house. She had to risk it. She needed Shannon to go on the record.

Nicola parked up outside the house on Lancing Drive. She rang the doorbell and waited. No reply.

She knocked on the door, and waited. No one came. She peered through the front window, but she couldn't see anything.

A neighbor came out. "You won't find 'em there. They're away now."

"Away where?" asked Nicola.

"Away gone. Piled all their stuff into one big van, and headed off. Mattresses, suitcases, kid's bike, the lot. I asked her where they were going, and she told me to mind my own. Woman said she'd had it with being round here."

"Was the little girl with her?"

"Yeah, it was both of them. I hadn't seen the feller before, but then it's been hard to keep track."

"And when was all this?"

"Last night?"

Nicola turned away.

Fuck, she thought.

CHAPTER FORTY-SIX

"Fuck!" she yelled, pacing the office.

Harry was watching Nicola's frustration. "It's not like we have nothing. We have the vehicle now. We treat what you learned from Shannon as information received."

"It's not that. I'm worried for her, Harry. She needed help, she needed protecting. And now we don't know where she is. I've been so busy with the case, I let that slip. That's how shit I am these days."

Harry didn't like seeing his boss like this and he wasn't going to let her self-lacerate without response. "You're not shit," he said.

"Oh, trust me, I am, Harry. I am so shit I couldn't even detect my husband having an affair under my own fucking nose!"

She stopped.

There was silence in the office. Harry looked straight ahead.

Nicola sighed.

"Forget I said that," she requested.

"Sure," said Harry.

"Not enough sleep," said Nicola.

"No," said Harry. He was suddenly unsure how to be.

A longer silence. Nicola broke it again.

"Anyway, there you are. You wanted to know why I came back here. Because I had to make a change."

She was quiet for a moment. Looked around, looked to Harry, and shook her head.

"I used to have a huge team around me. And resources; not endless, but more than this. I wouldn't have let Shannon's welfare go unchecked." She looked up at the ceiling. Work and life and tiredness and concern were all merging. "Everything that went on, it's made me doubt myself a bit."

Harry wouldn't let that stand. "Please don't. I'm not doubting you. I've not doubted you from the moment you got here. I mean, I might be a bit scared of you, but you're so good at this."

And just for a moment, Harry's comment made Nicola feel vaguely, fractionally, better. Somebody had actually been nice to her for a second.

"Aww, thanks, Westlife!" she said, and play-punched his arm. She loved the look of shock—*didn't know I knew that nickname, did you!*—followed by irritation, and then a grin that shot across Harry's face. And now they were both grinning as he shook his head. "Wait," said Nicola. "You're scared of me?" she asked.

"Sometimes, yeah. Cos I know I can't fuck up. You have high standards. And thank God you do. If you didn't, if you weren't here, we wouldn't stand a chance with this. I'm not just saying this cos you're my boss, but I really like working with you. I'm grateful to be learning from you. And we're nearly there, right?"

Nicola nodded. "Right." She couldn't say much more because she was trying to think of when anybody had last been that complimentary to her.

Harry continued, "Should we corroborate Eddie Godfrey's story about what happened at the end of the night, back in the pub, with Deakins?"

Have you got them?" Patricia Tiernan looked up from her sofa with hope in her eyes.

"Not yet. We're following a number of leads. When we have anything concrete to tell you, I'll let you know. We believe we're close," said Nicola.

"Well, that's good, isn't it?" asked Patricia. "Can you tell me anything more than that? Any names?"

Nicola swerved the question by getting to one of her own. "We wanted to ask you, at the end of the night on Tuesday, was there an incident in the pub?"

Patricia looked mystified. "Incident?"

"Jim had gone out, you were covering the bar—when he came back, did anything particularly unusual happen?"

Patricia thought for a moment and then realized. "Oh God, the bloody banjo! I'd forgotten all about it!"

"Could you just tell us what you mean by that, and what you remember?" nudged Nicola.

"Jim came back in a foul mood—something had obviously happened. I don't know whether it was something to do with the Skillett woman—I think they'd had a thing before—or something outside; I still don't know, but he was in a terrible state, and Mr. Deakins was playing his banjo, and Jim asked him to stop. Mr. Deakins doesn't really take to being asked to stop after a couple of drinks, it was getting a bit feisty, I tried to calm it down. Jim was really upset by this point. I think he even called me an effing witch or something like that, then Eddie got involved and Jim turned on him, and I don't really remember exactly what order it all happened in, but Jim broke the banjo and threw Mr. Deakins out."

"Was there a fight between Jim and Eddie?"

Patricia thought for a minute. "I mean, a little argy-bargy, but nothing . . ." She looked at them incredulously. "You're not suggesting Eddie had anything to do with Jim's death?"

"We're just going through every detail," smiled Nicola.

Going through every detail had also meant securing a warrant, and then conducting a search of Eddie Godfrey's house. Eddie Godfrey would be held overnight while they waited for forensic results, and Nicola and Harry spent the latter portion of the evening going through Eddie's property.

The house was sparely furnished, simply decorated. A large TV and a comfy sofa. A few books. A collection of CDs and cassettes. Old audio equipment. A fridge that had very little in it and a freezer full of ready meals.

Clothes, shoes, keys and files of bills—bank and phone statements; Eddie was definitely still an analog man—were taken away for investigation. Nicola found a small black notebook on the kitchen table, full of numbers and days. Other than that, Eddie's home yielded little that was immediately revealing.

As they drove away, at the end of another long day, Harry pondered Patricia's description of the barney at the pub. "Would Deakins kill Jim for a broken banjo? And then deliberately highlight the history with the fires and his family, to bring attention to himself?" said Harry. "Doesn't make sense."

Nicola considered, and after a moment said, "I mean, farmers are fucking weird."

Harry nearly spat out the water he was drinking and laughed. "Harsh!" He paused. "Some of them, maybe. Not all of them."

He liked the new guard-down Nicola. He had one final question before they parted for the night.

"Do you think it's Eddie?" asked Harry.

Nicola answered by not answering. "If it's not him in that van, who else could it be?"

CHAPTER FORTY-SEVEN

Frankie didn't want to go to work the next morning, but they had customers booked in: regulars who wanted their trims.

When Frankie arrived at the salon, they realized their regulars were going to be disappointed.

Arriving at the small shopfront down a side alley just off the high street, Frankie stopped in their tracks. The shop sign had been removed. There was no shop frontage anymore.

All the items on display in the window—the signs, the lights, the pictures, the products, the equipment, all the things Dino had bought but Frankie had carefully arranged—had also gone.

Frankie pressed their face against the window.

The salon was empty. The two chairs had gone. Mirrors had been removed from the wall. The equipment shelves below the mirrors were also no longer there. Hooks, clips, clippers, brushes. All bottles, jars, tubs, tins of sprays and clays and gels and thickeners and every possible variation had also gone. The display units, the shelving, the plants, the coffee machine, the kettle, the mugs, the glasses, the water cooler, the towels, the gowns, the combs, the hoses, the sinks, the sockets, the lights.

It was like a plague of shoplifter locusts had buzzed through, denuding everything.

Of course.

Frankie realized that they had underestimated the fallout from the events of the past few days.

What did you expect?

Frankie then had a flashback to leaving their flat earlier, before they'd gone and had a coffee, before they'd picked up some stuff for lunch, before they'd come to work.

The van parked across the road with a couple of guys sitting in it.

He wouldn't.

The front door of their flat was open. It had been kicked in.

Of course, thought Frankie for the second time that day. *He would.*

Drawers were scattered. The TV had gone. Their clothes were everywhere. Something brown was smeared on the walls. Frankie didn't need to guess what it was. The smell had hit them as they walked in.

They didn't want to move any further into the flat. They turned and fled. As Frankie down the stairwell, not looking back, their mind raced as well.

They would have to go to their parents now. Having to grovel to their father was a horrifying thought.

There would be the deadnaming and the misgendering, and that would be the first five minutes. Then would come the resentments, the complaints about the past, as well as the bafflement over the present.

Everything was falling apart.

How could a life change so fast?

Frankie ran out onto the street.

There was the van now, parked outside the property. The rear door on the passenger side was hanging open. Waving Frankie over was Dino.

Frankie checked their momentum. Braked. Began to step backward.

For the first time ever, they felt existentially in fear for their life. They felt that it was possible that soon they would be dead.

As dead as Jim Tiernan.

"Get in," said Dino.

It was not a request.

In a small town, thought Frankie, there was never anywhere to run.

CHAPTER FORTY-EIGHT

The seat belt across Frankie's torso felt like a straitjacket.

Dino was sitting next to Frankie. Two beefy blokes were in the front, one driving. Dino spoke quietly, as if it was just him and Frankie alone in the vehicle. Frankie realized with a jolt how naïve they had been about their boss, and what he might be capable of. They wanted to roll back time. But it was far too late.

"Why did you do that, Frankie?" Dino asked, right next to their face. "We had a nice thing going. You had a good job. It could've gone on for a long time."

"I didn't want to lie to the police," said Frankie.

Dino puffed out his cheeks in exasperation. "You're not gonna get very far in life with an attitude like that. I gave you a chance because I liked you. When things got a little tricky, I asked you to do one thing, and you refused."

"Hang on, I told the police what you wanted me to. I gave them the name of Theo Andrakis. It's not my fault he wasn't briefed properly. I did exactly what you told me. What happened afterward was not down to me."

The van was accelerating as if the driver was monitoring Dino's frustration in the rearview mirror. The force of the acceleration pinned Frankie back to their seat, the seat belt digging in even further.

"You need to learn when to stay quiet," said Dino, irritated. "Life is about knowing when to speak and when to shut up. Stop."

The driver slammed on the brakes at the sound of the word—the van smashed to a halt, throwing Frankie forward and then back. They thought they might end up with whiplash. Although if that was the worst thing that came out of today, it was possibly a win.

Frankie said, "I just want to cut hair. That's all I want to do."

Dino unclipped his seat belt and leaned across to Frankie. "You don't get to just do what you want in this life. Stop being a baby about it." He thought for a moment. "Take your shoes off."

Frankie looked at him quizzically.

"Take your shoes off," Dino insisted.

Frankie did so, trying not to shake.

Dino held out his hands. Frankie handed the shoes over.

"Now get out and put your palms face down on the bonnet."

Fear ran through Frankie as they got out of the van. The two big blokes in the front got out at the same time. Dino gestured to Frankie to do what he'd demanded.

Frankie leaned toward the front bonnet of the van and put their hands on it. The two beefy blokes held Frankie's shoulders, one each side. There was no chance of movement.

Dino kicked Frankie's legs apart so they were splayed.

Frankie said, "Dino, please—"

"Stay still," said Dino.

It was then that Frankie, now paralyzed with fear for what was about to happen, heard a buzzing.

They felt a hand on their neck, holding it.

And they felt the buzz of a tiny electric razor on the back of their head.

Frankie recoiled, but their head was held in place. They wanted to cry but were determined not to.

The back of their head was being shaven into. What was he doing? It felt clumsy. Dino was not gentle.

After a minute or two, it stopped.

"Wait," said Dino as Frankie tried to turn round. There was the sound of a picture being taken.

Frankie was released and turned round. Dino held up his phone. Shaven into the back of Frankie's hair was the word "GRASS."

Frankie refused to show emotion. That's what Dino wanted. So they just nodded and looked at Dino.

"Off you go," said Dino.

Frankie looked down at their bare feet, and then around at their immediate surroundings. They were at the top of the coast road, looking down on the winding bay and ancient cliffs.

It was a long walk home. It would be painful barefoot. It would be dangerous along the road, but Frankie had enough local smarts to know that the safe way would be along the shore. It would take a while.

Dino looked at Frankie and got back into the van without another word; his two silent blokes returned to the front and the van drove off.

Frankie stood on the brow of the hill overlooking the bay. A tiny figure in a vast landscape. The cloud was low, and it was beginning to rain.

Frankie crossed the road and moved down into the field.

The silent trudge back to Fleetcombe took hours.

CHAPTER FORTY-NINE

Reeta Patel was waiting for Nicola at the station first thing, merrily revealing that she (a) had been up all night working and (b) had therefore stopped off at a Marks & Spencer on the way in and bought a big tin of chocolate biscuits to go with the tea she insisted on making, and that she had information for them all.

"Biscuits for breakfast, and no one can stop us, Nic." Other than Mike, Reeta was the only person who called Nicola "Nic," and "Nic" realized she liked it.

As she settled into the sofa in Nicola's office ("This is a nice bit of furniture, Nic, how'd you wangle this? If I snuggle into the corner, it's like I'm being cuddled."), Reeta extracted papers and notes from the multi-section backpack-on-wheels that accompanied her everywhere she went. She laid the papers out on the low table in front of her, looked up at Nicola and asked, "How's spirits? All right? Hanging in there?"

"All the better for seeing you, I'm hoping," replied Nicola, failing to disguise the weariness in her voice.

"Long old slog these, aren't they?" grinned Reeta. "Have to keep your stamina up. We'll get 'em, don't worry. Harry!" she exclaimed with delight as he rushed in, a bit late. "Morning! We're having biscuits."

Harry looked momentarily confused, then pleased, and took one. The magic of Reeta, reflected Nicola, was that when she said "we'll get 'em!" you tended to believe her. "Everyone needs a little jam," as Nicola's grandmother—another one skilled in compliments to all and sundry—once told her. That was it—biscuits and optimism: despite being around the same age as Nicola, Reeta reminded Nicola of her nan.

Reeta flattened the pieces of paper with the palms of her hands and surveyed them. "Shall I jump straight in? The van we examined *is* likely to have been the vehicle used to transport Jim Tiernan's body to the site where it was left," announced Reeta.

Nicola felt her heart leap. Bullseye. First thing in the morning. She and Harry exchanged glances: they were in business, surely. "OK, good," she said cautiously, in case Reeta had caveats to follow.

"We found multiple traces of the victim's DNA in the back of the vehicle: hair and skin deposits. We also cross-matched and found traces of fabric and materials from the vehicle on the victim's body."

Shannon was telling the truth.

That was the main thought going through Nicola's head. This was not a story made up by a little girl. This was a traumatic experience accurately reported by a child. How could she know all this otherwise? She was a credible witness: her description was now backed up by hard evidence.

"Now, as for a match with the suspect you're currently holding . . ."

Reeta reorganized her papers elegantly, took a breath as if to speak and then looked puzzled at what was in front of her.

"Hold on," she said.

Nicola and Harry were very much holding on as Reeta rearranged her papers again, moving them side to side, and also taking sheets from under other sheets, cheerily muttering to herself, "Ah. Here we are. Now. We have multiple traces—and when I say multiple, I mean hundreds, if not thousands—of your suspect, Edward Godfrey, on the interior—and exterior, for that matter—surfaces of the vehicle. Steering wheel, door handles inside and out, gear stick, glove compartment, walls of the rear section, the lot."

Nicola nodded. It was Eddie's van and so that made sense, but she could feel herself already bracing, hoping there wasn't a "but" anywhere in her near future.

"But," said Reeta Patel.

Bollocks.

After Reeta departed, having donated the remainder of the biscuits, Nicola and Harry debriefed.

Reeta and her team had not been able to find any traces of Eddie's DNA on the body of Jim Tiernan. They had found traces on the deer antlers, but Eddie had already confessed to transporting the deer. Nicola wondered if this was due to the hazmat-style protective suit Shannon had said the driver was wearing. Reeta had allowed that could be possible. But it caused them a problem. There were also traces of Mick Donnelly in the van. Was that from when Mick drove it back from the pheasant shoot, when they were moving the deer? Or could it have been Mick who killed and deposited Jim Tiernan's body? But Reeta had confirmed there were no traces of Mick Donnelly's DNA on Jim's body either. Nicola's head was beginning to ache.

They could not yet connect Eddie Godfrey to Jim Tiernan's murder. They were tantalizingly close. But there was no smoking gun.

Nicola had asked one more thing of Reeta as she departed: "Please, take that van apart."

Now, she paced her office while she summarized to Harry. "We're confident this was the vehicle used to transport Jim Tiernan's body to where it was found. We have photographic evidence it was out on the road in the early hours of the morning, close to the place where the body was dumped. There are traces of Jim Tiernan's DNA in the van. There are multiple traces of Eddie Godfrey's DNA, which there would be, given it's his vehicle. But we don't have Eddie Godfrey's DNA on Jim Tiernan's body." She looked at Harry. "It's not enough to charge him."

Harry nodded. "CPS will want more."

"How else can we get at him?" Nicola thought for a second. "Talk to his employers. See if there's any issue with his performance, any disciplinary issues, anything over the past few weeks. Get a sense of what they feel about him."

Harry nodded again. "Will do."

Nicola took a deep breath. "We may not have quite what we want, but everything we do have is very bad news for Eddie Godfrey. Custody clock's running down—let's not waste it. Once you've talked to his work, we go back in. Tell him what we have and see how he responds."

As Harry spoke to Eddie's employers, Nicola gave her full attention to the notebook she'd found on Eddie's table. It was full of spidery black handwriting, dates and numbers. It seemed to be a daily record, going back seventeen months.

Each entry had a day, five sets of numbers, and a monetary value. And on Wednesday morning, it seemed Eddie had been experiencing some confusion, or angst. There were underlinings and question marks.

Nicola cross-referenced the book with photographs of the inside of Eddie's van. It did not take long for her to work out what the notebook depicted.

Nicola sat back, staring at the figures and the photographs.

Was this a smoking gun, laid out in Eddie Godfrey's own handwriting?

CHAPTER FIFTY

Sometimes the bravest thing you can do is get a bus.

The bravest, and the scariest.

CHAPTER FIFTY-ONE

Eddie Godfrey sat listening as Nicola reminded him of the interim conclusions of the forensic team that had been examining the vehicle he used for both work and leisure. It had, she told him, been used for transporting a dead body—the body of murdered publican James Tiernan. The detective explained that it would not surprise Eddie to learn that his DNA and fingerprints had been found all over the vehicle, given it belonged to him. Did he have anything to say on this new evidence?

Eddie leaned into the audio recording's microphone. "It wasn't me. I didn't kill him."

Nicola showed Eddie the notebook they had removed from his kitchen. "Do you know what this is, Eddie?"

Eddie blanched. He looked to his solicitor, then to the two detectives. "It's my logbook."

Nicola said, "I thought it might be. Can you explain to me how you use it?"

"I record the start mileage and finish mileage each day at work. So I know what's for work and what's outside of work. So I know what I spend on fuel, and what mileage I do."

"Every day you record the start and finish numbers for work. And the next morning, you record the start number again in case you've been out using the van for something not to do with work."

Eddie was very quiet now. "Correct."

Nicola showed him a page. "These are the pages for Tuesday night and Wednesday morning. There's a lot of scribbles there, Eddie. Calculations, crossings-out. Can you explain that?"

Eddie didn't say anything for a minute. Then he just said, "I didn't kill him."

Nicola persisted. "Answer the question, please."

Eddie looked almost defeated. "This is the total at the end of Tuesday." He pointed to another number. "This is the start number for Wednesday morning." There was a long pause. "There is a difference of twenty-one point three miles."

"To clarify," said Nicola. "After you finished work on Tuesday evening, and before you started work on Wednesday morning, your van drove twenty-one point three miles?"

"I *didn't drive it*!" said Eddie.

"Do you know the distance from Fleetcombe to Wynstone where Jim Tiernan's body was found, Eddie?" asked Nicola.

Eddie looked down, nodding.

Nicola said, "Twenty-one miles there and back, give or take, depending on the route. Taking the route which would have passed our traffic camera, we have it around twenty-one point one. But then you would have had to stop off at the White Hart first, wouldn't you?"

Eddie was shaking his head now.

Nicola looked to Harry. *Your turn.* Harry said calmly: "Do you ever black out when you're drunk, Eddie?"

Eddie looked up like he'd been slapped around the face. "Who've you spoken to?"

"Answer the question, please."

Eddie looked at Harry accusingly. "You spoke to Filbert, didn't you?"

Nicola asked, "Who's Filbert, Eddie?"

"My old supervisor. We used to do a lot of going out together. A lot of drinking. I don't do that drinking anymore. He shouldn't be telling you that. It was only a few times."

"He says when you drink too much you don't remember anything you've done. I confirmed this with Irina Bortnick at the White Hart. She said it's a running joke," said Harry. "You've also got behind the wheel of your van when drunk and not remembered the next day, Filbert says. He said he's had to lie to your boss for you. Is that true?"

Eddie was red in the face. He had the look of a man whose world was falling in on him. "I wouldn't black out and kill a man!"

"How do you know?" asked Nicola simply. "If we're to believe what you and your supervisor say about these lapses of memory? How can you be sure you weren't driving your vehicle at the time it was captured on our cameras? If you'd drunk as much as witnesses say you did in the pub that night, and alcohol has the effect of making you black out or stopping you remembering, then how can you be sure you didn't do it?"

Eddie was feeling cornered. "I was asleep on my sofa! I'm sure."

"You're tying yourself in knots, Eddie," said Nicola. "That's your problem here. Because the other scenario is you don't have blackouts at all. It's bullshit. You tell people that you do, but it's a cover when you've been caught doing something wrong. You know exactly what you did on Tuesday night. You planned and carried it out meticulously. The only thing you forgot to do was give yourself a credible alibi. And now you're asking us to believe that alcohol makes you black out. It doesn't, does it? You knew exactly what you were doing."

"No. It—oh God, I can't think straight here," said Eddie feebly.

Nicola looked to Harry. It was his cue. "Can you tell us about your issues at work, Eddie?"

Alarm filtered slowly but unmistakably into Eddie's expression. He tried to mask it, but the damage was already done.

"What issues?" said Eddie.

"There's been a number of problems with deliveries, hasn't there?" asked Harry. "With *your* deliveries."

Eddie shrugged. "Part of the job."

Harry nodded, looked at his notes. Nicola watched Eddie trying to read Harry's face for what was coming next. He didn't have to wait long.

"You deliver to homes and businesses, correct?" asked Harry.

"Yeah," said Eddie.

"There's quite a serious investigation at your work about a delivery going missing from Carter's Pharmacy."

Eddie sighed. "That was ages ago, and I told the warehouse guy, I told Filbert as well, that I delivered everything I was given and they signed for it."

"Yes," said Harry. "He said that was exactly the situation. Do you know what was in the missing consignments?"

"No, but I'm sure you're going to tell me," said Eddie.

"Liquid morphine."

Nicola sat forward. Harry slid his notes across to her, like the excellent pupil he was.

"Do you know how Jim Tiernan was killed, Eddie?" asked Harry.

Eddie shook his head. But, Nicola knew, he did know. At the very least, he had just worked it out.

"Injected with an overdose of liquid morphine."

Eddie Godfrey buried his head in his hands.

Detective Sergeant Nicola Bridge rearrested Edward Godfrey on suspicion of the murder of Jim Tiernan.

CHAPTER FIFTY-TWO

The bus journey had not been as scary as she'd thought. It had been long, but people had left her alone.

When she got off, it was in familiar surroundings. She felt like she could breathe again.

She walked to the building she had waited outside before and asked for Nicola.

When Nicola saw Shannon sitting by Mel, she stopped in her tracks. She could've sunk to her knees and praised the Lord, but that would not have been cool.

"I came on the bus," said Shannon by way of hello. "Nobody knows I'm here." She toyed with the zip on her coat. "It's not fair. Why does it have to be me who does this? Why can't it be a grown-up?"

Nicola said, "I agree. It's not fair. I'm sorry you had to be any part of this. Thank you for coming back here. You are truly the bravest, strongest girl I have ever met."

There was a silence. Shannon had been looking at her hands all through this. She kept doing so, and Nicola wondered if she'd gone too far, or said something that had landed badly. Maybe Shannon had misinterpreted what she was saying. Maybe the whole speech was too much for a girl that young.

After another minute, Shannon looked up. Her eyes were red, but her voice betrayed no emotion.

"Nobody's ever said anything that nice to me." Her eyes flicked past Nicola as she tried to remember her whole life. "Nobody's ever said *anything* nice to me."

Nicola wanted to scoop her up and hug her and tell her everything was going to be all right. But she couldn't. And she wasn't fully sure that everything would be all right for Shannon. But then and there, Nicola resolved to do everything she could for this girl, for however long it took.

Before they could even start on anything else, Shannon had something new she wanted to tell Nicola. "I remembered a bit more. There was a smell, that night."

"What do you mean?"

"Coming from the person."

Nicola said, "Like a scent? A perfume, or an aftershave, you mean? That sort of thing?"

Shannon nodded.

"Do you think you would recognize it again?" asked Nicola.

Shannon shrugged. "It wasn't strong, but it was definitely there. I was really close to them."

"Would you give it a try, just in case?"

Shannon nodded. "And also," she said hesitantly, "when we were coming back, something rolled through from the back, on the floor, under the gap. Right by my face. But then when the van braked, it rolled into the back again. And then when the van turned, I thought I heard it roll down the side or something. I didn't see it or hear it after that."

Nicola gently asked, "When you say *something* rolled away, what sort of something, can you remember?"

Shannon nodded. "A thing you use to inject people with."

Nicola stared at Shannon. *Oh, this girl.*

Nicola called Reeta: look for a syringe, it may have got lodged deep in the chassis of the van. Then she told the team: get Eddie Godfrey's aftershave.

But she also remembered something else. Dean "Dino" Jones. His aftershave arrived in the car before he did. They sold it in the salon. Frankie would know what it was. Who else? Mick Donnelly. And Ayesha Barton. A control—a random neutral scent. She would get Mel to call and find out what she wore.

Nicola allowed herself a moment's satisfaction. She had worked hard to gain Shannon's trust. Her instincts had told her she was important. And now this brave little girl was going to help them send Jim Tiernan's murderer to prison.

Nicola's instincts had been right. And Harry hadn't been just blowing smoke, earlier.

She was good at this job.

Her thoughts dwelled on this for a moment and, while an appropriate adult was being arranged for Shannon, she called her husband.

CHAPTER FIFTY-THREE

Nicola met Mike on the promenade down by the bay. The breeze was high and the waves were thudding onto the shingle. Seagulls circled the blue sky as they walked along with a cuppa and a sausage roll each. To the handful of other couples walking along the concreted promenade, they would have looked like they were out for a romantic stroll.

That was not Nicola's agenda. She had given herself half an hour to get some air and to say what she needed to say.

"This is nice," said Mike. "How's the case? Can you say?"

"I haven't been clear enough with you, and I want to be. I fucking hate you, Mike, I fucking hate you for what you did to me," said Nicola.

Her husband looked genuinely shocked. They stopped walking. After a moment he recovered slightly.

"OK. Fair," he said.

"You played me for a fool, and I am not a fool."

"I don't think you're a foo—" protested Mike.

"Shut up and *listen*!" interrupted Nicola.

"OK, sorry," said Mike. But he couldn't stop himself. "Do you think this is the best place to be having this—"

"Yes, it fucking is. I have clarity right now, and I need you to hear it."

"Right."

"I am good at my job. I can do this job. I was the best in Liverpool, I am the best here, and you made me feel like I couldn't see what was under my nose. You gaslit me, you lied, you forced me to detect *you*. You humiliated me."

"Babe, I never meant—"

"Please, Mike, stop talking! You're not here to talk. That's all we've done, since I found you out—talk talk talk, therapy, home, date nights—well, fuck that, now just listen. And understand. What you did to me. To us. You robbed me of myself. Not just as a wife, but as a detective. You made me doubt myself, and that is unfuckingforgivable. I didn't need you to make me doubt myself, I can do that perfectly well enough without your help. I resent what you did to me in my work. I was happy in Liverpool. I knew what I was doing. Some really tough men there were really scared of me."

"A really tough man here right now is pretty scared of you, too," said Mike.

"I just have to say to you, I hate you for what you made me think about myself."

Mike looked at her. "I'm sorry."

They walked on for a while.

Mike asked, "Is that . . . what does that mean, now?"

"It means: you still have to put a lot of work into me."

"I want to do that," said Mike. "Honest, I do. I've moved to bloody Dorset. I'm a Bootle lad. Look at this place."

"Fine. So stop acting like this is normal, stop pretending that everything's all right now. It doesn't leave us space to be honest, it doesn't give *me* space to be . . . angry at you, still. I want us to be truthful: with ourselves, with each other, with Ethan. Cos that's what we lost."

Mike was quiet for a moment, processing. And then he nodded. "OK, I'll do my best. And then, do we have a shout?"

She looked at him. "We'll find out, won't we?" It wasn't the level of reassurance he was asking for, but she felt it was all she could offer. She checked her watch. "I have to get back to work."

She shoved her empty wrapper and cup into Mike's hand and strode back to her car.

That afternoon, working through statements, rereading reports as she built up the paperwork, the dates, the information to present to the CPS in order to convince them that Eddie Godfrey was responsible for the murder of Jim Tiernan, she stopped, realizing she wasn't taking in the text in front of her.

She found herself uneasy. Where was Eddie Godfrey's motive? Why did he seem so bewildered? She just felt something was not right.

Those instincts again. Trust them, she told herself.

Her mind was flitting between the case and her conversation with Mike. But she knew it to be true: it was possible to love and hate someone at the same time. Part of her had even thought while looking at him: *I just wish you'd go away.*

She hated that her husband had presented as one thing—a loyal, loving partner—but had actually been another: a cheat. That's how he had played her for a fool.

As she sat there, the thought jolted through her body like an electric current.

Who in this case was playing *them*, Nicola and Harry, for a fool?

The thought stuck in her head. She could not shake it off.

Who was not as they presented themselves?

Eddie Godfrey presented as he was, she was sure of it. And he had no motive.

Her heart was racing. Her instincts were firing, and it was vital she listened to them, this time.

A thought was forming. She had missed something.

For all the looking, she had not been able to see.

CHAPTER FIFTY-FOUR

The blinds clattered down in Nicola's office, shutting out the rest of the office. She needed to sequester herself, to think and work fast.

She made a checklist, frantically scribbling tasks and questions, the bullet points cascading with clarity. She knew she had an array of documents to check back over.

She was looking for something new. Something specific.

She was both kicking herself and elated at the possibility of what she might find.

She loaded up with coffee, put in calls and pulled all the possible documentation she might need. It was all in the paperwork.

She went back through notes and statements. There was a phrase Irina Bortnick had used. An offhand comment that was haunting her, that she hadn't picked up on at the time but was now echoing.

She traced her finger along the lines of data. Cross-checked them, combed back through, chased up test results, unblocking them from the system where they were still awaiting delivery, rechecked call logs, submitted an urgent request for a phone triangulation. She had a hunch what the answer would come back with, but she wanted to be sure.

She spoke to the great Reeta Patel once more, working the idea through, testing a thesis, asking Reeta what might back it up. She asked for further tests to be expedited. She awaited the results.

Trawling through a number of different social media profiles, going back years, she tried to look at things from a different perspective. She was elated to find a post that backed up one aspect of what she believed. She was building a wall, and she had found a brick.

She made a phone call to a pharmacy to ask them one question. The answer to that led to a supplementary question. And the answer to the supplementary question gave her the information she needed. That piece of information formed a whole new set of questions.

She cast her mind back to a bathroom she had used in a house in the early days of the investigation, interviewing people. She had looked around. She had nosed in the medicine cabinet. Her greatest sneaky detective trick: go to the bathroom, assess everything, remember what's in there. This one, she remembered, had very little in there. But one brand, one scent.

She made a number of calls and spoke to a number of people. She set processes in motion, just in case.

Then she had Eddie Godfrey brought from the cells to the interview suite, where she interviewed him further.

Shannon sat before Nicola. Her appropriate adult, a retired teacher from Netherstock who'd performed this role a number of times before, sat in the corner.

Nicola offered Shannon a scent, sprayed on a piece of paper.

Shannon smelled it. She recoiled.

She smelled it again, of her own volition.

She looked scared. She stared at Nicola as if Nicola were a shaman.

Shannon nodded. "That's it. That's what he smelled like. Not as strong as that. But that smell."

Nicola's pulse was racing. She instructed the other officers to take care of Shannon.

From there, Nicola immediately became a one-person whirling dervish of investigation. If anybody had been watching her, she thought, she would have looked like a madwoman. But, for Nicola herself, the ensuing hours were a time of incredible industry powered by rare clarity. She was seeing the world, seeing the investigation, the case, the murder of Jim Tiernan differently.

And seen from a different angle, things were possibly beginning to fit together.

Further data came through: a new test result. Nicola read it through. Once. Then again. The final confirmation.

They had talked to so many people, and she had known all along that the answers were buried amidst the mass of information. The process of the job was knowing what information to discard so that the actual pattern could be discerned. The ratio of signal to noise, as her first boss had called it. The statue in the marble. The answer is in there, but it's obscured by everything around it.

Nicola felt she was starting to see the statue.

She was ready to call Harry in. Her neurons were fizzing. She ran through her thesis with a calm she didn't feel. It was late. Eddie Godfrey would have to be either charged or released first thing.

"We know he had the means, we know he had opportunity. But why would he do it? In all the conversations we've had with everyone, what has come out that goes to a motive for Eddie to kill Jim? There was no bad blood, there was no money owing or compromised relationships or past problems. Everyone says they got on. He was asking us: why would I do it?"

Harry said, "Agreed. So where does that leave us?"

Nicola adopted her best calm posture and tone. "Bear with me, right? Just go with this for a moment."

Across the years, she'd had to use that phrase, that tone, to skeptical bosses when she was positing new theories, or possible approaches, or actions in a particularly difficult case. Harry was not her boss, but she needed to convince him; she needed to take him with her if she was to be proved correct.

He was her first test.

"OK," said Harry.

"Let's flip it round for a moment, and *only* think about motive. Put means and opportunity to one side for a moment. What if, in this case, motive drives everything? If the motive is strong enough, hard felt enough, the killer finds the means and opportunity."

"Right," replied a confused-looking Harry.

DS Nicola Bridge talked DC Harry Ward through her new thesis. As she did so, she presented documentary evidence with a flourish, like a magician doing a practiced routine. She had a summary which, using the evidence they already had, reshaped where their investigation might now go.

At the end, Harry was quiet for a while. He looked over the documentation again.

He asked if he could take a break for a breath of air. She gave him a five-minute allowance. She watched him, from the window, pacing outside, running his hands through his hair.

When he returned, he stood in the doorway of her office.

"Yeah," he nodded. "It adds up."

At first light, armed with warrants, Nicola and Harry set out from the police station.

At a property in Fleetcombe, they waited for the door to be answered. Behind them were two uniform cars, and support officers.

Nicola rang the bell again.

After a moment, the owner of the property came to the door.

“Hello,” said Nicola.

“Have you got them yet?” asked Patricia Tiernan.

CHAPTER FIFTY-FIVE

Patricia Tiernan sat in the interview suite across from DS Nicola Bridge and DC Harry Ward. Next to her was a duty solicitor. Patricia had not elected a solicitor of her own. The only solicitor she knew, she said, was for conveyancing.

Nicola opened the interview. It was a tightrope she was about to traverse, and both she and Harry knew it.

“Patricia, we believe you were responsible for your brother Jim’s death,” said Nicola, “and we believe we have a pattern of evidence and witnesses to prove it.”

Nicola saw Patricia Tiernan’s eyes narrow ever so slightly at the mention of evidence and witnesses. “You hold the spare keys to the pub on behalf of your brother, correct?” she went on.

“I do,” said Patricia calmly.

Nicola nodded. “Thank you.”

She slid across the book Harry had discovered during Jim Tiernan’s memorial evening at the Fox. It was sealed in a plastic evidence bag.

“This book was found at the Fox. The pages describing a murder from 1925 where a body was left with stag antlers attached to the head were folded down. The book was otherwise unread. It seems like no one else ever picked it up, apart from DC Ward here . . .”

Pause, you might as well pause, Nicola. And now, off we go, finish the sentence:

". . . and you."

Once again, she looked up at Patricia. The eyes did not narrow this time. They blinked, three times in succession. Nicola knew from experience that Patricia was a starer, not a blinker. This was a tell. She carried on speaking.

"Your prints are on the book, and on those pages. There are no other prints on the entire volume. People don't really read books in pubs."

Patricia replied, "I'm not denying I've picked up that book in the Fox. That doesn't mean I killed my brother."

Nicola now placed a copy of a diary entry in front of Patricia. "Can you read out the late-morning appointment your brother had in his diary for Tuesday, September 17?"

Patricia picked it up. "It says 'TFW eleven thirty.'"

"Do you know what TFW stands for?"

"Should I?"

Nicola always took solace when suspects answered questions with questions. It was a clear defense mechanism. "Irina Bortnick told us that Jim used to call you a fucking witch."

Patricia flinched, the tiniest of gestures, but it did not escape Nicola. "Is that right?"

"And when I queried this with her yesterday, she said it was so much of a private joke between them you are actually in her, that is Irina's, phone contacts as That Fucking Witch. Or TFW."

Patricia Tiernan was very quiet for a moment. Then she said, "Well, it seems I have been more charitable to her than she has to me."

More distraction technique. But also, Nicola was interested to note that Patricia appeared wounded by it. Her brittleness was coming to the fore. "Can I confirm that you went to see your brother at eleven thirty on the morning before he died?" She knew she had Patricia cornered.

"I did."

Strike one for Nicola Bridge. "You didn't mention that to us in any of your statements. Quite an official, diarizing, with one's sister. What did he want to meet with you about?"

"He wanted what he always wanted from me nowadays. Money. A loan, he said. I declined."

"What was his response?"

"He was cross with me. He got angry. We had an argument. You can ask Irina what it was like. She was skulking in the doorway, thinking I couldn't see her."

"I did ask her. Thank you. How did the row resolve itself?"

"I left."

"But you spoke to him again later that day?"

"Well, obviously. I went back to the pub in the evening."

"Yes, we'll get to that, thank you," said Nicola. *I am running the order of things here. I am in control.* "I meant on the phone."

Patricia replied that she didn't think so.

Nicola brought out a phone log. Patricia was starting to look unhappy.

Nicola said, "You called him at 6:12 p.m. Why?"

Patricia looked at Nicola, and for the first time Nicola felt she could detect a "fuck you" behind Patricia's eyes.

"I can't remember."

Nicola nodded and brought out another document. "This is a screenshot of your Instagram page. Very nicely maintained. Not a frequent poster, but this one, a month back, is you and Ayesha Barton, arm in arm, you've tagged her, and you've also captioned it 'Good friends are worth more than anything.' Couple more of you with her across the profile. All very positive. A lot of hearts. That's nice. And then"—Nicola switched documents—"there's this post from a year ago. That's you, and this lady here is, I believe, called Diane. Am I correct?"

Patricia folded her arms. "You are. Why?"

"Diane is the bar manager of the Drayman's Inn. Diane told us you've known each other a very long time. She also said she spoke to you about twenty minutes before the time of your call to your brother. And she told you that she'd seen him at the Drayman's, going up to a room with Ayesha Barton."

Patricia's face was hardening. "Am I just here because of gossip? I don't understand what you think this adds up to."

"Did you phone your brother and call him out for sleeping with Ayesha Barton?"

Patricia took a moment. She thought.

"Fine. Yes. I believed he had betrayed Irina, I believed he had betrayed Mick, and I felt he had betrayed me. My relationship with Ayesha. I was close to her, long before he ever was. They didn't even like each other at first. I was much closer to her. She was mine, before she was his."

She was mine, before she was his.

Now Nicola began to understand a little more. She modified her tone to be gentler. "How strong are your feelings toward Ayesha Barton, Patricia?"

For the first time in the interview Patricia Tiernan looked down. She avoided Nicola's gaze momentarily. She looked back up quickly. "I'm two decades older than her, if that's what you're implying. I'm not a fool."

"I don't think you're a fool at all. I'm asking if you were jealous," said Nicola. "Because this had happened before, hadn't it? Irina stayed with you, but went to live with Jim. Ayesha and you were close, but you discovered he'd slept with her. Did Jim steal people from you? People you had strong affection for?"

Patricia remained silent for a moment, looking at Nicola as if she had just committed the most egregious invasion of privacy. Then she said, "Just wait. Give it twenty years. You'll know what it's like to be invisible and ignored then, too."

Bang. Silence.

Thank you, Patricia. Very helpful.

Nicola pressed on calmly. "Can we move to the evening? Despite having had words with your brother, you decided to go to the White Hart, correct?"

"I went to have a drink and read my book, and see who was around."

"Did you have any interaction with your brother?"

"Yes. I helped behind the bar while he went out."

"Where did he go?"

"The Skillett girl. She had come into the pub. She was always keen on Jim." She paused. "I can't be sure, but I think he previously had a dalliance with the mother. Possibly in the pub toilets."

Nicola took that in, mind whirring. "So, what did you think about him going to her house then?"

"I didn't have an opinion," said Patricia stiffly.

"Really?" asked Nicola. "You knew he'd seen Ayesha that afternoon, and now here he was, off to the house of another woman he'd been seeing, while you minded the bar?"

It was a deliberately goading question and Patricia bit.

"Fucking her once hardly constitutes seeing her!" she snapped.

Patricia's use of the f-word was like a firecracker going off in the room. Nicola had never heard her use it before.

"Did you suspect his motives in going round there that evening?"

"The little girl did need walking back. I try not to think the worst of people, but I'll admit he was giving me a run for my money that day. I was reeling somewhat."

"And yet you still helped out behind the bar."

"Not as a favor to him. To the other people there. They've come out, they deserve a nice night. And no one else was available. I've done it before. I quite like it."

Nicola asked about Jim's return and the argument that ensued.

"Which one? Inside or outside?" asked Patricia.

Nicola kept her poker face. "Tell us about both."

Patricia sighed. "I don't see what all this has got to do with anything."

"We just want to have all the facts corroborated," said Nicola.

"Fine," said Patricia briskly. "There was a to-do outside over money. I went to the door and heard some of it. Then Jim came back in, red-faced, and started taking it out on everyone else. Mr. Deakins, Eddie, me."

Nicola picked up on that phrasing. "Taking it out on you?"

Patricia looked back at Nicola. "He was raging and yelling at us all. I tried to calm things down by offering people spirits. It seemed to work. But it was clear Jim was in a mess."

Nicola made a note and pressed on. "What time did you leave the pub?"

"I should say shortly after half past eleven. I walked back, made myself some cocoa, and that was it."

Nicola smiled. "Well, we can agree that *some* of that is true."

Now she slid a set of car keys across the table, again contained within a sealed evidence bag. Patricia's eyes fell on them and she seemed unable to take them away.

Nicola consulted her notes. "You own a dark green Fiat 500, correct?"

"Correct."

Nicola patted the bag with the car keys in it.

"Do you recognize these, Patricia?"

"I do not." Curt, short.

"Because our lab tells us they have your fingerprints on them."

Patricia's hand moved to scratch an itch on the back of her neck that had not existed a millisecond before.

Nicola continued, "They belong to Eddie Godfrey. House and van keys."

For the first time, Patricia looked alarmed. As if she'd watched Nicola pull back a curtain.

"Has Eddie Godfrey ever lent you his vehicle?"

A long beat of silence. Sometimes, in these interviews, Nicola felt one could see behind people's eyes: the thought processes whirring. This was one of those moments. She could see Patricia evaluating: what was the best answer? What put her least at risk?

"He has not," said Patricia.

"Have you ever used Eddie Godfrey's van?"

"I have not."

"Then why are your fingerprints on his keys?"

Nicola watched Patricia hesitate again. And then she took the plunge. "I was walking home from the pub. My route goes past his house. He was slumped by his front door, completely blotto, with the keys in the lock. I woke him up, opened the door using the keys that were there, helped him onto the sofa, took the keys out of the lock and left him to it."

She sat back, satisfied with her own story.

Nicola nodded. She moved on. "You mentioned when we first talked that, after retiring, you took a couple of jobs in shops, but they weren't for you. Is it right that one of those jobs was at Carter's Pharmacy?"

Patricia checked a fingernail on her left hand. Her breath had become a little less steady. She looked up at Nicola.

"Yes. But I haven't worked there in a while."

Nicola checked her watch. "Thank you."

She produced a bottle of perfume in a sealed evidence bag. "We retrieved this from your house yesterday. Can you confirm it's yours?"

Patricia looked bewildered. "What has this got to do with anything?"

Nicola took a tougher line. "A simple yes or no, please."

Patricia shrugged. "Yes. It appears to be mine."

Nicola nodded. "All right."

She paused, very deliberately. Harry had been waiting for this.

"Patricia," she said. "I should tell you. When you took Eddie Godfrey's vehicle, you weren't alone in there."

Nicola watched Patricia lick her dry lips. The tells were coming thick and fast.

"I have no idea what you mean."

"You had a stowaway. A witness. In the back of the van. The whole time."

Patricia suddenly looked like a little girl lost herself. She didn't know where to put her gaze.

Nicola pushed home the advantage.

"I will say, you planned everything rigorously. You cleared up meticulously. But I think it was a long night. And an unfamiliar vehicle. And very dark, I would imagine. So, I'm afraid you missed something. Something that the other person in that van with you told us about. Something Reeta, our forensics expert, has worked tirelessly to find, within the panels of Eddie Godfrey's van."

Now she placed one final evidence bag on the table. It contained a syringe.

"One tiny syringe, with traces of morphine. And a match to your DNA. Tiny traces, but definitely you."

Nicola sat back and looked at Patricia Tiernan, staring at the final piece of evidence.

"It's taken us a long time, Patricia. We know it was you. We have evidence. We have a witness to you transporting the body. Now we can carry on like this. Or you can decide you want to tell us the truth, finally."

In the long silence that followed, Patricia took on the air of a boxer who'd been in the ring for too long, taking too many punches.

In the end, she said: "Where would you like me to start?"

CHAPTER FIFTY-SIX

Earlier

Patricia Tiernan stood in the cold night air, her breath visible in front of her.

She waited in the shadow of a tree on the other side of the road, looking up at the exterior of the White Hart. It was nearly half past midnight. She would wait for the light to go out.

She was calm and raging. Ice-ferocious.

In times to come, she would be asked whether something had snapped in her that day.

Nothing had snapped. Something had *built*. Over years.

It was a pool of resentment that had sat inside her for decades. The level of that pool rarely went down. With every thoughtless action, with every lack of consideration, her brother ensured that the level of the resentment pool rose once more. And across the previous twenty-four hours it had finally boiled over.

Something had not snapped. Something had finally *connected.*

Who else would stop this happening? Who else had all the facts at their disposal, as she did? Who else could see that there was no good ending ahead?

Patricia let herself in with the spare key her brother had entrusted her with. He often lost things. He'd turn up asking her if he could use it. He always returned it. He would call her a lifesaver.

She held the key in her protective-gloved hand. She reasoned that her prints were all around this pub anyway, but she preferred to leave no traces of her fresh presence tonight. She pulled the protective paper suit—she thought of it as her hazmat suit; she had a supply left over from self-fumigating her property from bedbugs brought by a particularly annoying group of renters—out of the rucksack she was carrying and pulled it on.

This done, she walked quietly through the pub, her soft shoes encased in disposable plastic overshoes. She wanted to leave as little to chance as possible. No sound, no trace.

She glided silently through the bar, not fully cleared and tidied from the evening's service, she noted disapprovingly. Jim had wanted them all out and said he would do it himself. Of course he hadn't.

She padded up the stairs. She could hear Jim snoring.

He was in bed. She knew he slept naked because he had told her more than once, almost as if boasting.

She did not relish going into the bedroom. She was relieved when she saw, through the doorway, that he was lying face down, the covers half off him.

She had researched the best places to inject.

Kneeling on the floor, she took out the syringe. It was fully loaded and she had the vial with her to refill it.

She injected the full syringe of morphine swiftly into his backside—the needle going in without any fuss.

She pressed the liquid through, calmly, cleanly and swiftly.

He started to moan, and his arm flailed. His eyes opened and he looked at her for a moment. She placed a soothing hand on his shoulder. "Sssh sshh shh," she whispered reassuringly. "It's all right."

He knew it was her. He was confused, but he knew it was her. He had seen her.

His eyes closed and he slumped back to stillness. Whether this was sleep or the effect of the morphine, she did not know. He fidgeted a bit, his backside still irritatingly naked, as she quickly refilled the syringe from the vial. Injected more. Less reaction this time. Less snoring. She did it again. And then, a fourth time.

She believed the fourth time was likely the fatal dose.

She left the room then. She did not want to be there when life stopped flowing through her brother's body. She did not want to see what that was like.

She just wanted it to be done.

She went downstairs to check the clock in the bar. The whole building was silent. No traffic passed outside. She did not remove the hazmat suit.

Patricia prided herself on her rational mind.

She had thought about this sequence of events for a long time. Initially, as a fantasy. But then it had begun assuming the air of possibility, before solidifying into reality. She had lived with the idea, refined the data points almost as a game, so that now she felt very calm executing it.

She went to the walk-in fridge, carrying the rucksack containing the tools she needed for the next section of her task.

She was already thinking of her brother as an object to be disposed of. She had to be efficient. It was a project. This would be the time when it would be revealed whether her planning was as good as she believed it to be.

She had ensured Irina would not return tonight. Irina knew about Ayesha Barton, thanks to Patricia. Irina always left after rows, often for days. This had been a big row.

The rest of the village would be quiet. It was a Tuesday evening, and everyone was asleep.

This was not a heat-of-the-moment crime of passion. She had thought about it for a long time. Patricia regarded her tolerance toward her brother's activities and their impact on her life as akin to the brake pads on her car. Over time, both had worn down, to the extent where remedial action was essential. For a while the refrain "I wish he were dead" had been a quiet, forbidden thought. That had become "the world would be better off without him." In recent months it had evolved further to "It would be better if he were put out of his misery" and its variation, "It would be better *for all of us* if he were put out of his misery."

Lives could be treated as data, to be analyzed. Forecasts could be made. Patricia could foresee what Jim could not: that the future was not viable for him. All the decisions he had made, the foolish things he had committed to or been involved in, were not fading away; they were spiraling downward. He was boxed in, all ways. The consequences of his life were going to overwhelm him, and now they were threatening to pull her in, too.

Today, and tonight, had simply confirmed it. It had been time to do something about it.

One night, when he had first returned to Fleetcombe, brother and sister had sat up drinking absinthe, at his insistence and against her better judgment. In the dark of the early morning Jim had confided to his sister that he could never go back to prison. That he would top himself before he'd let that happen. Despite the intoxication, she did not doubt him.

And yet. *And yet.*

His subsequent behavior, in the days and months and years that followed, showed no awareness of that statement and what he supposedly felt. He would tell her about the things he was doing, the people he was seeing, and she would point out the risks, the lack of wisdom, the possibility of difficult consequences, and the strong likelihood that he could not avoid such consequences forever. He brushed this away, as he had done all his life, living forever in the here and now rather than with an awareness of the past and an eye on the future.

They were opposite personalities, it was true, but she found it coldly infuriating that she could see what would be coming and he could not. Or would not.

In the moments when she was going about her preparations for disposal of her brother's body, Patricia justified it by telling herself that sooner or later he would have been back in a prison cell, for fraud or worse. And so this was, ultimately, an act of mercy.

She removed the antlers from the deer head in the fridge with a hacksaw from the rucksack. Also in it were rope and epoxy glue. She had combed many forums and watched many YouTube videos that day. She had bought supplies from a big hardware store ten miles away where she knew she would not be recognized. She cut just under the scalp, knowing how she would later affix the antlers with the glue and crisscrossed rope. Belt and braces, she thought to herself.

She had heard about the deer shoot and had been shown the deer's head by Jim earlier that day. It had been like a code unlocking in her mind. It was all laid out before her. Fate had intervened. *Prepare rigorously but stay alive to opportunity* had been the motto of the boss she'd worked for in a previous life. Tonight she was applying it in a manner that man could never have imagined.

Antlers removed—it had been harder and she had been clumsier than she had envisaged—she looked at the clock again. Forty-one minutes had passed, and she scolded herself for having not been alert enough. She had assessed timings and made a plan and needed to stick to it.

She moved quickly and quietly back up the stairs.

She found her brother unresponsive. She did not know if his life was yet irretrievable. She realized, calmly, that this was the pivot point where she could call an ambulance, if she had a pang of conscience, a change of heart. She could try and get someone to save his life.

She did not wish to save his life.

She looked at him for a moment. He was undignified, naked, on his stomach, but he had not suffered.

She stood for a short while next to his body, in silence.

Now, for the disposal. The more ambitious part of the plan.

She would not falter.

CHAPTER FIFTY-SEVEN

After Patricia had described her actions in the pub on the night she killed her brother, they took a break. All the participants ate, in separate places across the station. Patricia's food was brought to her cell in the custody suite in the police station next door.

Nicola and Harry ate mostly in silence.

After they had eaten, Harry said, "What made you look at it differently? Why did you want to try and start with motive?"

Nicola tried to put it into words. "It's our job to gather evidence. We use the evidence to prove the facts. And we have incredible scientific and technical resources at our disposal to do that. But in the end, we're dealing with the actions of people. And I couldn't square Eddie's motive."

She ate a little more, conscious Harry was not eating, just looking at her, waiting for her to finish explaining.

"Then, I started to think about two things. How people present versus who they are. We all do it, to a greater or lesser degree. I once read that the secret to happiness lies in the gap between how one sees oneself and how others see us. The smaller the gap between the two, the happier the person. I just kept thinking about everyone involved, what they wanted to project, what they wanted us to see, contrasted with who they might really be. That's at the heart of what we're trying to figure out."

Harry was just staring now, and Nicola was speaking quickly, in between mouthfuls. "And then I was asking: what *really* makes you want someone dead? And . . . so d'you know what calcification is?"

"Not really. Well, not at all," said Harry.

"I still remember it from science at school. It's when large deposits of calcium form in soft tissue, causing it to harden. So, go with me on this, think of love—any different form of love—as soft tissue. And there's a form of hate that is, well, calcified love."

Harry looked blankly at her.

"Look at divorcing couples. Why does it get so mean, so personal, so harsh? Love calcifies into hate."

Harry stared at her. "That's bleak."

Nicola thought to herself: you're so young.

When they returned, and the recording began, Patricia started by saying, "In some ways, this is a relief."

Nicola asked what she meant.

"I thought I'd be good at lying. I had planned this out carefully. Or so I thought. I had considered it over a long period of time. And I did not expect to feel any guilt. He had worn me down a long time ago."

She went quiet for a moment, then.

"But it's strange. It does change you. Almost immediately. You just carry something you've never had to carry before. You see the world differently. Because you know something no one else does. And also, you've been through something no one else has. It's very tiring, actually."

She looked across at them. "I suppose you think I'm cold."

Nicola said, "Tell us about the rest of the night."

CHAPTER FIFTY-EIGHT

If the murder of her brother was the result of an abstract thought evolving into a concrete plan across time and fueled by resentment, then the disposal of the body—not disposal, *placement*—utilized Patricia's whole skill set: diligence, rigor, the ability to gather and analyze data, and speed of thought when needed.

But even then, it did not go quite to plan.

At the beginning, when the idea of her brother's death was almost a game she played with herself, she had assessed the feasibility of dissolving a body in acid. That was clearly the most efficient disappearing act. But she was not confident of her ability to deal with all the chemicals without leaving any trace. Leaving no trace was fundamental to this whole endeavor.

There were certainly slurry tanks aplenty within the county of Dorset, and these would also be a good place to get rid of a corpse, but that would require gaining access to a farmer's property and equipment without being seen.

She had also considered that Jim suddenly disappearing might bring a missing person inquiry: people out searching, police continually checking in with her—she did not like the idea of that. And if the body were never found, it would be a long process. She worried that a prolonged grieving-sister act ("I just want someone to find him and get him back to us. We love you, Jim, we just want you home") was a mite beyond her.

She thought on it at great length, and over time. What if one didn't *need* to get rid of the body? What if there was a way to allow the discovery of the body—its positioning, its presentation—to become a piece of data in itself. An image so strange or shocking that it immediately created multiple possibilities as to *why* he had been murdered. The perfect diversion. It would also allow her to position herself in a simple way: bewildered, shocked, saddened. She felt she could do those.

She had thought about this thesis for many months. Even when she had decided that it had merit, she had then to consider what form the discovery could take. What would have the impact to achieve what she needed and desired?

It was when nursing a second gin and tonic one Sunday evening alone in the corner of the Fox that she began to browse through the books on the shelf there. She flicked through a few. They were hack jobs, she decided, cut and paste, poorly written and illustrated, often self-published and flimsily poor in construction.

There was one book, though, on which she was satisfied to spend more than a few seconds. It was a better-than-average recounting of local myths, mysteries and historic events—all of which erred toward the macabre.

Against her better judgment, Patricia became absorbed in the book. While the rest of the pub ignored her, she availed herself of another gin and tonic and some olives and submerged herself in the local history.

It was the image that caught her eye. An artist's impression of one of three unsolved murders dating back to 1925. A body laid against a stone hut, near the edge of the beach, with antlers affixed to its head. The superstitious interpretation at the time was that the Devil had come to Dorset, and left death in His Wake.

The mystery was compounded by the fact that the person who had been hanged for it maintained to their dying day that they were innocent. And even better, as she dug further into the case, there was a local connection.

Patricia appreciated the power of an outlier. She saw that superstition could help her. The power of the unexplained, laced with fear, religion and paganism would be a powerful mix. But she had always imagined it would be difficult to get it right.

Ultimately, fate gave her the final shove. When Jim began ranting about a deer head left in the walk-in fridge at the White Hart, the day his behavior finally went beyond the pale, Patricia realized that providence was offering her a gift.

As she carried her brother's wiry body over her shoulder down the stairs, Patricia smacked his head against a door frame, almost upsetting the whole balance of the carrying. She winced, and out loud she apologized. Then chastised herself for doing so—*he can't hear you anymore, you stupid woman.*

Patricia was practiced at the fireman's lift, having been an advanced first-aider at the company where she had spent the majority of her working life. She had done a number of advanced courses and always enjoyed them. There were not many tasks in life where she felt more equipped than others, but this was one. She took to it naturally, so much so that she sought out as many courses as she could. She looked into being a first responder. She raised money for a defibrillator and learned how to use it. She did a lifesaving course at the local swimming pool.

Disappointingly, nobody was ever in need of her skills.

She was pleased this evening that finally she could put them to good use. The fireman's lift, of course, was excellent for carrying an unresponsive corpse.

She walked through the kitchen to the back doors for staff use only and laid Jim on a battered chair that came inside at night but during the day was placed outside for staff (well, the cook) to sit and smoke on. There was a pile of empty hessian sacks in which potatoes were delivered. They would be useful, she thought.

She opened the door, exited and locked the door again behind her.

There was risk in this phase. She was gambling that no one would arrive back in the twenty minutes she now required for her plan to function correctly.

She knew the car park at Fleetcombe would be a fertile hunting ground.

She identified Eddie Godfrey's van early. He kept it well maintained—he had to. Also, he thought he was better than her. He was, like a lot of men, nice to her when he wanted something. But he had rebuffed her advances, as subtle as they were, a long time ago, and not in a particularly polite way.

When thinking about him, she formed a subset of her plan. Every section of it had to be covered. If he were to be implicated, she would need to see that there were layers connecting him to it. It would not be enough simply for him not to know what had happened. All routes would have to lead back to him.

That he delivered to Carter's Pharmacy felt wonderfully synchronous to her. She knew what drugs they received. She knew the haphazard way it was run. The morphine was pure, delightful opportunism, and she adjusted her plans accordingly. On the night itself, she made sure that his drinks were topped up and that his spirits were doubles.

She knew what happened to him when he drank, because he had bored her about it previously.

Eddie was the perfect target. A nightly drinker in her brother's pub. He lived not too far from her. She understood his routines. She understood he drank more when he was under undue stress. She observed that he wobbled home some nights. She noticed that he had one big key ring with everything on it. He often felt so at home in the pub he'd put them on the table next to his first pint, or even on the bar, when he was ordering it. What was it with men and their chunky, overloaded key rings? she wondered.

Before she arrived at the pub that evening she had checked Eddie's van was in the car park. She had a contingency if Eddie had a quiet night on the beer: she would try smuggling vodkas into his pints if necessary.

Eddie, of course, did not, ultimately, need her help. He was already there when she arrived from scouting his van. He was annoyed and venting at the bar. He was at least a pint down, and she suspected two. He had his keys in his hand.

She spent the evening watching him, and Jim. She found it hard to take her eyes off Jim, knowing she held the key to his potential future. What she felt more than anything was a sense of control. She was in control and nobody else knew.

At the end of the night, Eddie stumbled out. She waited, and then slowly followed him home. He was off his face. When he got to his door, he took out his keys.

He fumbled them into the lock. They did not make it. He dropped them. This was better than she could have hoped.

She stepped in. "All right there, Edward?"

He looked disappointed. "Oh, Pat."

"Need a little help?"

"No!" he said, and then looked around in the dark like a child. "I dropped my keys." The words came out slurred.

She helped him look. "Want me to open the door for you?"

He was like a grateful baby. "Mmmmhmmm."

She placed the keys in the lock and opened the door wide, gesturing him inside.

She watched him walk forward. This was the tightrope walk for her. She went in with him. She watched him go over and slump on his sofa. He was not looking at her. She was invisible to him, just as she was invisible to so many people.

She put the keys noisily on the side. "I'll leave the keys here," she said, louder than necessary. Her words covered up the small chink as she removed the keys from the side in one continuous move and slid them into her pocket. She would wipe them down later.

She turned and called out "Night!" She could see Eddie, already passed out with the TV on.

She left, closing and locking the door behind her. Even if he did wake, he could not leave.

She paused outside his door, waiting in case he woke suddenly and banged on the door demanding his keys. But there was only silence. She peered back in through the window. He had not moved.

She calculated she had less than an hour to wait.

She went home and made a cup of tea. She would look in on Eddie on the way back.

After that, she returned to the White Hart, to murder the brother she had grown up with.

She strode quickly to the car park, still in the hazmat suit. She gambled she would not be seen, and she was correct. She found Eddie's van and got in the driver's seat. The car clock said 01:17.

She drove without headlights the short distance to the back of the White Hart. She turned the engine off and left the door open so there would be as few slams as possible.

She moved the body from the chair inside to the rear of the vehicle. She tried not to think of it as her brother now. She simply thought of it as the object. She laid it down and got into the back of the vehicle alongside. It was cramped. She had to move quickly and efficiently. She applied the epoxy glue and placed the scalp of the deer on top of her brother's head, then took one length of rope and criss-crossed it in an X shape over the back of his head and the front of his face. She noticed that deer blood was dripping down his face. She could not do anything about that now. She hoped it would all stay in place and the epoxy glue (which sold itself as "five-minute drying") would work as billed. This next stage complete, she placed the chair flat in the back of the van. She closed the doors quietly.

She drove through the night toward a remote coastal spot she had earmarked as the perfect isolated dumping ground. It would echo the site where the bodies were found in 1925. She took a route that she knew avoided all speed cameras. She had found the most convoluted of routes, along twisty lanes and bumpy tracks, some of which were not even official roads. No one would drive this way making that journey.

After about fifteen minutes, she realized something. There was a problem. The fuel light had come on. Patricia calculated. She cursed Eddie Godfrey. There was not enough fuel in the van to get to her planned destination! The idiot. She had not thought to check.

She brought the van to a stop in order to think. Plan A was not achievable. She looked at the display telling her how many miles she had left. She kept a calm mind. What was the overriding purpose, what were the main principles she was adhering to? She needed this to confuse, to be as distant from her as possible.

There was another spot she thought of. She could see the image in her head. Not the same as 1925, but perhaps that didn't matter. Needs must. It was not as isolated, but isolated had been disallowed now, due to mileage. It did, however, have chutzpah. She would have to take a risk. She felt if she were quick, it could work.

She did not notice a traffic camera, almost obscured by bushes, on the unplanned route she now took.

She drove through the tiny hamlet of Wynstone and joined the A35, parking the van at the side of the road. She opened up the rear doors. She had laid out covers all over the back. She placed the chair in the middle of the road. She lifted the body and affixed it to the chair with rope. Once it was done, she stood back to admire it. She gave herself seconds. She needed to be out of there fast.

On returning Eddie Godfrey's van, Patricia felt, as much as could be allowed, that her gathering of data over time, her analysis and her planning had allowed her to carry out something almost exactly as she had envisaged. It might even have been better. She had erased the margin of error, apart from the issue with the fuel. But she had been so swift of thought, and then of action, that she felt even more proud of her achievement.

Later she would realize that not allowing for anything external beyond her purview was her downfall. She had not allowed for the unexpected stick in the spoke.

She had not allowed for Shannon.

CHAPTER FIFTY-NINE

Have you any idea," said Patricia Tiernan to Nicola, "how hard I've had to work to keep my life in order here? The world has wanted to push me further out from the center with every year that's passed. And I refused to be downtrodden. I've had no partner, no one to support me, financially or emotionally, or in any way whatsoever. I've had my job taken from me before I was ready . . . but I have survived. I thrived. People paid attention to me. Until *he* came back, and then, suddenly, he's putting himself at the center of attention, in my village, running the pub, of all things!"

She looked so exhausted now. "He was just so much noise, intruding into my life, always in some mess which I would get dragged into. D'you know, once I even had a man stop me in the street and tell me to tell Jim to do the smart thing with the money, *or else*. Can you imagine? I've never been threatened in my life! What's that phrase? Don't shit where you eat. Well, he did. Over and over. He shat where I ate.

"Because he's selfish. He only ever thinks of himself. And the selfish people, they never get held to account, do they? Not really. If you don't have a conscience, life is just fine. You never have to think about consequences. But his consequences played out in my life. Well, not just mine, he ruined others', too. There was Irina, there was the money.

And then him with Ayesha that day . . . it was the final straw. She was *engaged*. He was friends with Mick! And he had to go and . . . I just thought: this can't go on."

"But you'd already planned it, in your mind," said Nicola.

"It was a mix. Planning and opportunism. It was a kernel that grew. Idle bits and pieces that started to join up, and then, over time, a thought that just wouldn't go away. It lodged in the corner of my mind: what if you really did it, what would that feel like? It's like buying a house, isn't it? You imagine yourself living there. Well, I imagined myself living in a reality where my brother wasn't there to cause chaos and grief for everyone—including me—and I found I rather liked the idea of that reality."

Nicola asked, fascinated, "And how does that reality feel to you now?"

Patricia considered. "I'll tell you what's interesting. I thought I would be racked with guilt. That's not been the case so far. I wonder if it'll change. But how do I feel? I'm cross with myself, of course I am. I planned it well enough. But there were variables I didn't allow for. The fuel. I still blame Eddie for that. And then little silly mistakes. I don't know why I put that book back. I should have taken it home. That's an oversight. And the syringe. Well, that was unforgivable. I had too many things to think of. I think I was almost too pleased with myself to notice."

"And the fires?"

"Not difficult. They were part of the original legend. I knew the more I drew your attention to those, and to the Deakins family, the less likely it was that you'd look at me." She paused. "I had the second one planned from the start. I thought that was good. Did you think that was good?"

Nicola did not answer. She kept to her questions. "Why the antlers?"

"Isn't it obvious? It had to be an enormous distraction. Something supposedly full of meaning that would push everyone to look that way.

That it would just eat up your time and your focus. All that superstition, it's like catnip to a certain type of person. I thought if I pointed toward that, everyone would only see that, rather than me. I hoped the fact that I mostly pass through life invisible these days might finally be an asset."

She paused for a moment. "But also . . . I think one could argue . . ." Then she was quiet for a long time while Nicola and Harry waited. Patricia looked back at them. "Do you believe in the Devil?"

"No. Do you?"

Patricia's tone became matter-of-fact, as if she was discussing groceries. "I don't know, now. Some people believed it was the Devil who was truly behind those murders in the twenties. I think perhaps they might have a point."

Nicola said, "I don't understand."

"I mean, to murder my own brother. I must have been possessed by the Devil somewhat, mustn't I?"

The room went quiet for a while.

Nicola was rinsed. Even Patricia appeared tired now. She looked across the table.

"I knew I was in trouble when I first saw you," Patricia said to Nicola.

Nicola looked surprised. "Why?"

"My risk calculations were based on the information I had available. I thought I knew all the detectives who would investigate. They were old and tired, and arrogant." She looked at Harry. "Or young and green. They wouldn't have worked the way you did. My odds were good. But when you came to my house, the way you looked round it, the way you took everything in, the questions you asked, the way you asked them, I realized I might be in trouble."

Patricia was quiet for a moment. "Well done."

CHAPTER SIXTY

Over the next hours and days, the word spread around the small community that Jim Tiernan's killer had been caught.

For most, it came as a relief. For others, it was a chance to reclaim their lives. To figure out what came next.

Eddie Godfrey was released from custody without charge. Stumbling bleary-eyed and exhausted back out into the world, Eddie resolved never to touch another drop of alcohol ever again.

Or for six months at least.

Frankie had to allow time for their hair to grow back, before taking their CV into all the salons within a twenty-mile radius. They didn't want to travel, but realized they might have no choice. They tried to be selective. The last salon they went to was at the furthest end of town, heading toward the bay. It was new, opened and run by a twenty-year-old lad who had started his business at seventeen doing cuts for mates and booking appointments via Instagram DMs out of a shed in his parents' back garden. Three years later, he had become so popular he'd taken over a large empty retail space.

There was a line of people waiting. The lad cutting hair was making jokes and chatting, but Frankie knew from experience how stressed he must be. He seemed to be an hour behind on appointments. There was a second chair, and all the right equipment, but no one working on it today.

The lad looked up.

"Frankie, right? You were working up the road."

Frankie was surprised, nodded and proffered their CV, but the lad swatted it away. "What's that gonna tell me? Anyway, I've been inheriting your clients. Some nice trims." He looked at the line, then back at Frankie. "Give you a trial now, if you like."

Frankie did like. "Seriously?" they asked.

"Clear that lot—if they're happy, and you've got good banter, you're in."

Frankie grinned. Took their coat off. Looked around. Everything was in its place. They were at home. Frankie picked up a gown. Beamed at the line.

"Who's next?"

Nicola Bridge did not forget Shannon.

She spent time with her, listening in detail about exactly what went on at home. As Shannon recounted numerous examples of her mother's violence against her, Nicola wanted to hug the child to her.

During this conversation Shannon told Nicola of an aunt who lived on the outskirts of Lyme Regis, a dozen miles or so down the coast. When Shannon spoke of her aunt, her face lit up, as if describing a sanctuary. Her aunt and Shannon's mum had fallen out over Mandy

Skillett's treatment of Shannon and had not spoken for nearly two years. Shannon's mum had threatened her daughter with severe consequences if she ever tried to contact her aunt.

Nicola and Harry charged Mandy Skillett with actual bodily harm.

Mandy laughed and said, "You think that girl'll say anything against me?"

"She already has," said Nicola. "In detail. She kept a record. Including photographs on an old digital camera she found lying around at home."

Nicola watched Mandy Skillett's confidence shrivel very quickly.

For her own safety, Shannon went to live with her aunt Abigail, in a terraced house on a long street opposite a playground. Abigail was older than Mandy, unmarried, and unable to have children. "I've got stacks of room," she told Nicola. "She can have a proper life here."

When Nicola went to visit Shannon a few weeks later, drawings were already up on the fridge. Shannon was installed at a new school and attending at least most of the time. She had started to make new friends.

As they all ate tea together, Abigail nudged Shannon to tell Nicola what she'd told her teacher the week before.

Shannon looked at Nicola and said, "I'm gonna be a police officer like you, when I'm older."

Nicola beamed, not quite able to say anything, and Abigail handed her a piece of kitchen roll to deal with whatever had just got into Nicola's eye.

CHAPTER SIXTY-ONE

At the end of December, in that lull between Christmas and New Year, the lights were on once more at the White Hart pub in Fleetcombe.

That evening, Nicola entered the pub late.

It was a small gathering of old familiar faces. On entering she couldn't help but notice Deakins taking up his old position at the bar, separate from anyone else, a new banjo at his side, as if goading people.

Across the pub, she saw her husband, Mike, and her son, Ethan, with a girl who looked his age but who Nicola did not recognize standing next to him. Mike was chatting to Harry Ward. *Are they talking about me?* wondered Nicola, slightly alarmed.

As she made her way over, she was accosted by Christine Wilson from the brewery, who handed Nicola a drink and blocked her way to her family.

"So glad you could come! Such a sad night, but we wanted to do something."

"Thank you for asking me," said Nicola.

"I suppose I should give a speech at some point," said Christine. "I loathe giving speeches!"

Nicola did not think that was true.

She worked her way across the room, stopping to say hello to Ayesha Barton, who was standing with Irina Bortnick. Nicola was aware that in the months since Patricia Tiernan's confession there had been a rapprochement between the two women. So much so that Ayesha had offered Irina a job as duty manager at the Fox.

"How's business?"

"Busy," noted Irina.

"No Mick?" asked Nicola, looking around.

"Not anymore," said Ayesha pointedly.

Nicola clocked where the engagement ring had once been on Ayesha's finger. "I'm sorry," she said genuinely.

Ayesha shrugged. The pain was clearly still near the surface. "I fucked up. We tried, but he didn't have it in him to grant me a second chance."

Before Nicola could reply, Ayesha had grabbed the passing Frankie Winters and moved the conversation skillfully on.

"Hey! Congratulations on the new job," said Ayesha.

"Thanks!" Frankie smiled and said to Nicola, "I did your son this afternoon. He's well into his new girlfriend, isn't he!"

Nicola looked startled. Was that girl official? "He is! I didn't realize he was gonna be here. And I definitely didn't realize he was bringing . . . her." She nodded to the girl standing next to him whose name she didn't know. She felt both pleased and thrown.

As she was looking round the bar Nicola caught the eye of Eddie Godfrey. He stared at her coldly, then turned his back.

Nicola wondered, had she been too hard on an innocent man? She felt she'd been fair, but you could never be fully sure what people were left feeling.

Nicola felt an arm slipped round her waist and heard her husband's voice. "May I borrow you for a moment?"

Nicola didn't love either the possessive arm or the sense he was hers to borrow, but wasn't going to let that show. Things were better than they had been for a while. As they moved over, Mike said, "Be nice."

"Mum, this is Dani," said an eager Ethan as she came over. "She's in my psychology class."

"Hi!" Dani did a little wave and stepped forward, extending her hand to shake. She was seventeen, beautiful, shy, with a smile that could light up a room. Nicola saw the body language between Dani and Ethan, noticing instantly that these two seemed equally into each other. Oh my God, she thought, her son was no longer alone here.

"So nice to meet you, Dani. Was that you last week, 'studying' in Ethan's room?"

Nicola had walked in on Ethan and a girl she didn't know in bed together in his room the previous Tuesday. Both teens had buried themselves hurriedly under the covers when she came in.

"Yes, it was!" said Dani, guilelessly. "Awkward! Nice to meet you properly!" She was styling this out very nicely, thought Nicola.

"Oh God, Mum," said Ethan, laughing in disbelief. "I can't believe you went there straightaway. You even did air quotes."

"You solved this whole case, didn't you?" asked Dani.

All eyes were on Nicola. "It was teamwork," she said, and looked to Harry, who smiled back at her. Nicola noticed Mike watching the look between them.

They were interrupted by Christine Wilson tapping a pint glass with a fork. The small gathering went quiet.

"Thank you all for coming. As you all no doubt know, in the light of recent events, Wilson's Brewery has with a heavy heart decided to sell the White Hart for development. And as of tomorrow, the work will begin in converting this plot into multiple houses. I suppose it's at least good news for the housing crisis."

Nicola looked around, thinking about how many people had been through this pub over the centuries. Now, here they were. The last.

"The events of earlier this year," Christine bowled on, "were tragic and left a deep scar. But I would like to take a moment to mark the passing of a great pub, and to thank all of you as its patrons and regulars. You made it what it was."

"And Jim," came a voice from the back. "We raise our glasses to Jim." They all looked. Irina Bortnick was holding her glass high and defiant, tears streaming down her face.

"Yes. Exactly. Well said," replied Christine awkwardly.

Glasses were raised in the air. There was a heartfelt chorus of "to Jim."

At the bar, on an old stool, Deakins began to play the banjo, unbidden. He stared at Nicola as he did so. She looked back, unflinching.

Harry came over to stand by her and said very quietly, "Farmers are fucking weird," and they both laughed.

"Any news on the new offices?" he asked.

"Two-year delay, minimum. So, we may well be staying where we are for the foreseeable. Oh, and the acting chief constable resigned today. Apparently, the budget's even worse than was foreseen."

"Great," laughed Harry. Not for the first time, Nicola thought: cute smile.

She downed her glass, clapped Harry on the shoulder. "That's me done."

"See you tomorrow."

Nicola gestured to Mike with her head, and he met her at the door, as summoned.

For the final time, Nicola Bridge left the pub where Jim Tiernan had been murdered.

The drinking and talking and music and laughter and crying went on late into the night.

As the residents of Fleetcombe marked the death of the White Hart.

ACKNOWLEDGMENTS

This book began thanks to the encouragement of my longtime, incomparably wondrous agent Cathy King, subsequently flanked by the redoubtable Eugenie Furniss, both at 42 in London.

Two extraordinary editors—Joel Richardson in London, and Pam Dorman in New York—guided and cajoled me through the process of writing my first novel with wisdom, grace, diligence, demands for propulsion, forensic questioning, and plenty of wit and laughter. This book would not be half the thing it is without them.

I also want to thank:

The wonderful team at Pamela Dorman Books: Natalie Grant, Marie Michels, Brian Tart, Andrea Schulz, Patrick Nolan, Kate Stark, Tricia Conley, Tess Espinoza, Nick Michal, Diandra Alvarado, Alicia Cooper, Jason Ramirez, Dave Litman, Chantal Canales, Julia Rickard, Andy Dudley, and Rachel Obenschain.

The equally fabulous team at Penguin Michael Joseph in the UK: Louise Moore, Maxine Hitchcock, Philippa Walker, Ellie Hughes, Sriya Varadharajan, Courtney Barclay, Beatrix Macintyre, and Sarah Day.

At Imaginary Friends: the peerless Rebecca Roughan, Emily Grimshaw, and Caroline Cook.

In Dorset, three besties (and key pub companions): The Neils (Sentance & Hallows) and Kate Scott. Also, honorary Dorset residents: Roy Macmillan and Rachel Bavidge.

To my family: Mum, Dad, Cal, Aidan, Julie, Carl, Ben, Martha, Roni—so much love and gratitude, always.

And to Mads—for being my first, most trusted reader: your insight, vision, and notes on this were as perfect on this as they are on our whole life and family. You make everything better.